# The Encounter

## A Novel

## Carl Nichols, Jr.

iUniverse, Inc.
New York  Bloomington

**The Encounter**
**A Novel**

*iUniverse books may be ordered through booksellers or by contacting:*

*iUniverse*
*1663 Liberty Drive*
*Bloomington, IN 47403*
*www.iuniverse.com*
*1-800-Authors (1-800-288-4677)*

*Because of the dynamic nature of the Internet, any Web addresses or links contained in this book may have changed since publication and may no longer be valid. The views expressed in this work are solely those of the author and do not necessarily reflect the views of the publisher, and the publisher hereby disclaims any responsibility for them.*

*ISBN: 978-1-4502-1556-5 (sc)*
*ISBN: 978-1-4502-1558-9 (dj)*
*ISBN: 978-1-4502-1557-2 (ebk)*

*Printed in the United States of America*

*iUniverse rev. date: 4/7/2010*

*In loving memory of my sister, Chris.*

*And for Nan and Matty.*

# Part I

# Chapter 1

## THURSDAY

"Site's coming along well, Nick. Don't you think?" Emily Hastings asks.

As project manager, she needs him to say yes, but Nick Steele has his own punch list. This is the part of the job he loves most: visiting his company's construction sites at various stages of development. He takes particular pleasure in this stage—the superstructure, when the building is no more than a steel and concrete skeleton. Just vertical support beams, horizontal steel girders, and steel rod and concrete flooring, all reaching skyward with unwavering determination and resolve, holding the promise of something important, vital, and lasting. Since his promotion to president of the Rohr Corporation, he spends too much time behind a desk but still tries to make personal surveys of the company's building sites across the country.

"From what I can see, there don't appear to be any major issues," he says. Rohr owns and manages hundreds of commercial buildings around the country; this one, in Denver, offers a breathtaking, if distant, view of the Rockies. On the thirty-seventh floor, where Nick and Emily stand, downtown Denver's skyline shimmers against a cloudless blue sky.

"The usual hiccups, but we had uninvited visitors last night," Emily says. She is no one's idea of a construction boss—petite model-pretty, with stylish hair, flawless mocha skin, and manicured hands—but she is a slave to detail, and certainly no one's idea of a pushover. Nick considers her his best project manager.

"Visitors?" Nick asks.

"Vandals," Emily says. "Teenagers, probably. No structural damage, but they spray-painted graffiti all over the second floor. I mean *all* over." She shrugs. "Not the usual stuff, either. Fundamentalist punks, maybe."

Nick raises his eyebrows. "Let's take a look."

As they step off the temporary construction elevator onto the second floor, Nick stops abruptly. Before him, across the vast expanse of concrete flooring, are the words, "An eye for an eye. A tooth for a tooth," all precisely lettered in blood-red paint, as if by a graffiti artist. Nick is baffled but can't help wondering whether this is personal to him or to the Rohr Corporation. He's never seen anything like it before. Someone invested a lot of time and effort meticulously spray-painting the entire floor with this inexplicable biblical reference. *And for what? What could it possibly mean?*

Nick grimaces. This building is, as are all of Rohr's properties, very personal to him.

He's proud of the contribution this office building will make to the community: helping to strengthen the local economy, providing jobs, revitalizing the neighborhood, and adding to the city's overall architectural aesthetic for many years to come.

And it gives him great satisfaction knowing that when finished, it will be standing here for generations to come. Someday, his children, grandchildren, even great-grandchildren may stand on the side of the street, look skyward, and admire the looming edifice that their forefather played a role in creating. Although he'd be hesitant to admit it to anyone, part of what excites him about creating buildings is that each one offers the possibility of just a sliver of immortality.

"I've hired a security guard for the next week just in case they decide to come back," says Emily.

"Good. In the meantime, let's get it cleaned up. We've got investors, agents, and the architect visiting next week."

"We'll be ready."

Nick smiles at her. "I know you will."

She pauses. "Are you in town tonight?"

"Yeah. I have the Commerce City site to visit this afternoon, then meetings with our lead broker and his team."

"If you don't have any other plans, I'd be happy to buy you dinner. There's a great new restaurant a few blocks from here that's getting rave reviews."

Nick hesitates. "That's really kind of you, but I better not." He likes Emily, but it's in neither of their best interest to get too personal.

"Well, if you change your mind …"

"Thanks." Nick cuts her short.

Seconds later, Nick's Blackberry rings. The caller ID identifies his boss's assistant. "Hi Sally."

"Hi Nick. Something urgent has come up, and Johann needs to meet with you tonight. Over dinner."

"Where? In Chicago?"

"No, he'll fly down and meet you in Denver. I'll make the restaurant arrangements and e-mail them back to you. Probably be on the early side."

"Can't we just speak over the phone?"

"He said he needed to speak with you in person."

"What's up?"

"He didn't say. Just told me to make it happen. Said it was 'non-negotiable.' Couldn't wait."

"Everything all right?" Nick scratches the side of his head.

"I know as much as you do, Nick."

"Okay." Nick disconnects the call. *What's that about?*

"A problem?" Emily asks.

"No … It's nothing." He forces a reassuring smile.

He looks back over the floor—assaulted, violated, bloodied—and shakes his head in disgust.

"Let's wrap this up."

"Sure, Nick."

They both turn and head back toward the elevator bank.

# Chapter 2

The restaurant is cool and dark, a welcome relief from the dry mid-August heat. Nick sits alone in a quiet corner at a table covered with white linen set for two. His right index finger stirs an ice-cold vodka tonic, which has the inexplicable effect of cooling his entire body. His rumpled blue suit jacket hangs from the back of his chair, a red-striped tie dangles loosely from his open collar, and the sleeves of his white cotton dress shirt are rolled up to his elbows for maximum ventilation. His short, neatly clipped brown sideburns are damp with perspiration from being outside most of the day.

Gazing upward through the tinted glass window beside him, Nick fixes on a small grouping of thin clouds paintbrushed across the early evening sky, accentuating the expansive blue dome over the city. While the dry Denver mile-high heat may be intense, it's nothing like—and ultimately preferable to—the oppressive summer sauna back home in Chicago.

Nick is on the last leg of an eight-day business trip. *Just one more day*, he reminds himself, touching his lips to the cold, wet tip of his quinine-flavored finger. Tomorrow night he'll be back home with his wife and two teenaged daughters, whom he misses with a yearning that intensifies with each passing day, and even more with each lonely night. Of course they speak regularly on the phone and trade e-mails, but that only serves to stoke his longing.

It was easier when he was younger, being away on business for long stretches. Now at forty-six, with much of what he had hoped to achieve in his professional life well in place, his thoughts turn more frequently to his family. Though he tries, he can't shake the feeling that the longer he's away from home, the more he's sacrificing something—perhaps no more than the everyday pleasures of shared conversations and experiences—that can never be recreated and can't wait until another day.

Nick reaches into his left trouser pocket, pulls out his Blackberry, and checks the time—5:27. His boss and mentor—Johann Rohr, chairman of the Rohr Corporation, one of the largest commercial real estate development companies in the country—had scheduled dinner for 5:30. Throughout the day Nick had tossed around different possibilities in his head for the reason but couldn't put his finger on any one thing. This sudden request from his boss was out of character. In business, and indeed in all aspects of his life, Johann was deliberate, planning well in advance before making decisions or taking action on any matter of importance.

Nick knows this well enough, having a similar personality trait. Sometimes, just occasionally, despite all of the benefits that come with planning ahead, he wonders whether this trait prevents him from experiencing some of the effortless pleasures and rewards of spontaneity.

What could be so vitally important that Johann feels compelled to take the company G5 from Chicago to Denver for a last-minute dinner meeting? Especially when the two of them communicate every day by phone or e-mail?

*I'll find out soon enough*, Nick thinks.

He turns his attention to the entrance of the restaurant just as Johann arrives, greeted by a statuesque, young hostess, who he engages with a broad, authentic, and dazzling smile. Even from a distance Nick can see the sparkle in his eyes. He marvels at

Johann's natural ability to charm, especially pretty young women. As Johann makes his way toward the dinner table, Nick can't help but notice the youthful spring in his step, the smart cut of his gray pin-striped suit perfectly tailored to his tall, trim physique, and the still handsome, chiseled face belying his seventy-two years. As Nick pushes back his chair and rises to greet Johann, he glances again at the time on his smartphone—5:30. Punctual, as always. He can't help but smile.

"Nick, how are you?" Johann stretches out his right arm and grips Nick's hand. His voice is more paternal than professional.

Nick is comforted, but not relaxed. "I'm good. Good. A bit worn down, I suppose. It's been a long trip. But very productive. The two sites here in Denver are coming along well. No major issues. Tenant interest is good, leasing activity has had excellent results, and each project is nearly fully occupied. Much quicker than we anticipated."

"Excellent. Well done."

The waiter arrives and addresses Johann. "Can I order you a drink, sir?"

"Yes. I'll have a Dewar's on the rocks."

Nick holds his palm over his drink; he's fine for the moment.

A product of both German and American cultures, both of which value directness and no-nonsense pragmatism, Johann wastes no time getting straight to the point. "I'm sure you're wondering what this is all about."

"I'm a little curious," Nick says.

"I'm sorry for the lack of advance notice. I'm afraid this just couldn't wait." Johann shakes his head.

"Not at all. I welcome the company. Like I said, it's been a long trip."

"Always the diplomat." Johann smiles.

"I learned from the master."

Johann chuckles before assuming a more serious demeanor. "Nick, I need to tell you something."

"I'm all ears."

The waiter returns and places Johann's drink on the table.

Nick catches the waiter's attention before he leaves, tapping the rim of his glass with his right index finger. He's changed his mind; he is ready, after all, for another vodka tonic. His first drink is only half empty, but he has an uncomfortable feeling he's going to need another one.

The waiter nods and shuffles off.

Johann grips the glass of scotch and swirls the brown liquid around three large cubes of crystal clear ice. Nick catches a whiff of honey, peat, and oak, and notes the satisfaction—or is it relief?—on Johann's face as he throws his head back and takes a stiff swig of his drink. Nick has never seen Johann swig anything. He's a sipper by nature. Another first. *What's going on?*

"Nick, I have a board meeting tomorrow afternoon," says Johann, lowering his glass to the table.

"I know. I read through a final draft of the presentation last night. It looks good. You shouldn't have any problems. Is there something missing?"

"No. No. It's not that. Everything looks fine. As usual. Better than fine. It's been a good quarter. A *great* quarter. You've done a hell of a job. The board will be pleased. No … that's not it. That's not why I'm here. There's something else."

Nick looks into Johann's eyes, increasingly apprehensive.

"You see … Nick …" Johann looks out the window, takes a deep breath, and then turns back toward Nick. "I have ALS."

Nick checks to be sure he heard correctly. "Lou Gehrig's Disease?"

"One and the same, I'm afraid."

"Are you sure?"

Johann takes another swig, this time finishing his drink. "Confirmed by three separate doctors."

A loud, uncomfortable silence falls as Johann's words weigh heavily on both of them.

Nick is thankful to see Johann regain himself—for both of their sakes—before continuing. "Crazy thing is, with the exception of a strange tingling and weakness in my arms and legs, I feel fine. I first noticed it when I started to miss certain notes on the piano—first on more difficult pieces, then even on easier ones." He arches his back, steeling himself against any semblance of self-pity. "The doctors seem to think I could go on for another two years—less is more likely—particularly at my age."

Nick's eyes glaze over, visions of the illness racing through his head.

"Pretty nasty disease, huh?" says Johann, appearing to read Nick's mind. "Hard to fathom the idea, isn't it, that your mind will stay sharp as ever, right to the end, while every muscle in your body, one by one, stops functioning. Strange to think of being trapped inside your own body."

Nick shakes his head, at a loss for words.

The waiter brings Nick's drink—a welcome reprieve. Appearing to sense the dark mood at the table, the waiter departs without a word.

Nick grabs hold of the swizzle stick in his new drink and stirs slowly, gazing into the swirling liquid, searching for an appropriate response. His taste for the cocktail has suddenly disappeared. He looks up at the man who has meant more to him than anyone outside his immediate family for the last fifteen years. "I'm so sorry, Johann."

"Look, I've had a good life. No regrets, perhaps with the exception of my kids. As you well know, they didn't turn out exactly as I'd hoped. Perhaps I have myself to blame. Still, despite their shortcomings, I don't love them any less." Johann struggles to clear his throat.

"Johann, you still have a good deal of time," Nick says.

"That's true. Time perhaps to set a few things right. Despite the ... challenges ... of my plight, *that is* a blessing."

Johann reaches across the table and takes Nick's left wrist. "But that's only part of why I needed to see you tonight."

Nick braces himself.

"I need to pass the baton."

Nick nods.

"It's between you and Jim Franklin."

Nick tries to hide his disappointment.

"You know if it were just up to me, this wouldn't be a horse race. Of course, that's not the way things work. The board gets the final say."

Johann says, "I need to tell them tomorrow about my health, and the first thing they'll want to talk about is my successor. Of course, they'll offer perfunctory condolences. Oh, I suppose that's being unkind. A few of them will genuinely feel concern for my personal wellbeing. But what'll be most pressing on *all* of their minds, and rightly so, is the stability of the company. And that starts with the continuity of management. There'll be no issues or objections to you. We've discussed you as a lead candidate for many years. But we've also discussed Jim as a contender. I'm going to call for a vote next Friday. Of course, I'll be doing a bit of lobbying before then. As you know, I can be very persuasive." Johann winks.

Nick is silent, trying to absorb the implications of what he just heard.

Johann waves his arm at the waiter. "Let's get some food. We'll talk more over dinner. I've got to be out of here by seven o'clock." He turns back to Nick, appearing to be his old self again: confident, relaxed, and not at all ready to give up on the simple joys of living. "Let's find out what the specials are. I understand the food's excellent here."

# *Chapter 3*

At 7:00 sharp, Johann takes the white cloth napkin from his lap, tosses it beside his empty plate, slides his chair back, and rises effortlessly from the table. Nick stands as well, following his lead. They peer into each other's eyes. Johann reaches out to shake Nick's hand, embracing it with both of his own.

"Can I give you a lift back to your hotel?"

"No, thanks. I think I'll finish my coffee," says Nick.

"Nick, I want you to know how proud of you I am. Come Friday it's my hope and intention that you're elected my successor." He pauses. "As you can imagine, I'll have much to preoccupy me in the few short years I have ahead. So I'm counting on knowing that one of them will *not* have to be worrying about Rohr."

Nick shakes his head. "You won't."

"Good." Johann smiles and turns to leave as his eyes begin to tear.

Nick watches in admiration as his boss, his mentor and friend, strides to the entrance of the restaurant as fleet of foot as when he first arrived, flashes a charming grin at the hostess, and then heads out the door to a black Lincoln Town Car waiting on the side of the street.

Nick collapses back into his chair at the table.

It's potentially wonderful news—the achievement of his life's ambition, the gold medal he'd been striving for. But it's not his yet. There's competition. Always competition. And Jim Franklin, Rohr's CFO, is not one to underestimate. He, no doubt, will be doing some lobbying of his own prior to the board meeting.

And what about Johann? His misfortune is unfathomable.

Nick reaches for his phone, finds his wife's cell phone number, and presses the automatic dial. After two rings, he disconnects the call, suddenly remembering that she and his two daughters were going to the movies tonight, the 8:00 showing of the new Pixar film playing at the local town theatre. *Damn.*

What now?

He contemplates calling Tom, his wife's younger brother. Although they see each other only once a year during their annual family long-weekend get-togethers—rotating between Denver and Chicago each autumn—Nick has grown increasingly fond of Tom and enjoys his company. He especially likes Tom's harrowing tales of his adventures as a Navy Seal in the First Gulf War—a job he was lucky to survive, from the stories.

No point in disturbing him, Nick decides. He and his wife are probably settling into a quiet family night at home: reading to their three young children, tucking them into bed, catching up on household chores.

He then considers calling Emily Hastings to invite her for a drink. Not a good idea, he decides. She might take it the wrong way.

He's not ready to head back to his hotel room; he can't bear the inevitable loneliness that awaits him there, at least not yet.

Over dinner, Nick couldn't help but notice that the bar to the right of the restaurant entrance was beginning to come to life, mostly with young business types getting an early jump on the weekend.

After paying the bill, Nick gets up and heads over. Though alone, he suspects that he'll feel better around other people—at least for a while—absorbing their vigor and hormone-fueled vitality. Besides, he needs more time to think through his conversation with Johann. Somehow it'll be easier amongst a din of lively, happy people than isolated in his sterile hotel room.

He finds an empty stool at the stainless steel-covered bar. Purple lighting glows from behind the liquor bottles lined three levels high along the back of the bar, creating the impression of a translucent cityscape at dusk. A low-volume, repetitive techno beat infuses the cool air with a pulse that is as soothingly predictable as his own heartbeat. Two impassive bartenders, severely handsome, pouty James Dean wannabes, are dressed in ultra-tight black t-shirts, their thick, dyed black hair slicked back.

Nick orders a martini. It seems more fitting to the festive setting and to his contemplative mood than the vodka tonic he barely touched throughout dinner.

As he settles back and sips his clear, icy cold libation, his mind drifts—ushered away by the cacophony of voices whirring and buzzing round his head.

"Hi, can I join you?"

Nick is shaken from his trance. He swivels his stool to his right. A young Asian American woman is standing next to him. By Nick's reckoning, she's no more than twenty-six or twenty-seven. No thought is required to discern that she's attractive.

Nick answers, with some hesitation. "Sure. Please." Instinctively, he stands and presents the stool next to him.

"A gentleman. I like that."

They both sit down. She places her cocktail, pink liquid in a martini glass—a Cosmopolitan, Nick guesses—on the bar in front of her.

"Not that it's any of my business, but you look like you could use some company. You look ... a little sad," she says.

Nick raises his eyebrows, surprised by her presumption and the unearned stab at intimacy. He writes it off to the more open, confessional nature of the younger generation, who seem to put little stock in privacy. He wonders what happened to social discretion and finesse. Probably disappeared with basic manners. *My God, I must be getting old.*

"I hope that doesn't offend you. I just thought you looked like you could use some company."

"No, in fact I could."

She takes a sip of her drink. "Is Denver home?"

"No, Chicago."

"Is that where you grew up?"

"Everton, Illinois."

"Sounds like a small town. I'm a small town girl myself."

"Actually, Everton has the largest automobile supply manufacturing plant in the country—or at least it used to." Nick smiles. "But the town's real claim to fame is that it has more churches and bars per resident than any town in the country. Locals like to say that some people go to church for salvation, others seek it in bars, but only in Everton, with all those churches and bars right next to each other, can you double your odds of achieving deliverance."

The woman chuckles. "I could use a town like that."

"Amen."

"Is your family still there?"

Nick shakes his head. "My father worked in the factory, clocking in right after high school and clocking out the day he died. My grandfather, too. He was a Russian immigrant. My mother still lives there … in the same house I grew up in."

"What about you? You don't look like a factory worker."

Nick smiles. "No, I had different ideas about how I wanted to spend my life."

"So what do you do?"

"Commercial real estate."

"That sounds interesting."

"No complaints."

"How long have you been doing it?"

"Since I was nineteen," he says. "What about you?"

"Oh, I'm just a working girl."

Suddenly, Nick gets it: this is more than a friendly chat. This striking young woman is not acting purely out of kindness. He wonders how he could have been so naïve, so vain, so stupid as to assume she was actually interested in talking to him.

She reaches over and lightly touches his right thigh. "Nothing better than a little company, I find, when you're feeling down."

"No—no. Thanks, but no." He lifts his left hand, turns it around, stretches his fingers apart, and shows her the gold wedding band on his ring finger.

She chuckles and continues in a slow, sexy, breathy voice. "That's okay. We all need a little TLC sometimes. It doesn't have to mean anything. I'm sure you're not looking for a long-term commitment. And, frankly, neither am I." She smiles. "Just a little company. That's all. Nothing wrong with that, is there?"

Nick is speechless. Part of what she says, and perhaps too, partly in the way she says it—the soft, sensual tone of her voice having its own irresistible quality—seems to make sense to him. What's the harm, after all? It wouldn't have any effect on the close relationship he enjoys with his wife. That is solid. Untouchable. And no one would ever know—ever. This young woman was right about one thing: he sure could use a little company.

On the other hand, it doesn't feel right. It's not something he's ever done before, and he's not sure he wants to start now. It's been a matter of personal pride that, despite past temptations, he's remained faithful to his wife throughout their marriage.

She leans over and whispers in his right ear. "Come on. It'll be fun. You won't regret it."

The tingling of her moist lips on his ear, the soothing warmth of her fresh, youthful breath, the arousing sensation of her supple breast brushing across his arm as she leans forward, set his head spinning.

He takes a deep breath, conjuring up every ounce of strength he can muster.

Still whispering in his ear, she says, "You won't regret it, baby."

Nick leans back, trying to create some distance, a DMZ, outside the line of fire, where he's safe to recover his will to stand firm. Quickly, before it's too late, before she closes the gap again, before he loses his resolve, he says, "It's tempting—very tempting—but I think I have to pass."

"You think, or you know you have to pass?"

"I don't know anything for sure right now. You've done a pretty good job of scrambling my brain." He takes a deep breath. "As difficult as it is, I'm going to have to say thank you for your offer—but I'm afraid I have to decline." Nick looks down at his left hand resting on his lap, conscious of the fact that he's nervously twisting his wedding band. Without looking up, he says, mostly to himself, "I've always been faithful to my wife, and I'd like to try and keep it that way."

"Well, I hope you change your mind. Not about being faithful to your wife. I admire that. I mean about spending some time with me. I don't see any conflict there." Her voice carries the suggestion that Nick may be passing up a once-in-a-lifetime experience, and that if he doesn't come to his senses, he has only himself to blame—himself, and his dated notions of marital commitment.

Nick presents her with a determined smile; he appreciates her viewpoint, but he's resolved in his decision.

She steps back. "If you do change your mind, here's my name and phone number." She pulls a pen from her petite Kate Spade purse and writes the information on a bar napkin.

She leans over and kisses him on the cheek, a touch as light as butterfly wings, and then whispers one last time into his ear. "I've enjoyed meeting you. I'd love to get to know you better. Be nice, wouldn't it? I'm *very* discreet. Call me. I'm available ... tonight."

As she turns to leave and starts to work her way back through the crowd, Nick fights hard not to call to her to come back, to tell her he's made a terrible mistake, that he's reconsidered, and that yes, yes, please, he could use some company after all, and that he would, very much like her to come to his hotel room.

He slugs his martini back, throws $10 on the bar, gets up, and heads for the door feeling as horny and irritable as a teenage boy stuck in a classroom helplessly fixated on his relentless and painfully throbbing hard-on, powerless to relieve himself of nature's cruelest and most manipulative of forces. On the way out, he scans the bar area for his temptress, spying the mingling horde of young professionals. She's nowhere to be seen. Disappeared. Poof. Into thin air. Gone as fast and mysteriously as she arrived.

He's less than half relieved that she's vanished—much less.

Reluctantly, he shuffles out of the bar and wanders back to his hotel.

# Chapter 4

Nick Steele drags his body through the doorway of his nondescript downtown Denver hotel room, none too happy to have returned.

He scans the empty room. With the exception of the partial view of the majestic, distant Rockies, it's more or less the same as the last seven rooms he's stayed in; comfortably sterile. Today it's a Courtyard by Marriott. Yesterday it was a Holiday Inn Express. The day before that, it was a Hilton Garden Inn. Nothing's wrong with any of them, especially for one-night stays. They're just not home. More upscale hotels are within his budget, but it irks him to spend money needlessly, especially on something as straightforward as a decent night's sleep; he's still, and always will be, a product of his modest upbringing. Unfortunately, tonight, a decent night's sleep will not be easy to come by.

He unpacks the carry-on luggage bag he had dropped on the floor when he arrived that morning before running out to survey Rohr's building sites. In the narrow closet, adjacent to the bathroom, already congested with an ironing board, electric iron, and small safe unlikely ever to have seen use, he hangs his two lightweight summer suits, one tan, one navy blue, and three white, button-down dress shirts. He lays out his toiletries next to the bathroom sink: a toothbrush with worn bristles that his family hygienist would insist he replace; a two-ounce tube of regular toothpaste, small enough to pass though airport security without triggering suspicion; a razor with a dulled, four-mornings-old blade; a black hair-brush for smartening-up his full, neatly cut, wavy, brown hair; and a stick of roll-on deodorant to protect against his natural propensity to perspire. He doesn't pack shaving cream, preferring to lather with whatever soap is available in his room. Just one less thing to carry.

He turns on the faucet, waits till it runs cold, throws some water on his face, towels himself, and looks in the mirror, barely recognizing the stranger staring back. The bags under his eyes weren't there before he'd left home. And his face is gaunt, drawn, losing definition. He wonders, does he really look that old? Or is it just one of those "bad mirrors" making him look worse than he actually does? After years of travel, he's learned that some hotels have mirrors that make you look good, and some have mirrors that make you look bad. This is the kind that makes him look bad. *Wonderful.*

Looking for something to occupy his mind, anything, to take his mind off of *her* and the ache he still feels in his groin, he decides to boot up his computer and exchange day-old e-mails with colleagues and clients around the country. After that, he tackles a few budget planning documents he's been putting off for weeks. He has a hard time concentrating on any of it.

An hour passes. Next, he uncharacteristically lies on the bed, turns on the TV, and channel-surfs, completing six full rotations of seventy-nine channels in a matter of minutes, repeatedly searching for something, anything, to catch his interest. He flicks through what seems to be an endless array of crime shows—a novelist who solves crimes, a mentalist who solves crimes, a mathematical genius who solves crimes, a grandmother who solves crimes—twenty-four-hour news programs, testosterone-fueled sports commentators screaming into the camera, and reruns of old game shows that have been around since time began. Nothing of interest. It dawns on him why he barely ever watches TV.

Abandoning the TV, he leafs through the latest Jack Higgins novel he bought on the run at the airport a few days ago. It's not grabbing hold. Besides, he's tired of reading, having already devoured *The New York Times, The Wall Street Journal,* and two real-estate development trade publications on the plane ride from Dallas early this morning. On the bed, lying on his back, he peers around the disinfected, lifeless room and ponders what to do next. He feels a long way from home for what feels like way too long. He's bored and lonely—and horny. Not a good thing. His mind drifts.

Suddenly a thought, an impulse, enters his head out of nowhere. It's a mental intruder, unexpected and unwelcome. At first he dismisses it easily. But it comes back. He dismisses it again. Quickly, stealthily, it sneaks back. Over and over, again and again, his mind spars with itself as he tries to chase it away, to banish the thought forever. But it's strong and unrelenting and getting stronger with each successive return. Ultimately, after a few minutes, his defenses are beaten back, and he succumbs. He does something he's never done before.

He gets up, sits at the desk, opens his computer, goes online, and types in the URL www.craigslist.com. When the landing page comes up, he navigates his way to *Colorado*, then *Denver*, then *Adult Services*, and clicks W4M.

His closest friend since childhood—who lives no more than three miles away from his home—the one friend he speaks to and e-mails multiple times a week, Daniel, introduced him to the adult pages on Craigslist. It's where Daniel told him he goes to find women, to pay for sex, between failed relationships, ever since he stopped being attractive to women five years ago. That was when his wife of twelve years left him. He'd arrived home from work to find a note on the kitchen table. All it said was, "Gone to try and find happiness again. I won't be back." Since then most of his hair has disappeared, he's put on twenty-five pounds (half of it in his jowls), he bypasses basic hygiene, and he dresses like someone who simply doesn't care any more.

When Daniel told him about the adult pages on Craigslist, Nick never expected to visit the site himself. It was amusing when Daniel showed it to him. They laughed about it. They laughed at how easy it was to buy sex now, how above-ground this underground industry had become. They laughed at the bizarre postings, the sometimes blatant, sometimes thinly coded sex-trade language, the poor spelling and grammar, the ridiculously revealing pictures of women merchandising their body parts. They laughed, and then he forgot about it.

That had been a year ago. Now here he is, looking for something more than a good laugh.

No harm done in just looking, he reckons. He scrolls down the open page containing multiple listings of women and services for sale, finding himself immediately and unexpectedly aroused by what he sees and reads.

### Dominatrix—w4m—23
*Have you been bad? Well then I'll have to discipline you so you'll learn obidience. Or have you been good? Then I'll have to reward you, Service, Pamper, and Worship Me Mistress Adrianna, long dark hair to my waist, green mystereous eyes,5"7,120lbs Bondage,Dressup,R oleplay,cbt,h2ohumiliation,Fetish's nice&nasty,ect... AVAILABLE 24/7*

Whoa! He thinks not. Way out of his comfort zone.

### What Is Your FETISH ? w4m—26
*I offer all forms of fetish. Pain, torture, toys and other masochistic delights.*

He shakes his head in disbelief; hard to imagine anyone paying for pain.

Then one posting in particular grabs his attention.

### Discerning woman for a Discerning Gentlemen w4m— 25

> *My name is Jenna. I am an ideal companion for the most refined gentleman looking for the ultimate GFE. I offer upscale companionship. Giving you the best moment that you have ever dreamed of is my goal. But most important there is no rush here. I truly love my job and if I may say so, "I'm good at it"! Call Jenna for $225 for one whole hour (754-643-8769). Although I prefer older men if you are sweet age doesn't matte. OUTCALL ONLY NO EMAILS WANTED CALLS ONLY*

There is a picture of a scantily clad, petite, Asian woman, mid-twenties, looking trim and sweet with long black hair, streaked with blond highlights. Her skin is soft, lily white and unblemished. She looks shy but inviting. Her face is intentionally blurred, although he can see her bone structure well enough to guess she's pretty.

The picture immediately reminds him of the woman in the bar. Despite all his efforts, he can't get her out of his head.

He eases back in the faux Aron swivel chair and gazes at the ceiling, exploring, assessing, and contemplating his intentions. Nick has never been with a prostitute before, nor has he ever been unfaithful during his sixteen years of marriage. Of course, he's had impulses and opportunities, many, but he's always found the strength to deflect them, mostly because of a good marriage and respect for the institution. It's an old-fashioned notion, yet still an important one, at least to him.

So it's not clear to him why—right here, right now—sitting in this hotel room, just one of many over numerous years of travel, his fortitude is waning, why he's moving along an uncharted course over which he seems to have little control. Is it simply boredom? Is boredom powerful enough to make a cheater out of an otherwise honest husband? Is it loneliness? Is it the need to share his bittersweet victory today with someone—anyone?

His chest begins to pound. His pulse quickens. He leans forward and stares into the computer, at the photo, sensual and alluring. And he thinks of *her*. The woman in the bar. His loins stir, a desirous ache. He takes a deep breath. Then another. *Are you really going to do this?*

His hands make the decision for him. He reaches into his shirt pocket and pulls out the napkin with her name and phone number scribbled on it. He grabs his cell phone from his trouser pocket and taps out the number fast, no turning back. He holds the phone up to his ear and listens to five piercing rings. No answer. He pauses and then tries again. Seven rings this time. Still, no answer. He ends the call. His body deflates, relieved to have saved himself from himself. But also disappointed.

Over the next ten minutes, Nick tries to put it out of his mind. He tries to reason with himself: it's better this way. Better that he never got through to her. Better that his usually contained impulse was held in check. Better that—better, but ... He shakes his head, knowing full well that he's already crossed a line. He'd lost the battle with himself earlier, as soon as he made that call.

He picks up the cell phone and taps in the number again. After the second ring, a woman answers. "Hello."

He feels uncharacteristically clumsy and unsure. "Hi, it's Nick. We met at the bar ... at Mocean Restaurant about an hour ago?"

"Yes ... Nick," she says, sounding like the cat who caught the mouse. "I'm glad you called."

"I think I changed my mind."

"You think, or you know?" she says.

He pauses. "I know."

"Good. Where are you?"

Nick looks down at the phone on the desk, needing to remind himself what hotel he's in. "The Courtyard by Marriott. Downtown," he answers.

"Good. I'll be there in forty-five minutes."

"Great."

"Nick, my rate is four hundred fifty dollars for an hour."

He has no clue as to the fair market value for this type of thing. He senses it's more than he should be paying. But as he imagines lying next to her naked body, a surge of desire removes concern for expense from the equation. All powers of reasoning are now severely compromised. He responds to her question. "Yeah—yeah, that's fine."

All business, she asks, "How much is it going to cost you, then?"

Confused by the question and a bit taken aback, Nick hesitates before answering. "You just said."

"I know, but I need to hear you say it."

"You need to hear me say it?"

"Uh huh."

"Ah … let me see. That's four hundred and fifty dollars. Right?"

"Good." She brushes right past the sarcasm in his voice. "Now what's your cell phone number?"

"331-555-6478."

"The hotel phone number?"

"Mmmm, hold on a second. Let's see. Here it is—303-462-9299. I'm in room four fifty-seven."

"Now, what's my name?"

Nick looks at the napkin. "Mina, right?"

"It's pronounced Meena."

"Sorry. Meena." He pronounces it slowly and clearly, with extra emphasis on the eeee.

Silence on the other end of the phone. "It doesn't matter," she says.

"Just trying to lighten things up," he quips: "Meena, Mina, Major."

"Was that a joke?" she asks without emotion.

"Ah … yeah. Not a very good one. Sorry." He's trying to be nice, hoping for a connection, for some spark of intimacy and warmth, like he felt at the bar. This is hard work.

"Okay, I'll see you in a while," she says.

Nick presses the end button on his cell phone and thinks about their tryst at the bar, hoping it'll make him feel better about her than the phone call just did. He hadn't expected to pay so much but got caught up in the conversation, committing to spend more than he really wanted or felt was reasonable. Her voice didn't sound like the same person at the bar. There she had a softness, sensuality, submissiveness. Just now, Mina's voice was all business, lacking warmth, tenderness, delicacy. Still, he figures her businesslike manner will disappear once she's in the room with him. She's just protecting herself over the phone, he reasons, just playing it cool. He picks up his wallet from inside his suit jacket, grabs his room keycard, and heads out to find a cash machine to withdraw $500 from his checking account.

He's nervous and excited about his visitor. Adrenaline surges through his middle-aged body, creating energy and excitement. Will she be as sweet and generous as he hopes?

After retrieving his money from an ATM in the hotel lobby, he heads back to his room and waits. And waits. An hour passes. Nobody. No word. Growing impatient, Nick calls Mina's phone number. After just one ring, someone answers. A man's voice this time.

Nick tries to sound calm, unhurried, relaxed: "Is Mina there?"

A cold, harsh Russian baritone voice snaps back. "No, what you want?"

"We had an … appointment. I was just wondering where she is."

"I'm her friend. She on her way. I just speak to her." With admonition: "You be more patient."

"Whoa. Take it easy. I just wanted to know whether she was still coming, since it's been over an hour and she said she'd be here in forty-five minutes."

"She be there."

"Okay."

"Okay."

The connection goes dead.

Nick falls back onto his bed, wondering what he's gotten himself into. Who the hell was that? A friend? A pimp? The whole thing begins to feel like a bad idea. Doubt and guilt enter his mind and challenge his resolve. But a part of him remains committed, having come this far. Ultimately, after much internal debate, he decides to wait it out.

An hour and a half after having first spoken on the phone, Nick hears a faint, barely audible knock at his door. He jumps from his bed, approaches the door, and peers through the spy hole. Mina. At last.

He opens the door and is pleased to see she's as beautiful as he had remembered. She's changed her outfit, now in a simple white halter-top and tight-fitting jeans. She smiles perfunctorily, barely meeting his eyes, and then walks briskly, purposefully, into his hotel room.

Trying to sound concerned and caring, wanting a personal connection, Nick says, "Wow, that took a long time. Everything okay?"

"Fine. Do you have the money?"

Nick pulls $460 from his pocket, all of it in twenties. He hands her the cash, detecting a subtle smirk on her face. She counts it carefully, methodically, like a bank teller, two times, just to be sure.

As she's counting it the second time, he says, "There's ten dollars extra in there. Keep the change."

She doesn't respond. When she's finished counting, she announces, "I'd like to use your phone to call my friend and let him know I'm here. Can I do that?" It's more a command than a question. She's all business.

"Sure." Nick is hesitant but agrees to her request.

She steps to the hotel phone by the side of the bed, lifts the receiver, and punches in the number. Waiting for the connection, she tangles the phone cord around her right index finger, looking like a nervous teenager calling home past curfew. "Hi, I'm here. Okay. Hold on." She turns and speaks to Nick. "Can I use your bathroom for a minute? I'm going to leave the phone off the hook." Without waiting for a response, she places the receiver down and walks into the bathroom, closing the door behind her. After no more than a minute she returns, paying no attention to Nick. Strange. No sound of a flushing toilet. No sound of running water. No freshly applied make-up or perfume. What is she up to? Mina returns to the phone and picks up the receiver. "Hi. I'm back. Uh huh." Expressionless, she turns to Nick and asks, "Can I see your driver's license?"

Uncertain, he walks to the closet, pulls his wallet from the inside breast pocket of his jacket, removes his driver's license, walks back toward her, and hands it over.

She looks down at his license and starts reading from it over the phone. "Nick Steele, seven sixty-four Sunflower Lane …"

Nick reaches out and grabs his license, trying to wrest it from her.

She sneers at him with empty, black holes for eyes before releasing the license from her fingertips.

"Nick, I need to give my friend your license details for my own safety. I don't know who you are. You could be a killer. A rapist. You could be mentally unbalanced."

"Well, I'm not. And you have no right to share my personal information with anyone. Besides, I have no idea who that is on the other end of the phone."

Mina looks defiant. "Oh, I have a right. I have a right to my safety. And until I confirm who you are, I can't know I'm safe."

Nick tries to calm her. "Do I look like someone who's dangerous? Come on. I'm a decent guy. I'm just looking for some company. Christ, it was your idea. You seem like a woman who knows her way around. Trust your judgment."

"I don't know you. You could be anyone. Have you ever walked into a stranger's hotel bedroom?"

"No, and I don't intend to." Nick collects his thoughts, trying to make sense of the increasingly difficult and unpleasant encounter. "Look, I think you better leave. I'm sorry this didn't work out."

A long, uncomfortable silence hangs between them before Mina surrenders. "Okay, okay, take it easy. I'll let it go. I have your cell phone number, anyway." She says good-bye to her "friend" on the other end of the phone and hangs up. She sits in the armchair by the window, still looking distant and calculating, as if plotting her next move.

Nick notes a change in her expression. A light switches on in her eyes. She relaxes her face. Her lips pull back, and for the first time she smiles. She's being Miss Sweetness now. A new, improved Mina. The girl he remembers from the bar.

"Okay, Nick. Let's start again. Tell me what you're looking for tonight."

He looks at her in disbelief, barely able to process her mood shift. He knows she's play-acting, a spoiled child trying to get her way, but at least she's making an effort to be civil. *Okay,* he thinks, *maybe this can work out. Maybe we can get this back on track.* He eyes her tight, shapely young figure, her pretty, unblemished, smooth skin. She's finally here. She has his money. And she *is* unpredictable—a little dangerous. He doesn't want to cause trouble. He decides to get back in the game.

"Okay. You can stay. But let's try to be nice to each other. Okay?"

"Okay, Nick. So what are you looking for?"

"What do you mean, what am I looking for? You know. Otherwise you wouldn't be here."

"No, I don't know. Why don't you tell me what you like?"

"Why do I need to tell you? You asked me to call you. I did. Here we are. It's pretty clear what we're here for, isn't it?" Nick is working hard to keep the conversation light, to keep it from returning to its previous unpleasant tone.

"You need to tell me what you want."

"Look, I'm a pretty simple guy. I don't need anything fancy. Why do you keep asking me this?"

"You know, some guys like different things. I need to know what you like." She is unrelenting.

Nick sits across from her on an adjacent upholstered chair, within arm's reach. His frustration is mounting. He moves back to the side of the bed, further away from her. He needs to create some distance to think clearly. She is seriously starting to piss him off. How can he have sex with her? With someone he's starting to detest?

He takes a deep breath. Calmly, in measured tones, he says to Mina: "Look, this isn't working. This whole thing has gotten off on the wrong foot. I don't feel good about it. I don't know you, and we're already fighting."

"Nick, you sound hostile. I'm sensing a real anger and hostility coming from you."

Nick is stunned. "Hostile? What are you talking about?"

He gets up and returns to the matching chair next to her, closing the distance between them. He's bothered, upset at how unpleasant the whole situation has become. He leans over to her and says in as genuine and friendly a tone as he can muster, "Mina, Meena, or whatever your name is, you can keep a hundred dollars for coming here. But I think it's best if you leave now. Please give me back the rest of the money. And go."

Without hesitation, she says, "No, no, no. It's okay. Listen, some guys just like to do it different ways. I want to be aware of that. I want to be able to give you what you want."

Nick moves back to the side of the bed and puts his head in his hands. He wishes she would stop teasing him. He wishes he would stop being so weak.

"Come on, Nick. It's okay." Her voice is a siren's beckoning.

He looks up at her. She's smiling. Nick knows it's false. But still … God, she looks inviting.

He begins to cave again, his carnal drive overriding his better judgment. He's losing the fight, mostly with himself, and he doesn't like it, not one bit. Finally, he offers her this: "Okay, let me spell it out. I want to make love to you. Have sex with you. It's as simple as that. Nothing kinky, just good, old-fashioned man/woman sex."

"Good, Nick, very good. But," she addresses him as a fond but disappointed teacher might her star student, knowing he's capable of so much more, "I know you can do better than that. A big, strong, handsome man like you? You must harbor secret desires that your wife or girlfriend doesn't know about. Something a bit out of the ordinary. Every man does. Come on, use your imagination." She lowers her eyes, moistens her lips, and lifts her chest, seducing him to dig deeper into his hidden treasure of desire.

Nick chortles in disbelief, astounded by her persistence, wary of her motives, yet still shamelessly desirous. "What do you want me to say?" He decides to play along, hoping it'll help bring their conversation to an end and allow him to get on with the business at hand. "Okay, let me give it a try. Maybe this will make you happy." He looks down at the floor, gathering his thoughts; then he looks up.

"I want you to take off your clothes, wrap my belt around your neck like a dog collar, get down on all fours, crawl into the bathroom, and lap water out of the toilet. Then come back in here and hump the side of the bed until you come." Nick looks to see if this is more to her liking, wondering where in the world he conjured *that* from. "Is this what you were looking for?" he asks in a mocking tone. She smiles, the Cheshire Cat, and nods back. "Well, I'm sorry, but that's not what I'm into. Like I said, just good old fashioned man/woman sex is about all I'm good for. Still interested?" asks Nick.

Her expression hardens again. All the false sweetness is gone. Her eyes narrow and level squarely on Nick as she stands over him. She says flatly, "I'm going to call my friend again."

"What? You must be joking."

"He needs to know I'm okay, Nick. And I'm going to tell him you were getting hostile with me, okay?"

For the first time, Nick senses something is seriously wrong. Feeling helpless, he has half a mind to confront her physically. Instead he sits on the side of the bed and waits for her to make the next move, still not certain where this going.

As if she owns the place, Mina picks up the phone and calls her friend.

"Hi … Yeah. Well, I'm here with Nick and he's just asked me to have sex with him. He said that he wants to make love to me. He said some pretty disgusting things, too, like he wants me to act like a dog and drink out of the toilet bowl."

Nick rises from the bed and squares off in front of her, raising his voice in anger and disbelief. "I was fucking joking!"

Mina admonishes Nick with a steely look, then hands the phone to him and says, "Nick, my friend would like to talk with you."

He stares at her, wondering where this is all going. *Nowhere good, that's for sure.* Slowly he lifts the receiver to his ear as if it might scorch him if it gets too close. "Yeah?"

Like a prosecutor reading out the charges against a defendant—firm, fast, without emotion—the voice on the other end of the phone says, "Nick, you solicited Mina for prostitution. In Colorado this is serious crime. I record all Mina's phone calls to me. And she wearing a digital recorder. Everything you said evidence can be used against you."

Nick looks down at Mina's left jeans pocket. Her eyes guide him. He sees the silver metal head of a digital recorder. He recognizes it as the very same model he uses sometimes to record meetings. He slams the phone down on the hook.

"This is a fucking scam! I can't believe it."

Nick looks into Mina's empty eyes.

The phone rings. "It's for you," says Mina.

"No, it's not," Nick barks.

She picks up the phone.

"Hi, he's right here." Turning to Nick, she says, "It's for you."

"Nope, we're done with this. Go! Now!"

Unafraid, she says, "But it's Denise."

Denise is his wife.

He reaches for the phone.

He speaks into the receiver and answers guardedly. "Yeah."

It's the man's voice again, the one with the distinctly Russian accent. "Nick, do not hang up on me again. We record everything. All those bad, disgusting things you say to Mina. A police station right across street. Maybe we drop it off for them. You like that?"

Nick hangs up again. He turns to Mina, burning with anger, suppressing every impulse to strike her, to take the recorder from her pocket by force, but knowing this could make matters worse than they already are.

"What do you want?"

"I already got it."

"Give me that recorder!"

"Stand back, Nick."

"Give me that—now!" Nick takes one step closer.

"Back off," says Mina. She then reaches into her right pants pocket, pulls out a small canister of Mace, and fires pepper spray into Nick's face.

He buckles over, palming his eyes with his hands, trying to rub away the burning, toxic chemical.

Mina steps around him and heads for the door, as if he were a lamppost on the side of the street. Still on her own time.

"Don't follow me," she says. "And don't try anything funny. My friend will be calling you back to make sure you stay here."

She opens the door and exits as effortlessly as she entered, with his money and his pride.

Half-blinded, Nick feels his way into the bathroom, reaches for the sink faucet, throttles it on, and splashes cold water on his face and eyes. The burning in his eyes is excruciating. A hurricane of anger and confusion storms through his head.

Through the running water, he hears the distant ringing of the phone in the bedroom. It's Mina's friend—Meeeena's friend. The phone is poison. Each ring an insult, stinging, poking, spitting. He has no intention of answering it.

He wipes his face with a towel and despite the intense pain in his eyes, bolts from the hotel room, heads down the hall, and turns into the hotel stairwell, leaping downward two steps at a time, with speed, dexterity, and purpose defying his years, the extra weight around his gut, and his limited vision. He's not sure what he's doing. His body is leading him to a place he hasn't yet conceived. All that's certain is that he needs to get that recorder.

He enters the lobby and scans the blurry room searching for a familiar face, blinking and rubbing his watering eyes to help improve his eyesight. She's nowhere to be seen.

Without stopping, he heads out the sliding hotel entrance door and surveys the street. Still no sight of her.

A shiny new, black Mercedes sedan approaches. It's moving slowly, in no apparent hurry. He makes out the profile of a very large man at the wheel. He squints into the passenger window as it glides past, just feet away.

It's her. She turns directly toward him—relaxed, smug. She presents a grin that taunts him, skewers him. She waves, then blows him a kiss, as if saying good-bye at the airport before boarding the plane to a destination known only to herself.

As the car passes, he notes the license plate. He concentrates hard on the numbers, squinting his eyes to sharpen his vision: 5 … 7 … 6 … N … T … V. 5 … 7 … 6 … N … T … V. 5-7-6-N-T-V. He utters each character on the plate aloud over and over, etching it permanently into his head. The car is registered in Colorado. He doesn't know yet what he's going to do with this information. But it's something—something to work with. Maybe.

The car heads down the street and into the distance. His eyes remain fixed on it until it disappears from sight, his mind stuck on the recorder. He keeps thinking about it: how she recorded everything, every insipid, lurid, incriminating thing he said. Self-loathing consumes him. The conversation in the hotel room reverses and fast forwards through his head, over and over. *My God!*

His mind races. What was she going to do with it, the recording? Throw it away, along with all of the other recordings of her hapless victims? Blackmail him for more money? Send it to the police? Or would she send it to his wife? And who was the man she was with?

He remembers back to the hotel room conversation earlier: "It's Denise," Mina said, pointing to the phone with that smarmy, self-satisfied smirk. That cut deep. She has his cell phone number, his wife's name, and who knows what else. She's definitely a pro—cool, methodical, experienced. She and her male companion had controlled everything, from the meeting in the restaurant bar to the hotel room encounter to leaving him standing hopelessly at the front of the hotel, red-faced, half-blind, feeling like a pathetic fool.

A cold shudder runs down his spine. Not good. Not good at all.

Disgusted with himself, yet unable to decide, if anything, what to do next—at least for the time being—he heads back into the hotel and up to his room to tend to his wounds, and his shame, which at the moment stings far worse.

# Chapter 5

Back in his room, Nick collapses onto his bed.

It's beyond his understanding how he could have put everything at risk—how he could have been *so* stupid as to jeopardize all that he cared about, all that he's worked so hard to achieve. His marriage, his family ... his career.

His mind is a fog. Worried thoughts swirl about his head like a typhoon.

He had always been so careful and diligent about making the right decisions.

Now this happens, an uncharacteristic mindless lapse in judgment—at the worst possible time.

His mind drifts.

He remembers himself as an eighteen-year-old, proudly attending Northwestern on an academic scholarship with plans for studying law. It came to an end early in the second term of his freshman year, after his father died of a heart attack. Nick had felt a duty to provide for his mother and two younger sisters, who were left with a meager pension due to forced labor concessions at the factory over the years. Despite strong objections from his mother, he had known what he needed to do. Nick had left school and gone to work for his Uncle Leo, his father's younger brother, who had a small commercial real estate firm in Chicago. After a few years, motivated by a devoted desire to provide for his family, he was playing a key role in making the small firm a minor success.

When his Uncle Leo died of lung cancer, Nick was just twenty-three. He took over the small firm and after just eight years had built it to a decent size and reputation. He was proud of that.

The Rohr Corporation had bought the firm. Johann had made no secret of the fact that, more than Nick's company, he was looking to acquire a potential successor for himself. That suited Nick just fine. He was ready for a new challenge, something bigger. Johann confided openly to Nick that his two children had never showed the slightest hint of interest or willingness to participate in the family business. Nor, he freely admitted, were they capable. It was an enormous disappointment to him. He told Nick that his own father, the tough, contentious, but fair-minded founder of Rohr, would have reprimanded him, were he still alive, having always invoked the first generation immigrants' credo that the only people you can truly trust in business are family.

Eva, Johann's eldest, an abstract painter living in a luxury Manhattan apartment in Sutton Place, spends most of her time entertaining arty friends late into the night and sleeping most of the day. Her artwork, consisting largely of explosive, thick splats of colorful oil paint thrown on to large canvasses studded with bottle caps in the shape of spiders, rarely finds buyers, with the occasional exception of a few close friends and her beneficent father.

His son, Johann Jr., a bit-part TV actor still waiting for his big break (perhaps due in part to his well-known penchant for free-basing and young boys), lives in an oceanfront Spanish hacienda on Malibu Beach. Nick recently paid him a visit, at Johann's request, to review the status of his company stock holdings. It's quite a pad, replete with an in-home movie theatre; an attached cabana for Barry, his nineteen-year-old full time "personal assistant"; a custom-designed gourmet kitchen that appears never to have seen a pot of boiling water; a heart-shaped, saltwater swimming pool with an adjacent sunken Jacuzzi; and conceptual artworks from the so-called Young British Artists, including an early study of a dead shark submerged in a glass case of formaldehyde by Damian Hirst, prominently displayed in the living room overlooking the Pacific. "Bought it for practically nothing. Probably worth ten million dollars today," Johann Jr. had said smugly.

Thanks to a generous trust fund set up by their grandfather, which Nick knows he will be the executor of when Johann passes away, neither Eva nor Johann Jr. need ever worry about money or obtaining real work. Nick has never begrudged them this advantage. However, to his thinking, the old adage about third-generation wealth applies: "I was a soldier, so my children could be merchants, and their children could be artists." Nick doubts that whoever wrote that was thinking of "artists" in the sense of "idle dilettantes."

While always demanding high performance and ethical standards at work, from day one, Johann had welcomed Nick into his personal life. They enjoy a bi-weekly dinner together, Tuesday nights, just the two of them, hashing out business problems and on occasion, discussing personal matters. Their families often get together for Sunday lunch, devouring bratwurst, *Wiener schnitzel*, strudel, and pints of German beer, in the Rohr family tradition, proudly maintained and honored from the old country. After lunch, Johann often performs opera pieces on his baby grand piano, accompanied by his wife of fifty years, Sabina, an amateur mezzo-soprano who sang in her youth with the LA Civic Light Opera. Everyone is held spellbound as they perform the likes of Mozart's *Marriage of Figaro*, Rossini's *Barber of Seville,* and Johann's favorite, Wagner's *Siegfried*, especially Nick's two daughters who, sitting cross-legged on the living room floor, backs upright, peaceful Buddha-like smiles on their faces, appear transfixed. Nick likes to think that the music is transporting them, if only briefly, to a sublime place, far beyond the confines of their everyday lives, expanding their minds, their horizons, and their dreams. He thanks Johann for that gift.

Over the past ten years, Nick has worked side by side with Johann, serving as his right-hand man and ultimately the company president, overseeing all key investment, management, construction, and sales decisions. During this period, company revenues tripled. Johann openly credits Nick with this success. Although he deflects this praise and is quick to commend "the team," Nick knows that his contributions have been significant and that he's put everything he has into it.

Nick ponders how well he's been rewarded for his success and unwavering loyalty at Rohr. He enjoys a handsome salary, an annual performance bonus, contributions to a retirement plan, and company stock options. Right now, he already has enough money to retire on. But has no intention of playing golf every day; he enjoys work too much for that, and he loves Rohr.

What's more, since the day Nick started work at Rohr, his ambition has always been to become its chief executive. Nick has looked forward to this day for a long time. Taking the helm of this great company, where he has played a central role in building its size and stature, is now within his grasp. Beyond his family, it represents the pinnacle of his life's ambition.

And now this. This mess.

What to do?

For now, he can only hope that tape never resurfaces.

*Ever.*

# Chapter 6

## FRIDAY NIGHT

Driving home from the airport, Nick's car steers its way through the quiet, uncongested back roads of Oakwood, a wealthy suburb of Chicago, his hometown. It's 7:45 PM. He turns off the air conditioner, opens the car window, and inhales the organic scent of dry, freshly mown grass. Further on, he passes the entrance of Glencoe, the town's premier country club, where he enjoys a round of golf on many a summer weekend. He catches sight of the eighteenth fairway, running alongside the road, immaculately groomed—a velvety, plush carpet of green, awash in wide splashes of orange-red sunlight.

Heading into the center of town, Nick passes the train station, where he sees commuters stumble off the latest arrival, dashing for their parked cars or into the embrace of loved ones. Soldiers returning from the corporate wars.

He turns down the main street—quaintly named Main Street—home to expensive and fashionable clothing shops, upscale jewelry stores, over-priced restaurants, and the ever-present Starbucks. He sees no poverty, no high school dropouts, no teenage pregnancies, no homelessness, no murder. The only blight on this otherwise safe and protected enclave from the harsher realities of the outside world is teenage drinking. Based on the number of underage drinking infractions Nick reads about in the local paper each week, this appears to be a favorite pastime of the town's youth and a favorite collar of the town's cops.

As Nick leaves the center of town, dusk is beginning to darken the elm and oak trees overhanging the narrow, winding streets. The trees cast broad shadows on row upon row of wealthy homes: stately white colonials with immaculately landscaped gardens and grounds, owned by bankers and lawyers and corporate executives. Nick has been in many of these homes, invited to cocktail and dinner parties, where acquaintances come together and exchange pleasantries, often around the one uncontroversial subject they all share in common—their children: their trials and tribulations on the sporting fields, their teachers at school, their artistic passions and talents, their special skills, their challenges applying to elite colleges, their summer resume-building trips to Honduras or Guatemala or some other far away netherworld to help build lodging for the less fortunate, and of course, the difficulties of keeping them out of trouble, especially from drinking, lest they show up on the police blotter and tarnish the well-polished images their parents work so very hard to protect. While the conversation is always friendly, it's hard for Nick not to notice the latent competition between parents, who have a natural propensity to measure (sometimes ungenerously) other people's children against their own, though they disguise this well. He considers himself no exception.

Finally, Nick turns onto his street, Sunflower Lane, a small, tree-lined cul-de-sac. He parks his pre-owned Audi in the driveway of his relatively modest—by Oakwood standards—two-story white colonial with black shutters. As he steps out of the car, he takes in, as if for the first time, the lush front yard, the stone walls on both sides of the property, the rope hammock hanging between two old oak trees (ideal for lazy weekend afternoon naps that he never seems to find the time for), and the verdant flowerbed his wife tends, ripe, colorful, and aromatic with burgeoning petunias, geraniums, and roses. All this, thankfully, is just as he had left it over a week ago. He notices his daughters' bikes lying at the foot of the garden bed, thrown down as if in a hurry, eager to run into the house and announce some wonderful new incident, event, or revelation in their lives, however minor. They are always in a hurry, brimming over with energy and excitement, with so much life busting forth. He smiles. It's good to be home.

Weary from his long journey, yet energized at the thought of seeing and embracing his loved ones, Nick strides up the front steps, opens the front door, and enters his castle. He drops his bags at his feet in the entrance hall, looks around for signs of life, and calls out. As is his ritual upon returning home after a long business trip, his voice booming, he pretends to be calling for help across a vast, expansive canyon.

"Hello, hello, hello … is anybody out there, there, there … ?"

His wife, Denise, attractive, slender, and fit, looking much younger than her forty-two years, hurries down the stairs and wraps her arms around her husband's neck, planting a kiss on his lips. His two daughters, Charlotte and Sarah, close behind, come racing in from the den where they've been watching TV. They jump into their father's embrace. He knows he's been missed, and thinks *it doesn't get much better than this.*

Denise cradles Nick's face in her hands and draws him close until the tips of their noses are touching. She looks deep into his eyes and says softly, "Welcome home, baby."

Nick smiles without a word and kisses Denise back. "Thanks. It's good to be home." He stretches his arms around his daughters and his wife, his most precious accomplishments. This, more than anything, is what he's most proud of achieving.

After Nick unpacks in his bedroom and changes into more comfortable clothing—a pair of tan khakis and a blue polo shirt—the family gathers for a pleasant, lively dinner together. The girls are full of their lives over the past eight days, jumping from their chairs, arms flailing about, gesturing with enthusiasm, speaking over each other recounting their summer events, soccer team escapades, and social dramas. Listening to their stories, savoring their every word and expression, Nick also takes delight in the welcome-home dinner Denise and the girls prepared for him. His favorite: meatloaf, mashed potatoes and peas. Granny Steele's signature meal, passed along to Denise—her only son's ultimate comfort food.

After dinner, Charlotte and Sarah dutifully clear the dinner table, rinse the dishes, load the dishwasher, wipe clean the kitchen counter, and head up to their bedrooms. They've always been good with household chores and almost never complain. Nick knows that he has his wife to thank for this.

As they head up the stairs, Nick calls out to them: "Study hard, girls." Of course, this is the last thing they're going to do on summer break. Reminding them to study, even during the school year, is unnecessary, since they both are excellent, conscientious students—thanks, once again, to Denise.

"We will, Dad," Charlotte, his eldest, calls back. "After we smoke some pot and finish off our bottle of vodka."

"Save some for me, girls," he says.

Both are in their early teens—Charlotte is fifteen, Sarah, thirteen—and love teasing him this way.

"Sorry, Dad, you'll have to get your own, we're running low," says Sarah.

Nick smiles and turns his attention back toward Denise as the girls scurry upstairs. He pours the remainder of the bottle of Pinot Noir into their wineglasses. He takes pleasure in the simple, sensuous motion of the wine swimming around the sides of each glass, its warm, translucent, red hue like a liquid jewel. He savors the moment. Here, all is well. Here, in his peaceful and comfortable home, surrounded by the people and the things most important to him, all is right in the world. Here, with those he loves most, nothing is amiss.

Nick feels contented and is pleased that they, together, have created a life where the uncertainties of the outside world are kept at bay, where their close family thinks and acts as one. Denise leans toward her husband, places his left hand between hers, and strokes it.

"You glad to be home, darling?"

Enjoying the moment, he looks up from her hands into her radiant blue eyes. Her voice is a reminder of what a thoughtless fool he had been back there—back in Denver. All he sees before him is good and safe and permanent, right here, in the bosom of his family.

"You bet." The words slip from him effortlessly.

She reaches out and grabs his hand. "Nick, I'm so sorry about Johann."

"Me too. It's awful."

"Such a horrible disease."

"It is."

"What's he going to do?"

Nick shakes his head, a shadow across his face. "You know Johann … he'll carry on, I suppose, like he always does."

"Is there any kind of treatment? Anything to even slow it down?"

"Apparently not."

"How much time does he have?"

"He was told around two years, if he's lucky."

"Poor Johann."

Nick nods.

"Is there anything we can do?"

"Not right now. Just keep an even keel. He doesn't want this to affect how people treat him, you know, like he's sick or helpless or something. Most of all, he doesn't want to be treated like someone who's dying. He said to me at dinner last night 'I'm alive until I'm dead. And that's how I expect everyone to treat me.'" Nick smiles out of the corner of his mouth. "Classic Johann," he says, and then shakes his head. "So that's what we need to do."

"He must be relieved to know that you're there to take over the businesses."

Nick hesitates. "Remember, it's not a done deal yet. The board votes on Friday."

"I know, but Johann's pretty used to getting his way."

"We'll see."

"In any event, I'm very proud of you." Denise leans forward and gives him a kiss. "Did I tell you I love you today?"

He lifts his head and points to her adoring eyes. "You've been telling me ever since I got home." He leans over and kisses her back. "Don't ever stop."

They both fall back in their chairs, still gazing into each other's eyes. Nick is contented to be back with the woman he loves, sharing the same room, breathing the same air.

"I feel like I haven't seen you for ages. You didn't forget about us, did you?" asks Denise.

"Never. I thought about you every day, Susan."

Denise gently raps his hand. "So, how was your trip, *Norbert*?"

Nick pauses before answering. "Long, I guess, but good. I got a lot done. But I can't tell you how glad I am to be home. Eight days is too long. I don't want to go away for that long again. It wears on me, physically and mentally. I start to lose perspective. And I miss you and the girls too much."

"We miss you, too. You *do* look a little tired."

"I am. I may just sleep all weekend."

"I'm afraid there are a few manly things that need to get done around here this weekend," she says. "The gutter near the back of the house is leaking. We had a storm a few nights ago, and the water was streaming down the side of the house. And one of the kitchen cabinet doors has come off and needs fixing. Oh, and I got a call from Whitney yesterday—you know, Daniel's latest girlfriend. Boy, he really burns through 'em, doesn't he? Anyway, she's throwing a birthday party for him at his house on Saturday night. I told her I needed to check with you first but that I thought we'd be able to make it. I hope that's okay."

Nick willingly and happily accepts his homebound duties. "Sure, no problem. That all sounds good."

"Oh, by the way, a woman from your office called earlier today. She had an unusual name. I think it was Mina? She left a number. I wrote it down next to the kitchen phone. She was very nice. She even knew my name. Said she'd heard about me from you. Is she a new employee?"

Nick's throat constricts as he searches for a response. "Yeah—yeah, she started … a few weeks ago. Works in the human resources department and—did she say why she was calling?"

"She didn't say. She asked if you could call her back this weekend. I guess it must be pretty important, huh?"

"Can't imagine what it is." His mind is racing.

"Can't you let it go this weekend? I'm sure it can wait till Monday. What could possibly be so important?"

Thoughts careen through his head as he struggles to present a calm demeanor. "I don't know. I'm sure it's no big deal. I'll give her a call back tomorrow. Where did you say the number was?"

"Here, I'll get it for you."

Denise gets up from the kitchen table. She grabs the note by the phone and hands it to Nick. As he reaches for it, she pulls it away from his fingertips and then smiles at him playfully. "What are you going to give me in return?" she asks.

Nick can't hide his irritation. "Hey, come on … just give it to me."

"I don't know. If you're not nice, I may not give it to you at all."

More sternly, he says, "Come on, Denise, stop fooling around."

Denise ups the ante. "Boy, you must want this number pretty badly. Okay, one last time. I'll ask you again, what's it worth to you?"

Nick softens his tone, realizing he's overreacting. "Come on, Nise." He forces himself to lighten up. "You know, I'll give you whatever you want."

Her eyes light up. "Anything?"

He nods and smiles back at her.

"Well, let me see." She raises her hand to her chin and furrows her brow, imitating the Thinker. "Hmm … there are *so* many possibilities to consider here. I guess you can start by keeping calling me Susan. That's kind of kinky …"

Nick grabs hold of her arms, pulls her onto his lap, and kisses her glistening lips—deeply, passionately.

She emerges from the kiss starry-eyed and breathless, as if gasping for air after a deep underwater dive. "Wow, now you're talking, Mister."

He whispers in her ear. He tells he loves her more than anything in the world, and that if he can't have her right then and there, right on the kitchen table, he's going to go out of his mind.

She smiles and whispers back into his ear. "All this for that silly little phone number?"

He looks deep into her eyes. "What phone number?"

Nick gently lifts Denise and lays her down on the kitchen table. "Don't move."

He then walks to the kitchen door, eases it shut, and slips the shoulder of his chair underneath the doorknob, barricading it from his nocturnally peripatetic progeny.

Aching with desire, he returns to his wife, laying obediently in wait, casting an enticing aura of sublime sensuality. He glides his hands upward along the sides of her long, smooth legs. Once underneath her skirt, he removes her silk panties and senses the erotic release of damp, inviting heat. She puts a finger to her lips, then points to the ceiling and says, "Shhh, the children."

He enters her, and instantly, for both of them, the children disappear.

# Chapter 7

## SATURDAY

Saturday morning. Nick stirs from a sound, restful sleep in the comfort of his own bed. He reaches over to touch his wife and finds an empty space beside him. Thoughts of the night before arouse him, and he finds himself with a throbbing hard-on. He reaches down, grabs hold, and considers satisfying himself. He looks over at the digital clock on the side of his bed to check the time: *9:33*. He is amazed to discover that he slept nine hours. He really *was* tired. Next to the clock he notices a piece of paper. He sits up, leans over, and takes a closer look. It has a phone number written on it: *her* number. His penis wilts. Denise must have put it there when she got up. Payment for services rendered last night.

He holds the paper, staring at the phone number, then places it back on the bedside table, as if ditching a contaminated object. His head, heavy now, giving up all resistance to gravity, descends back into his pillow. He senses the weight of his body as it sinks deep into the mattress, the Posturepedic foam turning to quicksand. He gazes at the ceiling, looking for a lifeline to grab hold of, his pulse quickening.

He looks over at the piece of paper again. Anger begins to assert itself. That phone number has no place here. It's an intruder, as threatening as a thief breaking into his home. He glances over at the family pictures sitting on top of Denise's dresser. He sees a wedding photo of Denise and himself, framed in seashells they gathered from Bermudan beaches on their honeymoon; a photo of his two girls in their soccer outfits taken three years ago, their arms wrapped tightly around each other's shoulder, beaming sisterly smiles; and a photo of his mother and two younger sisters taken shortly after his father passed away, looking particularly vulnerable. Here in his bedroom, his sanctuary, shared with the people he loves most, an intruder has forced entry. Angry and disgusted, he crumbles the paper into a tight ball and pitches it into the corner of the room, hoping it will disappear into a black hole.

A minute later Denise shuffles into the bedroom, still in her knee-length, blue satin nightgown and comfy furry bedroom slippers, a gift from Nick last Christmas. She curls up on the bed next to him and kisses his forehead.

"That was nice last night," she says.

"If I'm going to be welcomed home that way all the time, I ought to go away more often." They cuddle up to each other, content in their silent embrace.

The phone rings, a harsh, unwelcome intrusion into their soft, glowing morning-after mood. Nick contemplates whether to just let it go unanswered. *Damn phone!* After the forth ring, out of frustration, Nick reaches over to the bedside table and picks up the receiver. "Hello," he barks.

"Hello, Nick."

"Who is this?"

"You know who it is, Nick. Why didn't you call me last night?"

Fast, instinctively, Nick responds. "I'm sorry, you have the wrong number."

"Remember this, Nick?" He hears the muted click of an electronic device. "'I want you to take off your clothes, wrap my belt around your neck like a dog collar, get down on all fours, crawl into the bathroom, and lap water out of the toilet ...'"

Shocked, he hangs up the phone. *Idiot! Why didn't I look at the caller ID before I answered?*

"Who was that?" Denise asks.

"Telemarketing call. Can you imagine? On a Saturday morning!"

Denise gives him a what-has-this-world-come-to look, pecks him on the cheek, and smiles. "Need to get the girls some breakfast before they head off to soccer." She rises from bed and heads downstairs.

Nick is beside himself with anger and worry, astounded by this brazen, threatening intrusion. First last night, now this morning. And that recording. What if someone else were to hear that? Denise? His daughters? Johann? The board? *My God.* And why hadn't she called his cell phone? Why the family phone? What is she up to?

He rolls over on his side and curls up in a protective fetal position, like a lab rat being poked and prodded, cowering in the corner of his cage. He lies stunned, lost in a swell of anxious thoughts.

After a minute or two, he decides enough is enough. He throws off the sheets, hurls himself from bed, marches into the bathroom, brushes his teeth, lathers and shaves his day old stubble, and jumps in the shower. He's in hyper-drive, lost in his thoughts, focused on what to do next. One thing he knows for certain: he can't solve this himself. He needs to speak with someone—someone he can trust, someone who can help him think this through, someone who might have had to get himself out of an ... unusual situation like this before.

His best friend, Daniel.

Toweling himself, he wonders what's compelling her to do this to him—to harass him, to taunt him, to jeopardize his very existence. Is it money? Revenge? Hatred? Madness? He peers into the fogged bathroom mirror and wipes his hand across it to clear a small window. Around the fringes, small pearls of water form and slide down the mirror, cutting clean, sharp trails through the moisture.

In the physical world, he half-remembers from his freshman physics course, gravity is the force that presses down on all things; photons are the force that keeps all things from falling apart; quarks are the force that keeps atomic things bound together. And so on and so forth down to the infinitesimal minutiae of sub-atomic particles, which are preyed upon by their own unique set of forces, many yet still unknown. He doesn't understand any of it, not really. But like the physical world, like those drops of water, he reckons, everything has a reason, and forces are at work, sometimes unknown even to ourselves, that motivate all of us. *What's driving her?*

Nick dresses and hurries downstairs, anxious to see his daughters before they head off to soccer practice. In the entrance hall, at the bottom of the stairs, is a small maple side-table where Nick parks his wallet, car keys, and Blackberry when he's home. As he walks by, out of habit, he grabs his smartphone and scans the e-mails that have arrived over the last twelve hours, searching only for those that might be of immediate importance. There are just two. The first is from his mother, always a priority. Nick makes a point of calling her two or three times a week. While financially settled—Nick having seen to this—her health and happiness, more fragile with each passing year, are of growing concern to him, the dutiful eldest child. He opens the message.

*Dear Nicky,*
*I hope you had a good business trip. I can't wait to see you, Denise, and the girls on Sunday night for dinner. Don't bring anything. Why don't you plan on being here by 6:00. Okay?*

*Love, Mom*

*Oops. Forgot about that.* He makes a mental note to tell Denise about the Sunday dinner he'd planned with his mother while on the road last week. Nick hopes she hasn't already made other plans.

The second priority e-mail is from Johann. With an uncomfortable mix of excitement and worry, he opens the electronic message.

*Nick,*
*Board meeting scheduled for Friday. One member asked if you had any skeletons in your closet. I assured him you don't even have a closet. See you Monday in the office at 9:00. Best to Denise.*
*Johann*

Nick feels sick to his stomach. How is it, he wonders, that after so many years of keeping his nose clean he may now actually have a *bona fide* skeleton in his closet? And not just any sack of dry bones, but the kind that destroys trusts and confidences and well planned and orchestrated careers. He needs to make this problem disappear … fast. He can't let Johann down, or Denise, or the girls, or jeopardize the support of the board and all that he's worked so hard to accomplish.

He hears Denise, Charlotte, and Sarah bantering in the kitchen. Their voices are pure and sweet and uncorrupted. He vows to put his … issue … aside, at least for the moment, to tuck it away, keep it as far removed from them as possible. He doesn't want them contaminated by it, ever. He heads into the kitchen to join the simple, unadulterated satisfaction of a Saturday morning family breakfast.

# Chapter 8

"Hey, come on in." It's Saturday evening, and Daniel's latest love interest, Whitney, greets Nick and Denise at the front door of Daniel's home. They've spoken to her on the phone a few times but never met. She's petite, with shaggy, dyed blonde hair, and cute—a lot better looking, Nick decides, than some of Daniel's past girlfriends. Since his divorce five years ago, Daniel has been through a string of women, each of whom Nick has a cold-hearted tendency to think of in terms of makes of cars. Denise begs him not to, but he can't help it.

Much to Nick's chagrin, over the years Daniel has confided in him regularly about his hapless romances, never sparing the intimate details.

First, there was Candice. Candy the Corvette: high-strung, stylish, well-coiffed, and deeply superficial. Daniel told Nick that her weekly news consumption consisted entirely of *People* magazine, *Entertainment Tonight*, and the celebrity gossip site, PerezHilton.com. Her most distinguishing physical characteristic was her blindingly white Crest White Strip smile, parked behind unnaturally large collagen-injected duck lips. She had taken Daniel for a fast drive into the postmodern world of middle-aged, suburban divorcee dating. Nick was convinced that Daniel never knew what hit him. Candy talked fast, walked fast, ate fast, and according to Daniel, fucked fast. She'd caught him off guard after his divorce, his defenses down; he'd barely had time to catch his breath.

Ultimately, she'd left him as suddenly and unexpectedly as she arrived. She told Daniel he lacked spark, was dull, and was getting fat. And why, she asked, didn't he whiten his yellow teeth? Daniel hadn't had an explanation, and he hadn't argued. Mostly, he told Nick, he was relieved to see her go.

Sophie was next—the VW Bug. She had a top-heavy upper body with short, spindly legs, a round, mournful face, and a kind and selfless nature bordering on what Nick felt was a Mother Teresa complex. It seems she had been attracted to Daniel's pain, his loneliness. Her mission was to nurture him back to happiness. She recognized in Daniel a kindred spirit, someone like herself, struggling with the sadness that comes from being deceived by someone you love. One night Sophie had discovered her husband having oral sex with her twin brother. She later learned they'd been having an affair for two years. She was devastated by the betrayal of the two most important men in her life. She claimed to have no idea her husband was gay. No idea her brother was gay. No idea that all the time they spent together in the downstairs den "playing poker" and "watching football" had actually been spent in each other's secret—and to her mind, sordid and repulsive— embrace.

After her divorce, Sophie said she didn't know who to trust. When she met Daniel online, she recognized a fellow sufferer, someone, like herself, unjustly done by. She'd been determined to ease her own pain by easing his. She smothered him with affection. She'd called him four or five times a day at the office and stopped by most nights to cook him dinner, clean his house, and wash his laundry. Daniel never invited her to move in. He told Nick he appreciated her kindness but found her overly attentive. He needed a companion, not a mother. Besides, he hadn't found her particularly attractive.

Eventually, Daniel had grown bored of their relationship and broke it off. Fearful of hurting her, he explained that he wasn't ready for a commitment and that he needed time to be on his own, to "sort things out." Giving, as always, she said she understood, obeyed his wishes, and moved on. Last Daniel heard, she'd moved to northern California and joined a new-age spiritual group called NAP (New Age Planet) that believed they could achieve world peace through collective meditation. Daniel had told Nick he hoped, at the very least, she'd find her own inner peace.

Next came Jackie—Jackie the Hummer. Truth be told, Nick had felt that Jackie might be a man. She had broad, hunched-over shoulders, stocky, muscular legs, a lantern chin, and a deep, husky voice—not the sexy kind. In fact, Nick could find nothing feminine about her. He couldn't imagine what Daniel saw in her. One night he watched her guzzle a full can of beer as if she were at a frat party, followed by a huge, roaring belch. The expression on her face was unmistakable: pure pride. Nick suspected she was a transsexual. Of course, he'd never told Daniel this because he'd seemed so happy with her. Indeed, they seemed so happy together.

The relationship had ended abruptly late one night. A deranged man showed up on Daniel's front porch at 3:00 am, weeping uncontrollably, pounding on the door, and professing his love for Jackie between gasps for air and sloppy, wet snorts and sniffles. When Daniel had opened the front door with Jackie at his side, the crazed man looked into her eyes and pleaded his case. He couldn't take it anymore. He missed her desperately. He couldn't live without her. He'd kill himself if she didn't come back to him.

Daniel was speechless, flabbergasted. Especially when Jackie, now also weeping, informed him that this was Freddie, her boyfriend from before she met Daniel, and that she, too, was still in love with him. She packed her bags and left that night, never to return.

After that, it was a while before Daniel went out with any other women. Indeed, he'd told Nick that after the Jackie fiasco he'd never allow another woman into his life, let alone his home.

So it comes as something of a surprise to Nick when Whitney opens the front door of Daniel's home, flashing a big, bright smile, assuming the role of mistress of the house, graciously welcoming her guests into her—their—home.

"Come in, come in. I'm so glad you could come. Daniel didn't want me to make a fuss about his birthday—forty-six. Wow, can you believe it? But I couldn't resist. He's so adorable. Don't you think? I just had to do something. It's so nice to meet you in the flesh. Come in. Come in."

Nick's not sure what kind of car Whitney is. Not yet, at least. But at the rate she's talking, he posits the possibility of a racy, little Fiat Punto.

Nick catches sight of Daniel at the far end of the living room, excuses himself, and brushes past Whitney to greet him.

Daniel is speaking with Tad Smith about their round of golf earlier that day, each recounting with perfect, almost obsessive detail every drive, fairway iron, chip shot, and putt. Nick overhears what they're talking about as he approaches and inserts himself into the conversation. "How is it that men can barely remember their wedding date, but have no problem recollecting every single shot of eighteen holes of golf?"

Tad looks at Nick with a guilty-as-charged grin. "I think someone once said: 'Golf is like a love affair. If you don't take it seriously, it's no fun.'"

"Yeah, true, but I think there's a second part to that saying: 'If you do take it too seriously, it breaks your heart.'" They all chuckle and nod.

"Serious or not, I just wish I could improve my game. I seem to be stuck. It's frustrating," adds Daniel.

"Don't feel bad, Danny." Tad seems to want to be empathetic, but his tone comes off as more didactic than reassuring. "Did you know that the NBA free throw average has been stuck at seventy-five percent for the last fifty years?"

"No way," responds Daniel.

"It's true. These over-paid pituitary cases spend hours every day practicing free throws but can't improve."

"Maybe they make too much money to really care," says Daniel.

"Nope, it's the same for college ball. They've been stuck at sixty-nine percent since 1965."

"No shit." Daniel shakes and scratches his head.

"Here's another one for you. Since 1980, the NFL's field goal average has been stuck at forty-six percent." Tad grins.

Daniel looks at Nick, pointing his right index finger at Tad. "A fuckin' walkin' talkin' statistician, right here in my house." He turns toward Tad. "Hey, buddy, you're not exactly filling me with hope that I can improve my game."

"Just trying to let you know that you're in good company, Danny, that's all."

"Appreciate the support," says Daniel, giving Tad a friendly grin. "Just promise me you won't try to cheer me up again about my game."

They all chortle.

Nick turns to Daniel. "Danny Boy, what's that you're drinking on this most auspicious occasion?"

"Margarita—and it's the first of many. I'm not going to stop until I forget how old I am."

"Oh, come on. You've still got the stuff. I just met Whitney. Very pretty." Nick raises his glass, toasting Daniel's good taste and good fortune. At the same time he imagines it to be simply a matter of time before she, too, vanishes from his life, just as her predecessors had. "And what is she, all of thirty?"

"Good guess. Twenty-nine. Clearly in need of a father figure."

"Do you have to spank her when she's naughty?" Tad asks.

Daniel gives Tad a don't-start-with-that look. Tad holds up his empty cocktail glass, taps it, and wanders off.

"So how are you, John Henry?" Daniel gave Nick the nickname in high school, a tribute to the legendary strong man, born with a hammer in his hand, who smashed tunnels through mountains. Nick had been a state champion boxer in high school, with a reputation for pummeling his opponents to the mattress. He first learned how to box from his Russian immigrant grandfather, quiet, unassuming, and understated, who insisted it was essential for a man to know how to defend himself.

"Not good, Danno. In fact, I need to talk with you. Tonight. Can we step outside for a few minutes?"

"Now? Sure—sure. Is everything okay?"

Nick waves his hand, indicating that Daniel should follow him outside before they speak.

They navigate their way through the living room, past the sea of partygoers. It takes them about fifteen minutes as they exchange hi-how-are-yous, great-to-see-yous, how've-you-beens, hugs, kisses, and handshakes with numerous friends and acquaintances.

Eventually they find their way into the kitchen, out the back door, and into the small gazebo in the backyard. Daniel's ex-wife had asked him to build it for them a few years before they divorced. She told him it would be romantic to sit there together on warm, star-filled, summer nights. After it was built, she never set foot in it.

"Okay, so what's so important that you drag me away from my own party?" Daniel gets right to the point.

"I've got a problem."

"What kind of problem?"

"I don't know yet. I … I met a woman at a bar while I was traveling last week. In Denver … I invited her to my hotel."

"Was she a working girl?"

"Yeah." Nick scratches his head. "Never done that before. Anyway … when she showed up, the whole thing's a scam. She pockets my money and threatens to call the cops if I raise a stink. She's got a recorder in her pants pocket. She taped the whole thing. When I asked her for it, she shot pepper spray in my eyes. Hurt like hell. And there's a 'friend'"—Nick holds up both hands and forms quotation marks with his index and middle fingers—"she keeps calling to tell him everything we're doing. Some Russian guy. He sounded threatening. It was so fucked up. I handled it poorly." Nick shakes his head.

"Okay, okay. Take it easy," says Daniel. "I'm not entirely sure what you're saying, but it sounds like you got conned. You're not the first guy in the world this has happened to, and you won't be the last. How are your eyes, by the way?"

"Fine. No damage. I can see fine."

"Good. You just lost some money. Right?"

"Not really." Nick straightens his back, broadens his shoulders, sucks in his gut, and looks squarely at Daniel. "There's more to it than that. She called my home last night. She spoke with Denise. Pretended she worked with me. Said she needed to talk to me about some business matter. Then she called again this morning. Thank God I answered the phone. She played a recording of one of the things I said. I said it as a *joke*, for God's sake—I was being sarcastic, pretending to want things I didn't. But it didn't sound that way. I don't want anyone to ever hear that, especially Denise.

"Anyway, I hung up right away. I don't know what this woman wants. But she's after something. And I don't think she's going to stop till she gets it."

Daniel rubs his chin with his knuckles. "Okay. Now I see your problem."

"There's more. Johann is sick. ALS. He just found out. He wants to retire and spend what time he has left with his wife, travel, get his affairs in order. I just found out a new CEO is going to be selected by the board next Friday. I'm one of two contenders."

"Fuckin' A, Nick, that's great news. Congratulations!"

"Yeah, thanks. Problem is, I don't think that Johann or the board would feel particularly good about one of their candidates if they heard that tape."

"Take it easy. Look, in the PR business, we advise our clients to get bad news off the table as quickly as possible; to control the message, not let others control it for them. The sooner the better, and the more complete the better. I know it's hard to imagine, but the best thing may be for you to tell Denise before she hears it from this woman—which, from what you tell me, sounds like a real possibility. She won't like it, that's for sure, but I think she'll eventually forgive you. Maybe not right away, but eventually. After that, you have a man-to-man talk with Johann. I'm sure he'll understand and most likely want to keep it to himself.

"I mean, come on, it was a fairly minor indiscretion in the vast, sordid world of potential infidelities. Nick, you've been a good, loyal husband, who, unlike a lot of guys we know, including yours truly, hasn't fucked around until now—or at least tried to. Of course, I've never fully understood that about you—this antiquated, puritanical notion of marital fidelity—but anyway, you slipped one time. It was one time, for Christ's sake! After how many years of marriage?"

"Sixteen."

"*Sixteen?* Shit. And you didn't even consummate. You're practically the Pope. Tell her flat out, 'I fucked up.' Just admit you were wrong. And stupid. I do it all the time. And beg for her forgiveness. Get it over with and move on. You don't want this thing to linger—or worse, escalate."

"That's true. But—maybe I should talk to this woman first. Call her back. Play along. Find out what she wants. At least as a first step. I'd really rather not tell Denise or Johann. Not until and unless I absolutely have to. Plus this woman is really pissing me off, and I'd hate for her to win."

"Nick, you're not in the boxing ring. There are no rules. And she has the black and white shirt and controls the clock. What you don't want is for Denise to find out about this from her. Who knows how she'll spin it? The fact that she's called you twice at home in the last twenty-four hours is not a good sign. She sounds … determined."

The outside kitchen door opens. A shadow approaches across the freshly mown lawn. "What are you two doing out here?" It's Denise.

Nick gives Denise a mild scolding look.

"I'm just having one," she says. She strikes the match and lights up before Nick has a chance to object further. She turns to Daniel, as if looking for support. "One of my few secret indulgences. Only when I drink." She shrugs.

"Fine by me," Daniel says.

"Right, honey? Only when I drink." She sits on Nick's lap and kisses his forehead, as if sealing the subject from any further discussion.

Nick can't help but smile.

"Well, now that you know why I'm out here, what about you two muggins?"

"Ahh … we're just catching up," says Nick as he puts his right arm around her back and strokes her thigh with his left hand.

Turning to Daniel, Denise says, "Danny, everyone's looking for you. They want you to open some presents."

"Oops, I better be off. It's gag present time. Now I get to pretend how funny it is getting old." Daniel hops up and returns to the party. Nick and Denise hear from a distance the muted, affectionate greetings he receives when he enters the living room. "Danny Boy!" "Dan the Man." "Daniel, where have you been?"

Denise looks into Nick's tired eyes. "You okay?"

"Me? Yeah. Daniel just wanted a bit of fresh air and asked me to join him."

"Sure?"

"Yeah! Why do you ask?"

"Your eyes look a little sad."

"Not possible. I'm never sad when I'm with you."

She kisses him gently and flicks her barely smoked cigarette onto the grass. "Enough of that. Come on, Prince Charming. Don't want to be unsociable." She takes his hand in hers and leads him back into the party.

# Chapter 9

By 10:30 pm the birthday party is in full swing, thanks in large part to the copious quantities of alcohol being consumed. Daniel has opened his joke presents to the delight of his guests, the cake has been served, candles blown out, wishes made, and an enthusiastic though mostly off-key round of "Happy Birthday" has been sung. There is much laughter and merriment.

On one side of the living room, Daniel is enjoying a friendly conversation with Denise. Whitney cuts a path through the bevy of guests, cocktail in hand, expressionless, eyes unblinking and cold. When she reaches Daniel, she drives an iron finger into his shoulder, followed by a firm pincer grip, and pulls him aside. Whitney's face is red and blotchy.

"Why are you flirting with her?" she barks.

"Flirting? With my best friend's wife?"

"I saw you whispering into her ear and touching her arm."

"*What* are you talking about?

"Stop it. I saw you do the same thing earlier with that cheap-looking blonde trying desperately not to look her age." She extends her arm and points a crooked finger at the woman in question across the room. Daniel pulls her arm down.

Her eyes narrow. "Get your hands off me. I know exactly what you're up to, Daniel. How dare you flirt with other women, right in front of me? After what I've done for you tonight—this is my thanks?"

"Whitney, these are good friends; wives of good friends. Give me a break." He takes a deep breath. "It's noisy in here. It's hard for me to hear. So I move closer to people. And they move closer to me. There's nothing illicit about it. It's very common, very natural. Don't be ridiculous," he adds.

"I know what I saw. Your face said it all. I'm not stupid. It's hateful the way you treat me." She looks around the room. "I want everyone to leave. Right away."

Daniel tries to calm her. "Look, babe, there's nothing to be jealous about. There's only one woman in this house that I'm interested in." He bends over to kiss her, but she pulls away.

"Actions speak louder than words. I want everyone to leave."

"Look, Whitney, you're mistaken. It's as simple as that. You've just got it wrong. You're acting like a child. There's no way you're going to chase my friends away. So just stop talking nonsense."

"We'll see about that."

She turns from Daniel and marches into the center of the living room. "Ahem … Excuse me. Excuse me, everyone. I'm afraid I'm going to have to ask you all to leave now." She sounds like an elementary school teacher giving her class a new assignment.

Daniel, standing in the corner of the room, is dumbfounded. A loud cry leaves his larynx. "Whitney, what the hell are you doing?"

"You know what I'm doing, Daniel. If you can't behave yourself—well, then, everyone has to go." Her voice is composed.

"You're absolutely nuts." Daniel turns to his guests. "Everyone, please just ignore her. Please, carry on having a good time." He levels his eyes at Whitney. "You," he says, "come with me upstairs. Now!"

She doesn't respond. Daniel raises his voice. "Upstairs—*now!*"

Whitney's pleased to have his full attention and seems attracted to his forcefulness. She follows him upstairs, looking like a scolded schoolgirl. *Christ, what have I gotten myself into this time,* he thinks.

At the top of the stairs, Daniel struggles to contain his voice to a whisper. Blue veins surface on his forehead, a red rash climbs up the side of his neck. "How could you do this? Why are you behaving so stupidly? You have no right. This is my home. These are my friends."

She throttles back inches from his face, screaming, spraying spittle and invective like snake venom. "You unfaithful low-life." She throws her drink. Glass and liquid smash against the wall, inches from Daniel's head. "You're a fraud. I know your type. I was so stupid not to have seen it earlier— you and your disgusting need to flirt with other women. No wonder your wife left you!"

Downstairs, the guests exchange uncomfortable, pitying looks. A few look horrified.

Nick and Denise, acting as a team, encourage everyone not to leave, trying to convince them—as well as themselves, perhaps— that it's just a temporary domestic squabble that will pass in a few minutes. Daniel wouldn't want them to leave.

Despite their best efforts, the discomfort in the room grows stronger, until two couples decide to leave the party. The ice broken, one after another, everyone else, anxious to distance themselves from the domestic brawl as if escaping a potentially contagious disease, leaves as well.

Noticing the quiet below, Daniel retreats from his battle with Whitney and runs downstairs to apologize to his guests.

Everyone is gone—everyone except Nick and Denise. Daniel looks across the once-lively, vibrant living room, now silent and littered with unattended wine and cocktail glasses, bubbling fondue pots, dipping prongs, plates of bite-sized pieces of bread and meat, and party hats and blowers strewn across the furniture and floor like abandoned orphans. The old-man gag presents he had opened to the delight of his friends seem cruel and mocking, more truth than satire.

"You okay?" Nick asks.

Daniel shrugs and shakes his head. "How fucked up is this?"

Nick nods. "Pretty fucked up."

"Poor Danny." Denise steps forward and gives him a sympathetic hug.

"Look, I'm sorry about this. I had no idea she was"—he searches for the right word—"disturbed. I sure know how to pick 'em, huh?" He looks across the ghostly room again. "What a disaster. How utterly, fucking embarrassing."

"Don't worry. These things happen," says Nick.

"Oh, do they?" Daniel asks. "When was the last time you witnessed something like this?"

Nick pauses. "Okay. Maybe never. You get the gold medal for the most fucked-up birthday party in the history of fucked-up birthday parties."

"Thank you," says Daniel.

As Nick and Denise head to the front door, Nick looks up the staircase and sees Whitney standing at the top, relaxed, looking back down at him as if nothing were unusual. Then Denise, close behind, glances up as well. Whitney's face turns sour, mean, and spiteful. Nick notes the hateful grimace and decides she's no Fiat Punto. In fact, he's not sure if there's any make of car for her. He reconsiders: maybe a Ford Pinto, a car taken off the market due to a history of sudden, violent explosions.

Denise exits the house and walks down the flagged stone path to the driveway, where their car is parked. Before Nick follows her, Daniel reaches over and puts his hands on each of Nick's shoulders, looking him in the eyes. "Thanks for staying. Not sure how I'm going to recover from this one. By the way, about that advice I gave you earlier? Forget it. Clearly, I don't have a clue about women. But you already know that. I'm the one who should be asking you for advice."

Nick gives him a reassuring smile. "We'll talk," he says, and heads to his car.

# Chapter 10

When they get home, Denise drags herself through the doorway and heads straight for the stairs. "I'm going up to bed," she says.

Before she reaches the first step, Nick grabs hold of her right hand. "You okay?"

"I guess so." She shakes her head and looks up into his eyes. "Well—maybe not."

Nick strokes her arm. "Pretty upsetting, wasn't it?"

"Yeah," she says. "It's just so awful to see two people do that to each other, to rip each other apart like that. I don't get it. I guess it all comes down to a lack of trust."

Nick nods.

She continues, "If there isn't mutual trust, what is there? How can a relationship survive? Right?"

Nick hesitates, anxious to steer the conversation away from the uncomfortable subject of the damaging consequences of a couple's eroded trust. "That's true … But on a more practical level, I also think Daniel has to find a way to avoid relationships with messed-up women in the future. A psycho's a psycho, trust or no trust."

Denise chuckles. While she may not exactly agree with his wording, he's probably right.

"She really was something, wasn't she?" she says.

"That's a nice way of putting it."

Denise gives Nick a hug. "Goodnight, my darling. And thanks for asking. I'll be fine." She turns and heads up the stairs.

When she reaches the top of the staircase, Nick aims straight for the kitchen. He grabs a tall glass from the cabinet, pitches a few ice cubes into it, reaches into the liquor cabinet, and pours himself a nightcap. He takes his time, waiting until Denise has settled into bed before checking the voice messages. Five minutes pass. He stands over the answering machine, staring at it, sipping his drink, postponing what he fears is the inevitable. He hasn't heard from Mina on his cell phone all day long.

He savors the golden color and peaty flavor of the single malt scotch, distilled, he imagines, in the barren, remote Highlands, a safe haven to which he would like, at this very moment, to retreat.

Persistently, annoyingly, the digital message display flashes two … two … two … two. He braces himself, inhales deeply, takes one more sip—this one closer to a slug, draining his glass—and presses the play button.

"Hi Nick, it's Mina—Mina from work." Her voice is calm, polite, friendly, that of a helpful co-worker. "Gosh, I'm sorry to bother you at home, especially on a Saturday night, but it's quite urgent we talk. You have my number. Please call." The emphasis she places on the last two words leaves little doubt as to their true meaning: *please call … or else.*

Nick deletes the message, fast, like a TV quiz show contestant racing to beat his opponents to the answer button. If he can delete the message quickly enough, maybe he'll trick himself into believing it never existed. No such luck. There's still another call left on the machine. The number one flashes, an imposing, insistent red warning sign. Nick presses the play button a second time.

The same voice. This time, though, harder, more determined. "Hi, Nick. Me again—Mina. Boy, I really am being a pest, aren't I? But you know I wouldn't be bothering you unless it was really important. Call me."

Nick stares out the window, into the night sky, the half-moon casting ominous, leafy shadows across the backyard lawn, looking for an answer to this madness.

"Wow, what's that all about?"

Nick, startled, turns toward the kitchen entrance where Denise is standing, leaning against the archway. She seems concerned. "I came down for a glass of water and overheard those messages."

Nick raises his hands, his palms facing upwards, and shakes his head in bewilderment. "I wish I knew."

"What could be so important that she calls you twice on a Saturday night?" Denise now seems irritated, but not suspicious; *why would she be?*

"You got me," Nick says, "but I'll find out first thing in the morning. It's too late to call back now."

"Is everything all right at work, Nick?" Denise asks.

"Yeah. Yeah, I'm as baffled by this as you. I'm sure it's nothing." Nick, vamping, tries to piece together a plausible explanation. "She's relatively new to the company, and young, probably just overzealous. You know these twenty, thirty-somethings. They're used to texting, talking on Facebook, and watching TV all at the same time. They're always plugged into something, seeking instant gratification. Nothing can wait. They have one speed, fast, and they're proud of it. They think nothing of e-mailing at two o'clock am, probably jacked up on Red Bull, and expecting an instant response. You know that magazine *Fast Company*? It's not just a magazine for them, it's a religion. Their work and personal lives aren't separate. Not like ours. It all blends together. They think nothing of taking personal calls in the middle of a meeting. I've seen it all too many times. They don't think in terms of work as a Monday to Friday thing, or nine to five, or—" Nick stops, hearing his own voice, realizing he's sounding disingenuous, defensive, rambling on like this. He remembers from a negotiating course a few years ago that people don't lie with their bodies. Everyone knows enough to look you in the eye to appear forthright, and to avoid crossing their arms and legs so as not to appear guarded and defensive. They lie with their words. If someone can't give you a yes or no to a simple question, there's a good chance they're hiding something, because, as he learned, liars have an uncontrollable need to verbally dance around the truth, to weave together elaborate stories to convince you of their veracity.

"Look … I'm sure it's nothing." He steps over and kisses her on the forehead. "Come on, let's go to bed."

Nick is doing his best to present a calm demeanor. Inside he's seething, and more than a little worried.

"Nick, are you sure there's not something you want to tell me?"

That question, the loving way in which it was delivered, is like a can opener piercing his secret, opening the seal that's kept it hidden away, airtight, the last two days. He wonders if now's the time to tell her, to just let it out. He thinks about the advice Daniel gave him earlier. Despite Daniel's pitiful track record with women, maybe he's right. Maybe *it is* best to just get it over with. Nick's always been honest with her. Why stop now?

"Denise, I—"

"Hi, Daddy." It's Charlotte, his oldest daughter. He's relieved to see her, thankful to have the gun pointing at his head taken from him. Having already said goodnight to her mother upstairs, she's come down to give her father a kiss goodnight.

Nick reaches out to give her a hug. His sweet Charley. His Angel in Distress. She nestles into his chest. He bends down and kisses the top of her head.

He's never understood how such a lovely, kind-hearted human being could have come from his genes. She is so … good. She's always seemed older than her peers, more aware, wiser in the ways of the world; more empathetic and selfless in her relations with others. Daniel, her godfather, jokes that she's an "old soul." He tells her he believes that after journeying through many previous lives purposefully lived, her immortal soul has ascended to the top of the human ladder, where worldly knowledge, spiritual enlightenment, and goodness reside. He lovingly calls her "Saint Charlotte." She enjoys reminding him that every sinner needs a saint.

"Goodnight, Daddy. Mom said there was a real scene at Uncle Danny's. Is he okay?"

"Yes, sweetheart. You know your Uncle Dan—he gets himself out of trouble as quickly as he gets into it. There's nothing to worry about. Although I will say that this latest girlfriend of his really is a piece of work."

"Why can't Uncle Dan just find a nice, normal girlfriend?"

"He will, darling."

Appearing satisfied that her godfather, whom she adores, will be fine, Charlotte gives her father a peck on the check. She turns to her mother, offering the same, and heads up the staircase.

Once Charlotte reaches the top of the stairs and closes her bedroom door, Denise levels her eyes at Nick. "You were about to say something when Charlotte came downstairs?"

"Oh," Nick shakes his head, "it was nothing. Look, I'll call Mina in the morning, and we'll see what's going on. In the meantime, there's nothing to worry about, I'm sure." He reaches out, takes her hands in his, and says again, "*I'm sure.*" He leads her upstairs, hoping she'll leave the issue alone.

Once in bed, Denise falls asleep.

Nick tries to read a cheap detective novel that's been sitting unopened on his bedside table for months, absorbing nothing, as if staring at foreign words. His mind is adrift, flipping through the pages of his life, thinking how precarious it's become, how everything he's worked hard to achieve seems suddenly so very exposed and fragile. He worries about guarding his good life—his good job, his good home, his good family, his good friends—how quickly it might all come tumbling down if he doesn't handle this situation the right way, and right away. Everything is now in jeopardy because of one impulsive, mindless lapse of judgment, in an otherwise carefully and cautiously orchestrated life.

He rises from bed and tiptoes to the corner of the room, so as not to awaken Denise, who's snoring gently. He picks up the crumpled ball of paper with Mina's phone number, which he'd flung in disgust that morning. He opens it, places it on the side table next to his bed, crawls back underneath the covers, and resolves, *Tomorrow—tomorrow—I'll call her, and bring this to an end.*

He turns off his light and closes his eyes, calling upon the gods of sleep to grant him peace, if only for a few brief hours.

# Chapter 11

## SUNDAY

Sunday morning, 9:15 AM. Dressed in a pair of jeans, a faded black, short-sleeved cotton sport shirt, and weather-beaten topsiders, Nick exits his kitchen door into the two-car garage. Denise and his daughters are attending their regular weekly church service. Nick joins them twice a year, on Christmas and Easter. Denise was raised a Presbyterian. When the girls were born, she told Nick she felt it was in their best interests to lead their lives guided by a faith in something bigger than themselves. Nick agreed. Despite being raised in a devoutly Methodist household, religion is something that never rubbed off on him. Sometimes he wishes it had. How much easier one's life would be in the hands of an all-knowing, all-seeing, benevolent God.

He steps into his car, pulls out of the driveway, and steers a course for the local hardware store, in need of supplies for the leaky gutter Denise mentioned when he first arrived home from his business trip on Friday night. Halfway there, Nick pulls the crumpled piece of paper with Mina's number on it from his right pants pocket. He unfolds it with both hands, while his knees steer the car through the deserted, winding suburban back roads—the town residents either being in church, in bed, or on the golf course. He stares at the number and commits it to memory.

He rolls down his window and lets the wind snatch the flapping paper from his fingertips. *I never want to see that again.* He taps Mina's number into his cell phone.

After six rings, just as he's about to give up and disconnect the call, a tired and apparently just awakened female voice comes on the line. If it weren't for the cocky tone, he wouldn't have recognized it.

"Hello, Nick." She coughs and clears her throat. "Thought you'd never call."

Determined to end the cat-and-mouse game, Nick goes on the attack. "What the hell are you doing? Why do you keep calling my home? What do you want? Wasn't my four hundred sixty dollars and the pleasure of humiliating me enough for you?"

"Whoa. Take it easy, big boy."

"Fuck you. What do you want?"

"I know this is going to sound hard to believe, but I want to help you … but only if you help me." Mina's voice is hushed.

"What are you talking about?"

"Nick, you're in some deep shit," Mina says.

"Enlighten me."

"He knows who you are."

"What are you talking about?"

"He's coming after you. He knows who you are, and —"

"*Stop!* Who's coming after me?" Nick is yelling into the phone.

"He is. That's all I can say right now."

"Look, I'm sick of this perverse game of yours. I'm sure you're having fun. But I've had enough. That's it. I'll tell my wife about Denver, and then it'll be over. Then if you want, go ahead and share that pitiful recording with the police or anyone else. Be my guest."

"Don't be stupid, Nick. This is *so* much bigger than that. Do you really think I get my kicks by telling johns' wives that their husbands are lying, cheating bastards? If that were the case, I'd be on the phone all day long. Please."

"Then why were you calling my home, and not my cell?"

"Because you might have ignored me on your cell. I knew calling your house would get your attention."

"Look, I'm going now. Leave me and my family alone. Don't call again, or I'll call the police. I have your license plate number, so don't think you can't be tracked down."

Mina's voice has a mocking edge. "Good for you, Nick. Well done. You must be very proud of yourself. By the way, have you checked your bank account recently? Why don't you take a look? Then call me back. And try to be nicer when you do." She hangs up.

"Wait," Nick yells into the phone.

He turns his car around before getting to the hardware store and races home.

He slams on the brakes in his driveway, runs inside the empty house, enters his study, and boots up the computer. *Come on. Come on. Goddamn Microsoft.* Minutes pass like hours. Finally it's up and running and he's able to get online.

He goes to his bank's URL and types in his user ID and password. As the details of his account come up, he stares into the computer screen, stunned. At 4:46 pm on Saturday, $76,400 was withdrawn from his account. He instantly recognizes 764 as the number of his street address. This ominous coincidence—or is it a warning?—shakes him to his senses.

He grabs the smartphone from his hip pocket, goes to Recent Calls, finds the last call he made, and presses send. He takes a deep breath, trying to quell his panic.

Mina answers as if preoccupied with the mundane task of filing her nails. "Oh hi, Nick. Long time no talk."

"Cut the shit. What do you want from me?"

"Are you going to be nice? 'Cause we can end this call right now."

Nick conjures up all the self-control he can muster. "Seventy-six thousand four hundred dollars has disappeared from my bank account. Can you please explain what you know about that?"

"Ahh, that's better. You know, you're not so bad, Nick, when you take that stick out of your ass. Now that I've got your attention, let me get straight to the point." She pauses. "I need your help. I know that's hard to swallow, but it's true. And if you give it to me, in return, I'll do everything I can to help you, although there are no guarantees I'll succeed."

"Get to the point."

"I need you to help me get out of here," Mina says. "I don't know how much more time I've got. He's gonna kill me, I know it. One of these days—probably sooner rather than later—he's gonna kill me."

"Who?"

"I can't tell you that. Not yet. Just bear with me and trust that when I tell you someone bad is coming after you, he's really bad, and he's really coming after you. And he's going to hurt you wherever he can. Your bank account, your retirement accounts, you credit cards, your mortgage. He'll wipe you out."

"You're insane."

"Maybe. But what I'm telling you is true."

"Okay. Let's just say, just for a minute, that I choose to believe you—although I have no idea what you're talking about, and given our brief past history I have no reason to believe anything you say. What would you suggest I do to stop this from happening?"

"It's simple. You need to get me out of here. And then I'll tell you everything you need to know to protect your finances—and yourself."

"What do you mean, myself?"

"Nick, this is personal for him. You hurt his family, and now he wants to hurt you. It's a matter of honor for these crazy Cossacks."

"Christ—you really are a nut case, aren't you?"

"You can believe what you want."

Nick decides she's too dangerous to set loose. "Go on."

"When you get me out of here, I'll explain everything. The problem is I'm never allowed to be on my own. He keeps me in this stinking apartment most of the time. He calls it *The House of Special Purpose*. He thinks it's funny. That's what the Bolsheviks called the place in Siberia where the last Tsar and his family were imprisoned—and murdered. Pretty weird, huh?"

"Are you telling me you're being held prisoner?"

"Yeah. That's about it. I'm not allowed to go anywhere alone. And when I'm in the apartment, there's always a bodyguard sitting right outside the door in the floor lobby." She takes a deep breath. "He's obsessed with me. I'm his prized possession, and he won't let anyone near me. It started when I was pulling tricks in one of his clubs. That's how we met. And that's when he fell for me. And the truth is, I fell for him too. Despite the fact that he's a psychopath, he can be pretty charming. At least he was early on. But after a few months, he got it into his head that he owned me, and he didn't want any other man to come near me. Christ, most men are afraid to even look at me. They're afraid he'll think they're hitting on me. He's nuts, Nick. Not like anyone you've ever met. We're talking prime grade psychopath here."

"Unlike yourself?"

"Cute. That's right. Unlike myself. If you want to save your ass you need to come and get me out of here. Fast. Use your money, use your contacts, use your influence—whatever. You're a big-time executive, right? But I need to get out of here and be hidden somewhere safe, assume a new identity, with enough money to get by until he's put away. Simple enough?"

"If he never lets you out of his sight, how do you explain meeting me alone in the hotel?"

"Once or twice a week, he lets me pull a scam, like the one I pulled on you. I get to keep the money I steal from the johns. What he's after is much bigger: your identity information."

"Was that him on the other end of the phone when you were with me in the hotel room?"

"Yeah. And driving the car when you came racing after me at the hotel. He likes to personally escort me on these little forays. He gets a kick out of hearing clean-living, all-American Tom, Dick, and Harrys like you shit your pants, scared to death you're going to fuck up your wholesome, make-believe Disney lives when you learn that all those nasty little things you said have been recorded. It's a good thing you didn't try to take it from me. He was right outside the bedroom door the whole time."

Nick is silent, trying to digest everything he's hearing, still largely confused and in disbelief. "This is absurd."

"Yes, it is. But I can assure you, it's for real. You do all that for me—get me the hell out of here and find a way to hide and protect me, get a new life—and I'll do my best to protect your money ... and you."

"How are you going to do that?"

"Because I know who hacked your seventy-six thousand four hundred dollars. And I'm the one who knows how they're going to come after everything else you own—which, by the way, will only take another seventy-two hours. So that's how much time you have, Nick, to get me the hell out of here."

Nick contemplates Mina's last statement, unable to fully process the destructive implications of what she's suggesting, looking for something, anything, to grab hold of that might bring clarity and reason to this anarchic intrusion on his well-planned, ordered, and sensible life. "Why me?"

"Because, Nick, you've got everything to lose. Shhh, he's coming. I have to go. I'll call you later and tell you more. It will be clearer then. In the meantime, I suggest you book a flight to Denver right away." The line goes dead.

# Chapter 12

Fear grips Nick as he sinks back into his leather desk chair, his eyes fixed on the computer screen in front of him—the bright, stark digital display of his once secure bank account, now largely depleted, the crime scene of a virtual hold-up. Nick's fear is palpable, gut-wrenching, well beyond any sense of foreboding he's known before. It feels … life-threatening, like peering into the great, cavernous, black abyss, knowing that there's no way back. He's known fear before, but nothing like this.

He was fearful when Daniel was carried out of school on a stretcher their junior year of high school, attended by emergency medical responders, unconscious after a two-day binge of Quaaludes. Thankfully, after having his stomach pumped, he was back on his feet the next day, fully recovered, back to his old self, as if nothing had happened. People never understood how Nick and Daniel, two total opposites, could be best friends. Their families had nicknames for them: "Salt and Pepper," "Sweet and Sour," "Light and Dark." Denise calls them "Yin and Yang."

Where Nick is reliable, Daniel is unpredictable. Where Nick instinctively puts others before himself, Daniel's inclination is to satisfy his own needs and desires first. Where Nick brings caution and deep consideration to problems and opportunities, Daniel flings himself upon anything new and exciting—including drugs—and asks questions, or just as likely doesn't, later. Where

Nick respects societal conventions and authority, Daniel lives by a different set of rules, mostly his own. Polar opposites in every way, yet the very best of friends—and the closest of confidants.

Of course, Nick knows the epoxy that binds them together. To be whole, fully realized human beings, they needed parts of each other that were lacking in themselves. They admire, value, and rely upon their stark differences, as good friends so often do.

Nick had been fearful when his father died, and he chose to return home from college to support his mother and sisters without any money, a job, or even a prospect of employment before his Uncle Leo took him on. Contrary to his prudent and prepared nature, he was forced to fly blind over all the careful plans he'd charted for his vigilant life.

And he was fearful when Denise turned down his proposal of marriage. They had met at Rohr the second week after he started there. She was a part-time executive assistant for Johann, working toward a master's degree in European literature at the University of Chicago. Focused on his work, Nick had barely noticed her— or, for that matter, any other woman in the office—despite her classic beauty, slender hourglass figure, and inviting smile.

One day, she strolled into his office with a file from Johann.

Slumped over his desk, absorbed in his work, Nick reached up, grabbed the file from her hand, smiled mechanically, and went right back to work.

"Are you a vampire?" asked Denise.

Nick looked up from his papers, for the first time taking note of the attractive woman looming above his desk.

"A vampire?"

"Yeah, a vampire. I noticed that you never seem to go out in daylight. You're the first one here in the morning. You take lunch at your desk. And you don't seem to leave until well after dark. I mean, look—I don't mean to be disrespectful. Don't get me wrong. I don't have anything against vampires. At least as long as they don't suck *my* blood and turn *me* into a zombie.

Frankly, though, I'm hoping you're not one of them. I think fangs would spoil your smile. And I can't really fathom you gallivanting around at night in a black cape. Black's not your color. And if, for example, you were inclined to ask me out to lunch, or maybe even dinner, I don't know of any decent restaurant that serves human blood—at least not *fresh* human blood, which I understand vampires are quite partial to, right? Me, personally, I need a more well-rounded meal."

That was the last time Nick failed to notice Denise. Indeed, since their marriage he has enjoyed telling friends it was right then and there that he started falling in love with her. Her bold, swift, and sweet intrusion had been like a bracing splash of cold water. Nick had been on automatic pilot ever since his father died, focused exclusively on work, determined to provide for his mother and sisters, making sure he'd never put himself, or them, in a compromised financial situation—not like his father had done, through no fault of his own. Success in business, largely measured in monetary terms, was everything to him. The downside of his blind ambition, though, was that he'd closed the door to life's everyday, simple joys and pleasures. Denise, on that memorable day, reopened that door for him—and it never closed again.

Three weeks later he proposed to her. Without reservation, he knew she was the first person he wanted to see in the morning and the last person he wanted to see at night, every day of his life. She brightened his life, gave him a peace of mind he'd never known before, and more than anything, helped him be a better, more complete man. He had bought a diamond ring from Tiffany's, invited her to his apartment, and poured them each a glass of blood-red wine from a bottle labeled "Vampire Vineyards." He knelt before her, professed his eternal love, and asked her to be his wife.

She reacted with an uncomfortable giggle.

"Nick … this is unexpected, that's all. I don't know what to say. Sorry, that's so trite. What I mean is, we've been seeing each other for less than a month. Don't you think it's a bit too soon?"

Nick replied, "I know I love you. I know I'll never love anyone else. I don't need more time to know what I know, and always will know."

"I'm sorry, Nick, but I do. I'm very fond of you—*very* fond of you. I may even be falling in love with you. But it's too soon, baby, it's way too soon. Let's just give this some more time. Okay?"

Nick was crushed and fretted that he might lose her. He feared that he might have moved too quickly, that she didn't or wouldn't or couldn't ever love him.

Just one month later, though, after spending most of their free time together, Denise invited Nick to her apartment one evening, poured them each a glass of Vampire Vineyards' blood-red wine, knelt before him, looked into his brown eyes, and allayed all Nick's fears. "If you'll still have me, I'm ready now."

The memory of these past events seems almost insignificant in comparison to the fear Nick feels in the face of this new crisis. They seem like a bad case of heartburn in relation to what he now equates to the sharp, excruciating pain of cardiac arrest.

Nick's first instinct is to call the police or the FBI, to pass on his problem—to someone, anyone, in a position of authority. Problem is, they'll likely compound his problem. The risks are too great. Law enforcement organizations are too bureaucratic, too slow. He thinks back to his earlier telephone conversation. What did Mina say? *"You have seventy-two hours."*

He makes the first call to his bank, to tell them about the theft—the incursion into his personal financial lifeline—and try to retrieve his money. He picks up the wireless phone on his desk, calls directory assistance, writes the number down on a pad of yellow legal paper, and taps in the number.

A cheerful, young man's voice comes on the line. "Hello, this is Roger. Thank you for calling Bank of America. Whom may I ask am I speaking to, and how may I help?" Nick struggles to hear through the thick Indian accent, bizarrely interwoven with an awkward, imitation American twang. The result is an odd, barely comprehensible garble of words, an amusing violation of the English language, sounding to Nick like a comic imitating an Indian imitating a Texan. Despite the seriousness of his situation, Nick struggles to suppress a chuckle.

"My name is Nick Steele."

Before Nick gets any further, Roger interrupts. "May I call you Nick?"

"Excuse me?" asks Nick, failing to understand Roger's incoherent Indian American distortion.

Roger repeats the question, making no attempt to adjust the tone or pace of his question to ensure clarity. "May I call you Nick?"

"You can call me anything you want, *Rog*. May I call you Rog? Look, I have an emergency. A large sum of money has been stolen from my bank account."

Impervious to insult, Roger continues. "Could you please tell me how much was taken from your account, Nick?"

"Seventy-six thousand four hundred dollars.. It happened yesterday. Someone hacked into my account."

Roger takes Nick through a series of standard questions to validate his account information and identity. "I am now opening your account, Nick." He sounds like a doctor explaining each step of a medical procedure to his patient. "I am now seeing your account, Nick. I am ... ah, yes, I see. Here it is. Would you please excuse me for a short moment, Nick? I would like to connect you with the appropriate person to address your issue. Please hold for just one minute. Okay, Nick?"

Nick waits on the line for five minutes, forced to listen to a Muzak version of "All You Need is Love," all the while thinking that if Roger calls him "Nick" one more time he's going to reach through the phone and rip his throat out.

Finally, a new voice comes on the line. This time an American, sounding as if she's in a position of authority.

"Mr. Steele, I'm Jennifer Warren, head of international customer security at the bank. I'm sorry to tell you, it appears you're a victim of automated clearinghouse fraud. That's essentially theft involving unauthorized electronic transfers. The good news is that since you reported this quickly, you have a sixty-day grace period. The bank will reimburse you in full. The only way to prevent this from occurring again is to close down your account and open a new one. Shall we go ahead and do that?"

Nick is relieved to have someone attending him who promptly and adeptly addresses his problem—in a language he can clearly understand. "Yes, yes, please do that. But can you track down whoever did this?"

"We *will* try, sir. But I have to be frank with you; the odds are low. Cyber criminals are getting better and better at erasing their electronic trails. But of course, we'll be investigating and will certainly let you know what we learn."

"Do you see much of this? I mean, I thought banks were supposed to have impenetrable security systems and firewalls."

"Not a lot, but still, it's an ongoing problem. We do everything we can, but as you know, technology is changing so rapidly. And as much as we may wish it were otherwise, there are those who are determined to find new ways of breaking even the most elaborate security systems; sometimes for sport, sometimes as a livelihood."

"So how can I be assured of preventing it from happening again?"

"In order to break into your account, someone had to have had your routing number. I have to ask you, do you know of anyone who has or could gain access to that information?"

Nick knows full well who perpetrated the crime but has no idea how Mina got his routing number. "No one, other than my wife."

"I don't know for sure, but you or your wife may have been 'phished.' Typically, this involves receiving an official-looking e-mail, maybe with a header that looks like a bank—maybe *our* bank—that's loaded with spyware. The spyware then seeks out private information inside the computer, things like user IDs, passwords, and personal banking information, like routing

numbers. You or your wife may have inadvertently opened
something like this and infected your computer. You should look
into this right away."

"I will. Is there anything else I should know?"

"Not at the moment. As soon as we know more, we'll contact
you. In the meantime, I'll put you back on the line with someone
who can help set up your new account."

"Thank you for your help."

"You're welcome, Mr. Steele. I'm sorry for your
inconvenience."

Nick is reconnected to a Muzak version of "Strawberry Fields,"
which seems bizarrely appropriate, given that nothing at this
particular moment seems real.

"Hello, Nick? This is Roger."

Nick can't help but smile at the cheerful, impervious voice
imperfectly programmed to emulate the cordial tone and manner
of an old acquaintance. Succumbing to his affability, Nick
responds in kind. "Hello, Rog. This is Nick."

After they close his old account and open a new one, Nick
presses the red button on his phone.

*Now what?* He's relieved to have the stolen money back in his
bank account but knows this isn't the end of his troubles.

Sitting on top of his desk, he notes, there's the 365-day tear-off
calendar Denise gave him last Christmas, highlighting daily quips
and quotes from famous authors. It's been two weeks since he last
looked at it. He reaches forward, grabs hold, and one by one tears
off fourteen days' worth of insight, wisdom, and inspiration before
arriving at today's quotation from Victor Hugo.

*Life is the flower for which love is the honey.*

He reads it twice, slowly the second time, allowing its meaning
to sink in, marveling at its auspiciousness, its prescient wisdom. It
is clear to him: *It's time. I need to tell Denise.*

# Chapter 13

"I want to tell you a story about someone we both know."

Nick and Denise sit side-by-side on the living room sofa, comfortably positioned in front of a granite stone fireplace nestled between two floor-to-ceiling red cherry bookshelves, spilling over with Denise's favorite novels.

Denise arrived home at 11:00 after attending church with the girls. Upon entering the house, Nick asked her to join him in the living room. He had something he needed to tell her. No, it couldn't wait.

Whenever Nick gives her bad news, which isn't often, or wants to tell her something particularly important, he presents it in the form of a third-person story. It started off as a joke when they first met, an homage to Denise's literary studies, and somehow, over time, managed to stick.

"Okay, so there's this guy, right? All in all, he's pretty decent … at least he tries to be. He's a good father, a good son, a good brother. And he's worked hard at being a good husband. Not that it's hard, because he loves his wife. Anyway, he's lived a pretty honest life, mostly doing the right thing.

"Except one day he does something *really* stupid. You know, right out of the blue. He doesn't even know why he does it. It's so *weirdly* out of character he barely recognizes himself. But still, there it is. He does it.

"He's on a business trip. Gone for days. He's feeling a little lonely ... a little horny." Nick scratches the back of his head. "He meets a woman at a bar. She asks if he'd like some company. The kind you pay for. At first he declines. He's never done something like that before. Doesn't want to be unfaithful to his wife. But then he caves in. Eventually he figures, what the hell, no harm done. There's nothing emotional about it. Just like scratching an itch. When it's over, he'll simply goes back to his work, back to his life, as if nothing ever happened.

"Except it doesn't turn out that way. The woman is a scam artist. She records their conversation in his hotel room and threatens to share it with the police. Before they have sex, she takes his money and leaves. Our friend feels like a fool, a total ass. Since no one was hurt, though, and he swears to himself he'll never do anything idiotic like that again, he tries to forget about the whole thing.

"Except he can't. The woman starts calling his home. He doesn't know what she wants." Nick shakes his head and shrugs. "He doesn't want to know. So he tries to ignore it. But that doesn't work, because she won't stop calling. Finally, our friend speaks to her. Tells her to go away, tells her to leave him alone—leave his family alone—or he'll call the cops. She ignores him—tells him that she's part of a group of ... professional criminals ... who are coming after him. That they're going to steal everything he has, his savings, his retirement fund investments, everything. And that his only hope is to help her escape from an apartment in which she's imprisoned by one of the thugs."

Nick notes the incredulous look on Denise's face. He realizes how ridiculous, how utterly ludicrous and divorced from reality this all sounds. He can hardly believe the words coming from his own mouth as he hears them himself. He has no choice but to get it all out.

"Of course, he doesn't know if he should believe her. Why should he? It's all so surreal, so fictional—like something out of a cheap detective novel. But when she tells him that they've already stolen money from his bank account—and it turns out to be true—she has his attention."

Denise's eyes narrow.

"So he decides to tell his wife. On a practical level, he needs her to know about the stolen money—*their* stolen money—that the bank will reimburse it, and that there's a new account number and password. He also needs to tell her that their computers may have been infiltrated with malicious spyware and that they need to be cleaned right away."

Denise shakes her head, in apparent disgust.

"But more important than that, he needs her to know he's sorry for what he's done—for his stupidity—for creating this mess. He wants her forgiveness. He needs her to know how much he loves her and needs her—how deeply devoted he is to her and his family—"

Nick pauses mid-sentence and looks into Denise's steady, unblinking eyes, hoping for a glimmer of forgiveness, for some small indication of absolution. But there's nothing. Her pupils are fully dilated, glazed, impenetrable shells. He feels like a poor, weary prospector mining for gold well after everyone else has moved downstream.

"Pretty wild story, huh?"

Her head falls downward, her long blond hair dangling over her expressionless face and slumped shoulders.

Determined not to give up, Nick searches for a button to push, any button that might evoke a response. "Please, Nise. Please say something. You need to talk to me." No movement. More silence. Reaching for straws, Nick continues, "If nothing else, just say something witty and urbane like you always do … for example, what would your great classic literary heroes have to say about this?"

As if awoken by a full-body shake, Denise jolts upright, braces her back, tightens the muscles in her jaw, purses her lips, and levels her eyes at Nick. "I see, so you'd like to discuss this on an intellectual level." Denise takes on an air of contemplation.

"Okay, I can see the benefit of that. Let me give it a shot." She pauses to load her thoughts, then fires. "Of course, I could say, Nick, it's okay, everything's fine. I'm not upset or offended. I forgive you. What you did is understandable, and in the overall scheme of things, not a big deal.

"We live in a time of human paradox and moral uncertainty, a time of moral relativism, where there is no absolute truth that guides our lives. It's all subjective now, right? There's no longer a need for a common set of laws or rules or ethics or values. No, that's *so* old fashioned. The circumstances dictate everything. As long as no one gets hurt, we should all just do as we please. Live and let live. How am I doing so far?"

"Please, Denise —"

She drives on. "I could also say—since you're specifically interested in hearing from my 'literary heroes'—that true enough, in some classic novels it's not uncommon for *men of the world* to cheat and yet still be able to build an impenetrable wall between their adulterous and domestic lives, to isolate and secure the sanctity of their homes, wives, and children from their less scrupulous side. This, no doubt, should give me comfort, since you are clearly an accomplished man of the world who loves his family."

"Please don't do this," Nick says.

"I could also say that many of the famous adulterers in literature aren't men, they're women: Anna Karenina. Madame Bovary, Lady Chatterley. Of course, they generally mess around for reasons that go beyond the need to *fuck* someone new. Their infidelity usually stems from a deep unhappiness with their marriages, typically to dull, socially inept, and sexually unappealing elderly husbands. Since this girl—this woman—you fucked, *or tried to,* is a professional, I should also take comfort, or at least feel no competitive threat, since her aim was a quick, easy buck. It was nothing more than a simple business transaction. Hey, I think I'm getting the hang of this. Is this what you were looking for? Your smart, well-educated wife of sixteen years able to intellectually rationalize, and ultimately dismiss as insignificant, her husband's *indiscretion*?"

Nick shakes his head in surrender.

"There's just one problem. I think it was Tolstoy who said, 'Emotions can be blocked, temporarily, but never denied.' I can certainly think my way to forgiveness, Nick. I can do it as well as any other devoted wife—and we can go on with our lives just as before, like nothing happened. But I'd be lying to you if I didn't tell you"—for the first time, Nick sees an opening in Denise's eyes—"my heart aches. And I'm not sure my mind can simply override that—or this old-fashioned feeling of betrayal—as quickly as you'd like.

"Oh sure, I'll get over it. I'm not naïve. I know this shit happens. I know it's not the end of the world. But I guess I truly thought in our case ..." She pauses, catching herself in mid-sentence. "I guess I *am* naïve."

She takes a slow, deep breath, closes her eyes, and continues in a softer, somber, more contemplative voice. "One of the things I love most about you—always have—is your moral certitude. You've always known right from wrong. Better than anyone I know. And you've always, as far as I know, lived your life honorably, and to a large degree selflessly. Your example has inspired me, and given your daughters an invaluable role model. Do you know how rare that is, Nick? In this day and age?

"But you also need to know it's the betrayal to your daughters that bothers me almost as much as your betrayal to me. They're young, vulnerable women themselves, just starting to figure out how they're supposed to connect with members of the opposite sex. And I can tell you from experience, it's not easy at their age; especially for their generation, with so much confusing sexual crap in the media. You're their male role model, Nick. It's one of the most important roles you can play for them—showing them what it means to be a real man."

Nick grimaces.

"Oh, you mustn't worry," she continues. "I'm not going to stop loving you for what you did. And the girls will never find out. And I'm not going to leave you. Our lives will go on much as before. At least I hope so, given all that you've said about this woman and her associates and their … malicious intentions. But I *will* need some time. And honestly, *you* will need to win me back some. I don't have to believe in a lot. But I do need to know that we believe in each other."

The ticking of the grandfather clock in the corner of the room punctuates the long silence between them. Nick leans over, takes her hand in his, and kisses it. He meets no resistance. He pulls her toward him and wraps his arms around her shoulders as she curls up into a ball in his lap. Red rings circle his eyelids, and water springs from his pupils. As she lies nestled against him, two bodies now melding into one, he resolves to shed all fear and do whatever must be done to protect that which is most dear to him.

# Chapter 14

"Come on in. Door's unlocked."

Nick opens the black front door to Daniel's small, white colonial, obeying the instructions of the distant bellow coming from inside, and steps into the front hallway. Having tried to phone Daniel on both his home and cell phone numbers, and getting no answer by e-mail, he drove over, Daniel's home being just three miles from his own; this after confessing everything to Denise, whom he left at home in a somber, contemplative mood, at her request, for some time alone.

After stepping inside, Nick swings the heavy wooden door shut behind him. The entrance hallway is tiled with black-and-white flooring, giving the impression of a checkerboard awaiting his next move. Standing there, Nick looks around for the source of the beckoning voice. The sparse, formal dining room to his left is empty as usual, unattended by anyone other than Daniel's twice-monthly Colombian cleaning woman. She occasionally dusts the oak dining table and Windexes the vacant floor-to-ceiling glass cabinet that once proudly displayed Daniel's wife's extensive Herrend porcelain collection, which disappeared when she did.

Straight ahead, the entrance stairway, with its white-posted handrail running along its left side and an unadorned white wall on its right, shows no sign of life. With only one place left to turn, Nick calls into the living room on his right. "Daniel?"

"Yeah—over here."

Nick follows the flat, lifeless voice, a beacon whose battery appears to be running low. As he steps through the archway between the entrance hall and living room, he catches sight of his friend, still in pajamas, lying on his back on a coffee-colored sofa in front of the fireplace. Daniel is stretched out, sunk deep into the sofa's soft cushions, looking as if he has no intention of ever leaving this snug, safe crater of comfort. Surrounding him are the remnants of last night. Nothing has been touched. The after-party squalor he left behind now looks to Nick more like the aftermath of a natural disaster that may take days, even weeks, to clean up. Daniel's head, propped up on a small pillow wedged against the sofa's side arm, is hidden behind the Sunday *Chicago Tribune*, which he appears to be reading intently.

Once in the living room, Nick sits down on a white linen upholstered chair adjacent to Daniel's sofa. He asks, "What you reading there?"

"I'm reading the wedding announcements."

"Ah. A new area of interest?"

"Hardly. Not after last night. But still, it makes for fascinating reading. You ever read the wedding announcements?"

"Nope. Don't believe I have."

"Me neither." The paper remains propped-up in front of Daniel's face. He continues to talk through it, as if too preoccupied with what he's reading to lower the paper and engage his friend face-to-face. His voice carries an air of nonchalance, as if he's trying to appear effortless in reading and carrying on a conversation simultaneously. "But I think I'm going to start reading it regularly from now on. There's so much happiness in here, so much hope … After last night, well, I need a little of that. It doesn't matter that in time fifty percent of all these newlyweds are going to *detest* each other. Right here, right now, they're blissfully happy.

"I realize this looks like a perverse fascination. Probably is, but I'm in a particularly perverse mood, given my particularly perverse display of domestic dysfunction last night. Still you might give it a try; kind of picks you up. Here you go … tell me, how can this not put a smile on your face?" He reads from one of the announcements. "'Richard Cochran and Richard Boehner were married Saturday afternoon in Boston.' Isn't that great? You can't make this stuff up. The headline should read: *Two Dicks Wed.*"

Nick half-smiles. "Hey, you gonna come out from under there?"

At first, Daniel doesn't respond. An anticipatory silence hangs in the air. Then, slowly, he lowers the paper to his lap, revealing a large contusion above his left eye and three bright red, surface-deep gashes running parallel down his right cheek.

"Danny—what the hell?"

"Whitney."

Nick looks at his friend with genuine concern, trying to assess the severity of his wounds and determine whether he needs a doctor.

Daniel jump-starts himself with a long, slow, deep breath. "Don't worry, I'm fine. After you and Denise left last night I went back upstairs, and with as much calm and reason as I could muster, decided—you won't be surprised to hear—to tell Whitney it was over, and to ask her to pack her things and leave in the morning. Before the first words left my mouth, she threw a left jab … right here." Daniel raises his left index finger to the point of contact above his left eye, a golf ball-sized purple welt of flesh. "Unfortunately for me, she knows some martial arts. She went for my face, trying to rip my eyes out with her fingernails. I mean she was literally trying to *rip my fucking eyes out!* I pushed her away with every ounce of strength I had. She bounced off the wall sideways and fell down the stairs. Tumbled down the steps like a rag doll. When she landed on the hallway floor, she didn't move. Not an inch. I thought for sure I'd killed her.

"I was panicked. I ran down the stairs, knelt beside her, and put my ear to her mouth. I was praying—praying to whatever benevolent force in the universe might be on duty at that moment—to make her breathe."

Daniel registers the look of shock on Nick's face. "Hard to believe, right?"

Nick nods, too stunned to answer.

"Anyway, it gets better. As I'm leaning over her, suddenly, she grabs my crotch—I mean she's got my whole fucking fruit basket in her grip, clutching real hard, and she won't let go. I don't remember ever feeling anything as painful. I couldn't breathe.

"Something primal overtook me. I wrapped my hands around her neck and began squeezing as hard as I could. I was determined to choke her until she either let go or died, whichever came first. Her face turned beet red, her eyes looked like they were going to burst from their sockets, veins popped out of her neck. And Nick, I have to tell you honestly, I started to like the idea of killing her. It actually started to feel good. For a brief moment I was lost in the pure pleasure of murdering this woman.

"Fortunately for both of us, she let go pretty quickly. And I came to my senses. I released her and fell over on my side—curled up in a fetal position, grabbing my crotch, trying to breathe, sweating like a pig, rolling around the floor, back and forth, in total agony.

"In the meantime, Whitney gets to her feet, stands over me, staring down in utter disgust—I remember that look all too well—and drop-kicks me. POW! Right in my gut, a forty-five-yard field goal attempt. She coughs up some phlegm, leans down, and spits right in my face." Daniel adds, "And without so much as even a simple good-bye, or a 'thanks, it's been swell,' she opens the front door and leaves." Pointing to the newspaper on his lap, he says, "Do you see now why I need those happy Dicks to help lift my spirits?"

Speechless, Nick gets up and moves to Daniel's side on the edge of the sofa. He reaches out his hand to examine his friend's face closer, first checking the bruise, then the scratch marks. "Look, I think we should get you to a doctor. You might be concussed."

Daniel says, "I'm not. The only thing that's concussed is my dick."

"You remember in high school when I walked around for a week before I found out I had a hairline fracture in my skull?" Nick asks.

"Yeah, but you're tougher than I am. You know I'd run to a doctor if I suspected *anything* remotely might be wrong. Look, let's please just leave it. I don't want to talk or even think about this anymore. It's over. She's gone, thank God. These are surface wounds, and they'll heal soon enough."

Nick concedes the point. There's no profit in arguing with Daniel when his mind is set. He's probably also right about having no serious injuries.

"Okay, you win. But could you at least promise me that you'll stay away from dangerous women for a while?"

Nick sees the disbelief in Daniel's eyes and realizes he's hardly in a position to criticize him about spending time with questionable women. "Sorry. That was a stupid thing to say." Nick extends his right hand to Daniel, palm facing upward, who smoothly low-fives it.

"So what brings you over here? Shouldn't you be on the golf course or home with your family?" asks Daniel.

"Well … I tried to call, but couldn't get you. I'm thinking about going to Denver. I was going to ask you to come along—but that doesn't make any sense now. You're in no condition—"

"Whoa, whoa, what are you talking about? Denver?"

"Yeah. I guess I'd better back up. A lot's happened since we spoke last night."

Nick proceeds to tell Daniel the details of his conversation with Mina: her demand for help or else, her forced detention, her fear for her life and need to escape, the crazy Russian intent upon destroying him, the online theft of his bank account, and the threat of more to come. He then tells of his confession to Denise.

As Nick recounts all of this, Daniel listens with a stunned expression. When he finishes, Daniel scratches the side of his head. "And I thought I had it bad."

"Anyway, I need to deal with it. I'm thinking the best way to determine how real this whole thing is to get myself out there."

"What about just calling the cops or the FBI?"

"I've thought about that, a lot, but I'm worried they'll take too long to deal with it. Besides, I don't want this to get back to Johann or any of the board members or any one else I know. Once it's in their hands, it'll be beyond my control.

"Hell, Danny, I don't even know if this whole thing isn't just some elaborate scam on her part. The only thing I do know is that I can't sit around and do nothing, and there's no one else to turn to I can trust. So I'm thinking of going out there myself, and figuring it out along the way. If what she says is true, and that's still a big 'if,' I don't have much time to waste."

"Wow. This is very unlike you. All impulsive-like."

"They say the secret to getting ahead is getting started, right?" Nick says under his breath, mostly to himself.

Daniel looks at Nick quizzically.

"Mark Twain, I think."

"I'm not complaining. I like it. Going on instinct. Mr. Spontaneity. This is a side of you I've never seen," Daniel says.

Nick lowers his eyes and chuckles through his nose. "I know."

"When are you thinking of going?"

"Don't know yet."

"Well, when you do, I'm coming with you," says Daniel.

Daniel rises from the sofa, appearing newly energized.

Nick's cell phone rings. He recognizes the number. He waves to Daniel to sit back down: "Hold on, it's *her.*"

# *Chapter 15*

Nick presses the speaker button on his smartphone. He places it on the glass-top coffee table directly in front of the sofa, facing both he and Daniel, now sitting side by side.

"Hello, Mina." Nick speaks toward the phone in a casual, conversational tone, as if sitting directly across from her. He wants to create the impression of addressing an accomplice, rather than an adversary, there being, he believes, no further benefit in appearing anxious or contentious, despite the hatred he feels. Before committing to go to Denver, he needs more information—much more. For that, he well knows—after many years in business where he's learned knowledge is indeed power—he needs to earn her trust.

"Hello, Nick. Sounds like you have me on a speakerphone. Is someone else there I should know about?"

Nick answers, trying to sound reassuring. "A friend. Someone I trust."

Mina snaps back, reminding Nick who's in charge. "Well, I don't know your friend, Nick. So perhaps you'd be kind enough to introduce us."

Daniel leaps into the conversation. "Daniel. My name's Daniel. I'm a good friend of Nick's. He's told me everything."

"Hello, Daniel. Nick's told you everything, huh? That's interesting, because Nick knows hardly anything—not yet. That's why I'm calling. Tell me, Daniel, do you have any connection to the police, the FBI, the CIA, the military, or any other governmental agency that might prove helpful in this situation?"

"No. I'm a PR guy."

Mina gasps. "A PR guy? Well, I suppose this should make a pretty good story when it's all over. In the meantime, though, how is a 'PR guy' going to help your friend get me out of here, and help me disappear?" Mina's voice turns harsh. "Somehow, Nick, I thought you understood the seriousness of the situation. I certainly thought you could do better than this."

Nick holds his arm up in front of Daniel, like a traffic cop instructing a car to stay put until he signals for it to proceed. He interjects, "Look, Mina, I simply don't know enough. You said that's why you're calling, to tell me more. Right?"

"Fair enough." Mina breathes heavily into the phone. "Okay, let's start with who you're dealing with. His name is Vladimir Yurovsky. He's Russian mafia. The real deal. He runs his own syndicate out here in Denver. He's rich, well-connected politically, and very well armed. Do some homework. You won't have to dig too deep. As I told you before, he's crazy. Certifiable. And very dangerous. He keeps me cooped up in here—this awful apartment—most of the time."

"Where's here?"

"You'll learn that when you get to Denver. Have you booked a flight?"

"No. I need more information."

"You're messing with fire here, Nick. And you are running out of time."

"Maybe. But I need to know more."

"Okay. Maybe this will convince you. Vladimir does most of his business right here in this apartment. He has a nice home just outside the city, where he lives with his wife and two kids. But this is where he handles business. This is where he and his crew do all their scheming." A hint of pride now filters into her voice. "Well, guess what? Remember my little digital recorder from our brief encounter in your hotel room last week? For the last six months, I've been recording all of Vladimir's conversations: all of his illegal plotting, all of his endless, fat-headed bragging about who he's robbed, who he's beat up—and who he's killed. When I know a meeting is about to take place, before everyone arrives, I hide the recorder under one of the couches. It has a built-in memory stick so I have hours—maybe days—worth. I have enough evidence to put that sick fuck in jail for a lifetime, maybe two."

Nick is too bewildered to react, working hard to process this vital, new information. Mina continues with a mix of anger and excitement. "You getting this, Nick? This is my salvation—and yours. You get me out of here. We take the recordings to the Feds. They arrest Vlad and his cronies. End of story."

"I don't want to sound like I'm not happy for you, but where exactly is my 'salvation'?"

"Oh, you'll be safe once Vlad's out of the way. His issue with you is personal. It's a matter of honor. He needs to deal with you on his own."

"How so?"

"You ready for this? He thinks your grandfather killed his grandfather—back in Russia, too many years ago to count. Shot him in the head. Do you know anything about this? About your grandfather's past? Any of this ring a bell? Anyway, Vladimir's really into his ancestry back in Russia. Studies it endlessly.

"He's been searching for you for years. And now he's found you: the living direct bloodline to his grandfather's killer. He wants to avenge his grandfather's death, and you're his target. He doesn't just want your money, Nick. That's just the fun part. He wants your life. You have to keep in mind that revenge is like sex for these guys, these crazy Cossacks—maybe better. I can't tell you how sick I am of hearing them recite the same old Russian proverb, like they're poets or something." She puts on a thick Russian accent, intentionally making it sound imbecilic. "*Revenge ... is the sweetest form of passion.*"

Nick is stunned, still trying to process everything he's heard.

"*Hellooo*, Nick. Do you think it was just coincidence that we met in Denver? He's been tracking you for a year. Notice any strange clicks when speaking on your cell phone? Notice an increase in spam that isn't getting filtered, for things like Russian girlfriends, investment opportunities, time-shares, gambling vacations, gay liaisons? How about unexplained charges on your wife's store cards? I'm sure there are other things he's been doing to you I don't even know about. He's been surgically stalking you. Playing with you. This is like sport for him. You showing up in Denver was like a birthday present."

Mina changes the subject. "I've got to go. Just in case you need more proof of what I'm telling you, I'd advise you to look into your bank credit card account."

"Come on, don't start that again."

"'Fraid so. You don't seem to appreciate that this is a racket you're dealing with. These guys are a sophisticated, well-organized business that just happens to specialize in stealing other people's money. They're smart, well-educated guys—guys you'd hire, Nick. Except you could never afford them."

"Okay, I get it. What about my credit card?"

"This one's easy. Real low-tech. Remember when I came into your hotel room and the first thing I did was ask to use the bathroom?"

Nick delves into his memory, searching for an impression. Yes, there it is—she's speaking on the phone with her friend, who he now knows was Vladimir, and then inexplicably asks to use the bathroom, but she doesn't hang up. "Yeah, I remember."

"Well, most of you road warrior types carry your wallets on the inside of your suit or sport jackets. And you also, either through upbringing, or because your wives have trained you well, hang your jackets first thing when you enter a room. When I went to the bathroom, I simply reached into your closet and pick-pocketed your wallet from your jacket. I learned how to do that from Vladimir. I figure it's one of those valuable life skills I can take into retirement. Anyway, in the bathroom, I wrote down the number of your credit card, put it back in the wallet, and slipped it back into your jacket on the way back. Usually, guys are so transfixed on who's on the other end of the phone—that's part of the set-up—or preoccupied with thoughts of what they're going to do with me when they get my clothes off, they don't pay much attention to what I'm doing.

"The rest is simple. We take your credit card number and emboss it on dummy cards. Then it's charged against phony merchandise at phony merchants. Pretty soon, I'm sorry to say, these bogus purchases are about to trip an automatic security call from your credit card company."

Nick is frozen in silence, wondering when it will end.

"Bye for now. Better get your ass out here. Fast!"

# Chapter 16

Sunday evening, 6:00 pm. Nick watches with affection as his two daughters fall into the loving embrace of their grandmother on the pouch of her modest home. Denise, following close behind, receives a similar show of affection and returns it in kind. Nick's mother reserves the biggest hug of all for her baby boy, her pride and joy. At five-foot-one, a full foot shorter than Nick, she wraps her arms around his waist and nestles her gray head into his chest.

Rosemarie—Rosey to her friends and family—comes from pure, honest to goodness, no-nonsense, tell-it-like-it-is, straight-shootin' Midwestern stock. There was never any doubt where you stood with her. Things were either black or white. "In between's when you don't know what you mean," she used to say to Nick.

She had no time for mopers or hangdogs, provided no quarter to idlers or complainers. That was a weakness she simply wouldn't abide. "No good for anyone," she'd snap. When it came to doing household chores, homework, even dealing with illness, one needed simply to get on with it.

Growing up in the Steele household, Nick learned that he wasn't going to get much sympathy when he came down with a cold or flu, cut his finger, or banged his head. Oh, Nick's mom was kind about it: "Poor baby," she'd say, but she wasn't going to give him what he wanted most, which was all the attention in the world. She pretty much expected him to suck it up. Complaining? That was like speaking in a foreign language. It got you nowhere. Had the opposite effect, in fact. Nick learned early on how to recover remarkably fast from whatever ailed him.

She sure did, though, show her love in other ways.

Although working hard every day as a math teacher at the local high school, she managed to save most of her energy for her children. She greeted Nick and his sisters whenever they arrived home as if they'd just returned from a long journey, helped them each night with their homework, celebrated their victories, no matter how small, attended all of their sporting events, read to each of them in bed at night, and listened … listened to what they were saying as if it were the most important thing in the world to her.

Rosy lives in the same compact, brick house Nick grew up in, built in the 1920s, no more than a forty-five-minute drive from his own home outside of Chicago. After stepping up onto the screened-in front porch, there's a small living room to the right and an inter-connected kitchen and dining area to the left. A small, steep, narrow staircase directly ahead of the front door leads upstairs to two and a half bedrooms—Nick's used to be the half—and one shared bathroom on the second floor. A pull down retractable ladder provides access to the attic used for long-term storage.

Of course, the house always seemed so much larger to Nick as a kid. It never really felt claustrophobic—all of them living on top of one another, his father, his mother, his two sisters, himself, the family's gregarious black lab, Sally, an aloof, semi-feral cat named Shadow, a freakishly large pet goldfish, Orangy Bighead, and two gerbils, Frosty and Sunshine, who seemed to exist for the sole purpose of mass reproduction—until, that is, he entered into his teens, and his budding manhood yearned for privacy and an occasional place to hide.

After enjoying a delicious, rib-sticking dinner—Nick's mother had prepared his favorite meal, as she often does when he visits, meatloaf and mashed potatoes, just as Denise had two nights earlier—and vibrant conversation, everyone retires to the living room where Rosy serves homemade chocolate pudding and coffee.

While Denise and the two girls dig into the chocolate indulgence and engage in conversation about returning to school in early September, just a few weeks away, with all that needs to be prepared, Nick senses a free moment to speak to his mother privately, without distraction. He leans in close, taking one of her hands in his.

"How are you feeling, Mom?"

"Oh, not too bad. You know, the arthritis. I have good days and bad."

"What is it today, good or bad?"

"A *gad* day. A little good, a little bad."

Nick chuckles. He loves how she often puts two words together to create a new one, none of which are likely to gain a place in the English dictionary.

"Born too long ago," she adds.

"Nonsense," Nick says. "You'll live to be a hundred."

"God willing." She lowers her voice. "Is everything okay at home, Nicky?"

"Yeah. Why?"

"Oh, nothing. Just that Denise seems—distracted. Has most of the evening. Not her usual vibrant self."

Nick hesitates. "Oh, she's fine. Probably just needs a good night's sleep. We were at Danny's birthday party last night."

"Okay, sweetheart." She gives him a good motherly looking-over that Nick recognizes all too well.

He says, "Listen, Mom, I need to ask you something."

"Sure, sweetheart, what is it?"

"You know, you and Dad never talked about Grandpa Steele—about his life in Russia before immigrating. And frankly, up until now it hasn't been something I was particularly interested in. But I am … sort of interested now. Do you know anything about Grandpa's life in Russia?"

"Not really. He never talked about it. I always thought it was a bit strange. It was almost as if he wanted to forget about it. You know how first-generation immigrants are often nostalgic for their home country? Can't stop talking about it? Not your grandfather. He never said anything. It's like he shut it out."

The expression on Nick's face conveys that this isn't the answer he was hoping for.

"You can look in the attic, sweetheart," says Rosy. "There may be something up there. Just before he died, Grandpa Steele gave your father a small cardboard box of some of his personal things. I'm embarrassed to say, I never looked through it. And your father never spoke to me about it."

Nick isn't surprised to hear this, that his mother didn't know the contents of the box. She was never one for looking back; hardly ever took photographs or movies of his sisters and he growing up. She even threw away the lovingly handcrafted birthday, Mother's Day, and Valentine's Day cards they made for her each year—sentimental items mothers often store away and cherish for years. For whatever reason, she's always been focused on what's ahead, not behind. Nick suspects that it might have something to do with losing her only sister when she was a young girl. Toughened her up, somehow. They had been thick as thieves. "Onward and upward" was a common refrain heard around the Steele household. Nick's father was the collector, the soft touch, who tucked away the family memorabilia for safekeeping.

"I think I'll go up and take a quick look," says Nick.

Nick gives her a kiss on the check, rises from the sofa, and swiftly, light of foot, heads up the stairs. Denise and the girls, deep in their return-to-school planning mode, fail to notice his stealthy exit.

On the hall landing at the top of the stairs, an old hemp rope dangles from a door in the ceiling. Nick grips it with both hands and pulls hard, forcing open the creaky door. A wooden, spring-controlled, foldout foot ladder automatically extends to the floor. As he ascends into the attic, he's struck by the strong odor of aged cedar and the hot, still, stale air, hanging in limbo, clotted for years, infused with an oppressive, sauna-like humidity. Nick begins to sweat and gasp for the fresh air rushing up from the floor below as if were supplying emergency artificial respiration.

As he scans the congested, sweltering room, he sees before him smatterings of the tokens that families save throughout their lives but rarely look at again, gathering dust until a death or move or nostalgia inspires someone to dust it all off and travel back in time.

Nick steps onto the attic floor. Directly in front of him is a shelf full of his boxing trophies and his last pair of boxing gloves dangling from a nail. He grabs the gloves, lifts them to his nose, and takes a deep whiff. He remembers it well: the pungent, sweaty scent of his opponents. He slips on the gloves, assumes a boxer's stance, knees bent, fists held high, and throws a few jabs at the invisible foe before him. It feels at once familiar and strange; it's been a long time.

Removing his gloves, knotting them back together, and then returning them to their appointed nail, he proceeds with his search. The attic is littered with cardboard boxes, each labeled by his father many years ago in bold, black magic marker. Some are marked "Books," others "Clothes," others "Photos." Nick and his two sisters have boxes of their own—containing mementos their father had collected for them over the years, including report cards, family photos, boy and girl scout badges, local newspaper clippings of their sporting and community activities, and many of their handmade cards their mother, after reading, had thrown away, or at least thought she had.

Next, Nick turns his attention to a beaten-up, dark green military trunk with his father's first and last name stenciled in white on the top. He kneels down, unhinges the two side latches, and opens the not altogether unfamiliar container. As a young boy, Nick loved to come up to the attic and dig into his father's musty old trunk from when he was stationed at Camp Lajeune in North Carolina during the Korean War. He reveled in the touch of his rough, scratchy woolen marine uniform, and the heroic suggestion of his two brass medals. He'd slip on his father's oversized black, still spit-and-polished boots, wrap his leather holstered pistol around his waist, stand erect, and present a sharp, crisp salute, imagining himself, along with millions of other adolescent boys, making similar forays into their father's military trunks, hidden away in attics of their own, a brave and much-acclaimed war hero.

This time, though, Nick is focused on the many letters in the trunk, which were never before of interest to him. He rifles through them looking for anything that may be related to his grandfather. Unfortunately, most of what he finds are love letters during his parents' courting years. Out of curiosity, he opens a few his father had written to his mother, marveling at the strong, handsome penmanship and surprising eloquence of his romantic musings. One in particular catches Nick's attention. It's a Valentine's Day card his father wrote to his mother.

*To my darling Rosy,*

*One year. That's how long it's been since I first saw your smile. A smile like no other. Full and generous and inviting. Like a gift. One I've been waiting for my whole life.*

*You took me by surprise. I had no idea something as simple as a smile could win my love. But yours did. Instantly. One glimpse of your bright moonlit face and I was gone. I never stood a chance. I wanted that smile because I knew I'd never find it anywhere else.*

*It said everything about you. Had you never said a word, that enchanted night a year ago, I would have known you still, if only from your smile. It told me you were kind and intelligent, tender and loving, selfless, honest, and good. The same things your smile tells me today.*

*If I'd never met you, never gazed into your welcoming blue eyes, never been swollen with desire by the sweet softness of your sensual lips on that still, star-carpeted evening one short year ago, I would be half the man I am today, incomplete and heartless for having never known the joy of loving one so sweet as you.*

*With all my heart,*
*A secret admirer*

Not bad, Nick thinks with admiration, for a factory worker with a high school education. He knows, too, very well, about the special smile his father was referring to. Everyone who knows and loves his mother knows it still today. It's a smile that he never wants to let down.

After searching from box to box, reading each label, hoping to stumble upon something of relevance, he finds nothing and decides to head back downstairs. As he steps onto the first wrung of the ladder and reaches to his right to turn off the light switch on the side of the wall, he notices a small shoe box tucked back, barely visible, hidden between two diagonal roofing joists. Deciding to take one last look before he goes, he crawls into the tight, narrow space, extracts the shoebox, and blows the dust off the lid. On top, written by his father, in large letters in black magic marker, is the word "DAD."

Nick takes the shoebox, walks back to his father's military trunk, and sits down on it. He places the box on his lap, gently, reverently, as if it were a precious jewelry case. Slowly, he lifts the lid.

He's struck by how sparse it is. A few personal trinkets, including an inscribed Timex watch his grandfather had received upon retiring after forty-five years at the factory; picture postcards from friends and family mailed from exotic places, at least considered exotic at the time—places like Fort Lauderdale, the Jersey Shore, Reno and San Francisco; and a few *Life* magazine covers featuring monumental events that must have held particular meaning to his grandfather, one being Stalin's death. And one last thing. Hard to see at first, standing upright, flush against the side of the box. A white envelope without a postmark. Addressed to "My Son." Nick's heart skips a beat.

He pulls the letter from the envelope and unfolds it. It's written on three pages of yellow, lined notebook paper. The handwriting, in blue ink, is large and flowery. Unrecognizable. A woman's. Nick vaguely recognizes the date on the top of the first page as the month and year of his grandfather's death. He dives in, hoping, praying, it'll provide some clue to his predicament.

*To My Oldest Boy,*

*I'm writing this with the merciful help of my nurse, Elethea. God bless her. She knows I'm too weak to write on my own—angel that she is. I was never much good with a pen anyhow. Course, you know that.*

*Well, let me get right to the point. There's something I got to tell you.*

*I been thinking, here in the hospital. Staring into the Lord's Kingdom of Glory, hoping he'll invite you in does that to a man, I suppose. Anyhow, I been remembering way back. Taking stock. Sizing up my life. I guess I should rightly say lives. Cause I had two of 'em—one growing up in Russia, the other right here in America. Two lives lived by two different people. Two strangers. This ain't making sense, I know, but it will in a minute, so don't go getting impatient on me like you do sometimes.*

As Nick is reading, he hears his grandfather's voice in his head, as if he were sitting next to him, an odd, unique and appealing blend of his distant Russian accent, permanently imbedded from youth, along with the more dominant plain talking, early 1900s, working class, Midwestern vernacular and twang of his adopted country. He remembers, too, his grandfather once explaining to him that the factory had what they called a Sociological Department of Americanizing Immigrants. Workers were expected to attend daily English and civics lessons designed to erase national and linguistic differences between the masses of immigrating Poles, Russians, Italians, Austrians, Hungarians, Mexicans, Ottomans, and Japanese. They would all be blended into one big American stew.

*As I'm heading for what I hope and pray is eternal peace, God willing, I need to confess something to you. I need you to know who I was before you came along, or your brother, or your mother or my grandkids. I kept it to myself till now cause of feelings of shame.*

*But it's time now. I don't want to hide from myself no longer. And I don't want to carry the burden of my sins with me into the next world. I need to leave them right here, back on earth where they was born and where they need to be good and buried.*

*Since I never spoke to you none about my past, or nobody else, I suppose it's best I start from the beginning.*

*I was born and raised in Solnyetsvo, a small city outside of Moscow. I grew up poor, dirt poor, as most of us did back then, back there. First the Tsar took everything we had, then the Bolsheviks. They was both equally bad. World War I didn't help much neither. Wiped us out. Like nothing you ever seen. What the Russian people went through, My God, how we survived at all I'll never know. If nothing else, we surely know how to suffer. That we do real good.*

*Anyhow, my parents and me lived in a single-room basement apartment. There weren't no running water or electricity. I know I never provided much, and I'm sorry for that. I'm sorry I couldn't give your mother and you boys more. But this was a kind of poor you ain't never seen before, and by the grace of God, never will. We had to share one toilet and kitchen on the second floor with all the other tenants in the building. And there were lots of them. Seemed like the plumbing was always clogged or over-flowing. Our apartment floor was bare cement. Froze your toes whether it was summer or*

winter. Didn't make no difference what the temperature was outside.
Had just a few beat-up old pieces of furniture, if you could even call
them that. There was three dirty mattresses on the floor, one for my
mother, one for my father, and one for me, three wobbly three-legged
stools, a rickety old card table for eating, a cracked mirror none of
us spent much time looking into, and a wood-burning stove. That's
it. The whole kit and kabootol. Thank God for that wood-burning
stove. Without that we'd a turned to human icicles in the winter.
And it was dark, real dark, all the time. Only natural light we had
come from two narrow, ceiling windows, at street level, looking out
at people's boots walking by. Couldn't see much of nothing without
candles, even during the day, though none of us was around much
before evening come round. Who'd want to be?

My father's job, well, he sold iron pots and pans at the local
market. Stored 'em on one side of the apartment at night. A big old
pile of wood for the stove took up most of another side of the room.
Had to be restocked all the time. We'd burn anything we could find.
Even if we had to steal it, as was the case often as not. Planks from
city benches, floorboards from abandoned buildings, you name it.
My mother was a housemaid for a family of boyers. Boyers was rich
people. Paid a slave's wage, she was. I'll tell you what, they treated
her like one, too. May she rest in peace.

Early on, I knew, no doubt about it, just knew, deep down in my
bones, that I was going to find my way out of this gutter rat's existence.
Like other kids in my situation, and there was plenty of us, turning
to crime was the quickest and easiest way to improve our lot. The
Russian mafia was our role model, or at least that's what they call it
now. Controlled most of the trade and government in Solnyetsvo. The
way most of us poor kids saw it, crime was the norm, lawful living
the exception.

I'm sorry to say, yours truly was no exception. When I was just
eight, I was the lookout for older kids on the block, watched their
back while they burgled stores and homes. By twelve, I was a pretty
darned good pickpocket. I ain't going to lie to you and say I weren't
proud of it. I was. It was the most admired trade among the thieving

*class. At fourteen, I was a full-fledged member of a notorious street gang named—you'll get a kick out of this—Terror Incorporated. Can you imagine that? All the gangs had bad-sounding names like that. By eighteen, I was the leader of the gang.*

Nick looks up from the letter and stares at the ceiling, finding it extremely difficult to square all of what he's reading with his quiet, reserved, mild-mannered Grandpa Steele, who had never once so much as raised his voice in anger. He takes a deep breath and continues.

*We was pretty bad. My gang, that is. Mainly interested in one thing: going from neighborhood to neighborhood and beating the dickens out of other gangs. Sounds stupid, I know, and surely it is, or was, but when you come from nothing, when you got nothing, sometimes, it's the only way for a young man to prove his worth, to show folks how fearless and deserving of respect he is. That was the only currency we had. Course, we stole plenty, too.*

*You still with me? Now I'm getting to the important part.*

*I remember the exact date and time like it's iron branded into my head. It was 6:15 pm on September 20, 1919. Can't never forget it. I was walking down a side street in my neighborhood, minding my own business. Suddenly, I was jumped. Someone sneaks up behind me, leaps over my shoulder, and goes for my throat with a kitchen knife. Manages to cut a pretty deep gash in the left side of my neck, just missing my windpipe. Somehow I was able to break away. Drew a German Luger from my hip pocket and shot him. Point blank. Right between the eyes. I never had intended to use that gun. There was plenty of 'em lying around after the war. But it was just for show. Or at least, that was my thinking at the time.*

*Course, I knew who he was. We grew up on the streets together. A rival gang member. Sergey Yurovsky. That was his name. Nineteen years old. A year older than me at the time. Had a wife and a six-month-old son. I don't know for sure why he did it.*

*But I got a hunch. My father had a bit of a reputation—as a philanderer. People used to joke with me, or tried to joke with me before I knocked 'em flat, that I had siblings all across town. Never believed it none. But there was something about Sergey, I got to say. We did look kinda alike. Maybe even like brothers. Same features and all. Sometimes I wonder if he mighta been trying to get revenge against my father by killing me. Being a bastard, forgive me for saying, but back then, it meant a whole lot more than it does today, none of it good.*

*Anyhow, hearing that I was a marked man for killing Sergey, my parents set their minds to getting me out of town fast. They knew someone who knew someone who knew someone in the secret police, or some other such corrupt government service ... well, I suppose it doesn't really matter ... who claimed he could get us out of the country. Course, only on condition we "donate" to him every last ruble we had, which I can assure you weren't nothing, except what I stashed away from my illegal dealings. Took our apartment and all my father's inventory of pots and pans too.*

*After going through Ellis Island and settling briefly on the lower East Side of Manhattan, we moved to Everton. Good old Everton. We heard from other immigrants that good jobs was available at a new Ford parts factory there, even if you didn't speak no English. That was sure us all right. Two days after we arrived in Everton, my father, brother, and me we all went straight to work in that factory.*

*And the rest, as they say, is history that you already know.*

"Nick, are you up there?" asks Denise, calling up the attic staircase from the floor below.

"Yeah, sweetheart. I'm just going through a few of my father's old things. I'll be down in a minute. "

"Okay. We've got a long drive and the girls are getting a little restless."

"Just a few more minutes."

Nick turns to his attention back to the last page of the letter.

*I never told no one about none of this 'cause I never wanted to dwell again on killing a man. Trust me, that's not something you want to carry with you. Especially when that man just mighta been a relation. Most of all, though, I wanted to start a new life. America saved me. It surely did. It saved me from killers and from a life of crime that woulda ended up with me dining nightly on rat stew in a Siberian Gulag. I got me a second lease on life, and I had no intention of wasting it, no how, no way. Building a safe and happy life for your mother and you kids, that's all I wanted. Hope I got that right.*

*Hand to heart, from the day I stepped foot in this great country, I lived each and every day a law-abiding citizen. And that's the honest to God's truth.*

*So there you have it. Now you know. Where I come from, why I did what I did, and why I spent my entire adult life trying to hide from it.*

*I feel good telling you this. Shoulda done it sooner, I know. I hope you don't hate me for it or for hiding it from you. I was just trying to protect you all, and myself, too, I suppose, truth be told.*

*I'd appreciate you keeping what I told you here to yourself, you being my eldest and all. No need for anyone else to know. What's done is done. I just needed to get it off my chest 'cause I'm not taking it with me. No, sir. It's staying right here, right where it belongs, just as Pastor Johnson used to say, right here in the 'realm of earthly sin.'*

*'Fraid I'm getting tired. And I already imposed enough on Alethea's kindness.*

*Fondly,*

*Your loving father*

Nick remembers the pronounced four-inch scar on the left side of his grandfather's neck, just above the shirt collar line. As a child, he never thought twice about it. Why would he? It was just a normal part of his body, no more remarkable than his round, tortoise-shelled eyeglasses, his spiky head of shortly cropped gray hair, his ubiquitous oily factory smell. As far as Nick knew, he was born with the scar, along with his belly button.

He takes a deep breath, folds the letter, puts it back into the envelope, places it into the shoebox, and slides it back into the squirrelly nook where it was hiding. Looking down at his shirt, he realizes, for the first time, that it's drenched in sweat.

He steps down the creaky wooden ladder and after reaching the floor landing, lifts the attic door. As it closes, he feels like he's placing the final marble block on a burial tomb to be sealed for eternity.

"You find anything up there, Nicky?" asks his mother when he returns back downstairs.

"No, not really."

"Did you find the shoebox?"

"Yeah, but it didn't have much inside. A few old trinkets, letters, magazine clippings."

"Well I suppose it's all for the best. He was probably hiding something, but clearly he didn't want to share it with anyone."

"Suppose not." Nick has half a mind to tell his mother the truth, to confess that he did indeed uncover an amazing truth about his grandfather, a remarkable deathbed letter revealing a dark secret about his covert past. But he doesn't. He chooses to respect and honor his grandfather's wish that his past be buried along with himself. Besides, like his mother, Nick has little interest in hidden family treasures. He found what he was looking for, and that was enough: the reason why, as strange as it sounds, a man remotely connected to his ancestral past is hunting him down.

# Part II

# Chapter 17

## MONDAY

"Stay here. Don't move. I be back soon. You be ready," commands Vladimir Yurovsky. Crouching in the back of a beat-up, gutted 1999 Ford van, he double-checks the firmness of the rope he's knotted around Mina's hands and legs.

Mina sits on a dirty mattress on the floor of the van, her back leaning against the ribs of its hard metal interior wall, hands and feet tightly bound. There is no escape. She feels no pain or fear. Fear left her long ago. She knows all too well what's about to happen. She's been here before, enough times to lose count. Hatred and repulsion surge through every synapse in her body—and hopelessness, though she always fights this emotion the hardest.

"You need to take pee? If so, you pee now. I take you outside like doggie. You pee on sidewalk. When I come back from business, my Tsaritsa, I not want you to say"—in a squeaky woman's voice—"'Vlad, I need go pee-pee now.'"

"Don't worry," Mina responds, her voice a blend of insult and challenge tempered with surrender, born of a primal desire for survival.

"But I always worry 'bout you. You know that. You my princess. If I not worry 'bout you, who else?" He reaches out to brush her hair in a show of affection, but she turns her head away. "Oh, don't be like that. You hurt Vlad's feeling." Without moving her head, Mina looks back at him defiantly from the corner of her eyes.

"Okay then. I like it better when you angry anyway." With both hands, he takes hold of her head, as if grabbing a large melon from the supermarket shelf. Leaving no doubt who's in charge, he jerks her head toward his. He moves to within inches of her face, close enough that she can smell the putrid blend of vodka and cocaine on his breath. He lifts his right index finger to his lips. "Shhhh … be good girl. I go now." He grins, pinches her cheek, crawls to the back of the van, and steps onto the street. Before closing the van's back doors, he looks back toward Mina. She knows what he's thinking, having seen the expression on his face too many times before. He's aroused by the sight of her vulnerable, bound body, excited by what awaits him upon his return.

He blows her a kiss, *"Au revoir,* my love," grabs the keys from his hip pocket, and then closes and locks the back doors.

Standing on the side of the street, Vladimir surveys the surroundings of the quiet Denver inner-city neighborhood. It's 3:30 on Monday morning. Curtains and shades are drawn across the windows of the small, identical, closely nestled, two-story semi-detached townhouses running up and down the street, behind which, at this late hour, darkness is a welcome guest to its sleeping inhabitants. Overhead, fluorescent streetlights illuminate everything in mesmerizing high definition, creating the impression of a movie set. A motley assortment of parked cars lines the treeless street; empty sidewalks littered with neglected garbage cans; small patches of un-mown grass and weeds glistening with moisture from the cool, night-air. Vladimir loves this time of night. It's his time, in his city, when he imagines everything belongs to him.

Vladimir prepares himself for the evening's festivities. He checks the contents of a small traveler's day pack strapped around his waist, then lifts his right pants leg to reveal a sheathed bowie knife strapped to his calf. He then grabs a comb from his back pocket and pulls it though his long, oily, jet-black hair, styling first the top of his head, then the sides. He's worn his hair slicked-back ever since he saw the movie *Thelma and Louise.* He loved the movie, loved Thelma and Louise's lawlessness and chutzpah as they rampaged across the county brashly averting the law. They reminded him of strong, resilient Russian women, women he remembers from his home town outside of Moscow; not weak, spoiled American girls.

But most of all he loved Brad Pitt's beautiful, long, full-bodied, slicked-back hair. That's what he remembered most about the movie. And that's what he himself was determined to look like ever since. Especially on special occasions, like tonight. Trouble was, despite having a full head of hair like Brad Pitt, Vladimir was six-foot-four and weighed three hundred pounds. And unlike Brad Pitt, he knew people didn't think of him so much as sexy, as scary. That was a good thing.

Finished coiffing his hair, Vladimir turns toward the house directly across the street and slowly, purposefully, strides toward it. He continues along a narrow paved walkway skirting the side of the house, until he reaches the backyard.

He finds and kneels before a small cellar window. He pulls his tools from his travel pack. He first puts on a pair of surgeon's gloves. He then attaches a glass suction cup to the center of the windowpane, traces its parameter with a carpenter's glass cutter, and pulls the window pane outward without a struggle. After he slips through the window—moving with speed and agility not ordinarily associated with such a large man—and lands on the cellar floor, he straps a small, lightweight camper's headlight on his forehead and begins silently winding his way up the cellar stairs, through the kitchen, across the downstairs hallway, and up the main staircase to the master bedroom. Standing in the bedroom doorway, he listens with envy to the deep, rhythmic snoring emanating from the bed. Sleep is not something that comes easily to Vladimir. For a moment, he imagines how wonderful it must be to rest so soundly. A shame to have to disturb it.

Vladimir steps to the side of the bed and lingers overhead, eyeing his prey, savoring the moment, inhaling the aromatic invitation of a gourmet meal before digging in. After a few minutes, an aching hunger swells up inside that he can no longer contain. He leans over and places the edge of his Bowie knife against his victim's neck.

"Wakey, wakey, Misha."

The man stops in mid-snore, choking on his own saliva, and looks with terror into the blinding beam of light.

"Were you having a good dream?" asks Vladimir.

The man squints through the light, trying to identify the intruder, although the terror in his eyes shows that he has a pretty good idea who has come to call. "Don't do it, Vlad. *Bozhe moi.*" My God. "You have to believe me. I had nothing to do with it. You know that."

"*Konechno, nyet.*" Of course not. "But still, Misha, you know rules good as me. You fucked up. You tried take from me what is mine. And now, I must take from you. Please to get up. Now."

Misha rises from his bed to his feet as Vladimir embraces him from behind. The bowie knife remains pressed against Misha's neck, penetrating deep enough to create a necklace of dripping blood. Vladimir whispers in Misha's ear. "Misha, you think you are *boyar?*" A nobleman. "You think you have special privilege? Let me tell you, *tovarish*"—comrade—"you do not. People need to know they cannot fuck with me, Misha. You know that. If I say, 'Okay, I forgive you, Misha,' what will people say about me? I will tell you. They will say, 'Vlad is prostitute-loving, cock-sucking pussy.' Is that not true, Misha?"

Misha struggles to respond. "No, Vlad, that's not true. You know there's too much respect for you. Look, I have an idea how we can work this out."

"We not at gym, Misha. I not need work out." Vladimir chuckles. "And is too late for ideas. You should come to me with ideas before you get in big trouble like this."

Vladimir turns Misha about, still maintaining a wrestler's constricting hold, and whispers in his right ear. "It is time now, Misha, that you pray for your sins to be forgiven."

As Misha begins to struggle, Vladimir thrusts his Bowie knife deep into his chest, just below the sternum. As he carves the knife downward to his lower gut, then up and across the center of his belly in the shape of a cross, he savors Misha's paroxysms of pain, the warm blood oozing from his belly, the panicked look of horror and shock in his eyes. After shaking violently, Misha's body begins to weaken. Vladimir leads him back to bed, lays him down, and gently pulls the covers up to his neck, as if tucking a child into bed for the night.

"Go back to sleep, Misha."

Once Misha stops breathing, Vladimir takes off the bloody surgeon's gloves and throws them on Misha's head, closes the bedroom door, and strolls back down the staircase, through the kitchen and out the back door of the house as effortlessly and quietly as he entered.

Vladimir checks that the street is clear before crossing and returns to the parked van. Of course, he knows he needn't worry about the police, having made the necessary payments to ensure the street is unpatrolled this evening. He unlocks and opens the back doors, and looks at Mina cowering against the side of the van. He crawls inside and closes the doors behind him. He looms over Mina, his breathing heavy, his eyes fully dilated, his body taut with anticipation: a salivating wolf ready to devour its prey. Without a word, he unties the rope from Mina's wrists and ankles. Vladimir knows she's not stupid enough to fight back. He rips the light cotton summer dress from her body and claws away her panties. Unable to stand, he drops his trousers as he kneels before her. He cups his hands under her buttocks and lifts, guiding her onto his throbbing member, thrusting into her, over and over, deeper and deeper, half wanting to fuck her, half wanting to rip her apart.

Forty-five seconds later it's over. His face contorts grotesquely. His body shudders violently, then wilts. Exhausted and sweaty, Vlad drops Mina's midsection back on the mattress and falls by her side. He is filled with a warm, blissful glow. The perfect end to a perfect evening.

# Chapter 18

"Knock, knock." Nick peeks around the doorway of Johann's office.

"Nick, come in," says Johann, looking well-rested, bright, and cheerful, appearing to be a man without a care in the world.

Though working together for many years, and as personally close as they are, Nick has never allowed himself the presumption of simply strolling into Johann's office unannounced. As a formal show of respect, he waits to be invited in. Johann, in turn, has never encouraged him to do otherwise. Just one small shared ritual that serves to subtly reinforce their respective positions in the company.

It's 9:00 am on Monday. The morning light casts a warm glow over Johann's elegant corner office. An antique mahogany desk, the perimeter of its surface inlaid with elaborate handcrafted mother of pearl floral patterns, sits to the left of the doorway. It holds no papers, no notepads, no letters, no calendars, ledgers, paperweights, pen holders or photos; none of the usual desktop fare. One might reasonably deduce that the magnificent desk is only for display. But Nick knows better. A stickler for neatness, Johann's father relentlessly drilled the old aphorism about a cluttered desk being a sign of a cluttered mind into his son's head. Behind the desk is a long, antique credenza upon which silver framed pictures of Johann, standing side-by-side with various luminaries, are neatly and proudly displayed. Above the credenza perches a commissioned abstract oil painting of Johann's musical idol, Johann Sebastian Bach. On the right side of the room a large leather couch, two matching armchairs, and a rectangular coffee table imbedded with ancient Tuscan tiles make for an inviting and comfortable seating area. A charcoal etching of Johann in his forties, posing smartly in suit and tie, a half-smoked cigarette casually propped between his dangling fingertips, looking every bit a man of dignity and gravitas, hangs on the wall above the couch in a handcrafted wooden frame. An oriental rug covers most of the office floor.

Standing next to Johann is Jim Franklin.

"Morning, Nick." Jim extends his hand and flashes a bright smile. Brighter than usual, Nick decides. "Heard you had a productive trip."

Nick shakes Jim's hand and smiles back. "It was."

"How was your weekend?" asks Johann, looking relaxed and confident, with no hint of preoccupation.

"Restful, thanks."

"Good. Please, have a seat for a minute." Johann directs Nick and Jim to sit side by side on the large leather couch. He sits down in the armchair to their right and leans forward.

"As you both know, I've arranged a board meeting on Friday. The purpose is to vote on my successor. That'll be one of you. No other candidates were considered. They'll have an hour with each of you before the vote is taken." He looks them each in the eye. "On the basis of performance, ethics, and leadership, you've both excelled. Consequently, this will be a very difficult decision for the board. Whatever the decision, I know Rohr will be in excellent hands."

Johann clears his throat.

"I know you two haven't always agreed, but you've always been a good team. I don't know how we could have come this far without you both. Whatever the outcome, I don't want to lose either of you. On Friday, one of you will be disappointed—rightly so. Perhaps you'll feel slighted, underappreciated, undervalued. Your first instinct may be to resign or run off to a headhunter. Please don't. This company needs the stability —"

Suddenly, Sally, Johann's executive assistant of thirty years, sticks her head through his office door. "Mr. Rohr, Rick Hastings is here. He says he needs to see all of you right away. He says it's very important."

"Can't it wait?"

"He says not."

"Okay. Send him in."

Rick Hastings, Rohr's twenty-seven-year-old boy wonder IT director, who earned his doctorate in computer science at MIT at the tender age of twenty-three, bounces into the room.

"Have a seat, Rick," says Johann.

Rick sits down in the armchair across from Johann. He starts shaking his right leg and drumming a pen on his thigh.

"The floor is yours," says Johann.

Rick instantly steadies his quivering body parts. "We've got a huge problem with our Web site … well, maybe it's not a *huge* problem, but it's big one, that's for sure."

"What is it?"

"About an hour ago our site went down. I've never seen it before. I mean, I've *seen* it before, but not like this."

"What do you mean?"

"Hard to tell. I mean, I can *tell* you what I think, but it's hard to be certain what's going on. Here's my best guess—not that I'm guessing, 'cause I've been trying to diagnose the problem for the last hour, so I have a pretty good idea. Ready for this? I think we've been sabotaged."

"How?"

"It's called D.D.O.S—distributed denial of service. It's a cyberweapon usually used in politics and war. I don't mean *usually*, since it's become more commonplace than that. Actually, it's happening more and more to companies these days. Someone's spraying huge packets of random data at our site from botnets."

"What the hell is that?" asks Johan.

"Reflective amplification. A number of zombie attack computers are generating huge streams of data and choking our network. We've got a shock absorber built into our system, but it wasn't big enough to defend against an onslaught this large. Looks like a forty-gigabyte attack. If we're lucky—I don't really mean *lucky,* 'cause luck's got nothing to do with it—our system can withstand a ten-gigabyte assault, max."

"Can you get us back up and running, Rick?" asks Jim.

"Shouldn't be a problem. Actually, it won't be a problem. It'll just take a lot of work, probably a few hours. I've already called my team together. I'm hoping—not *hoping*—I mean, my goal is to get us back up by no later than noon. I've already sent an e-mail out to the organization."

"Make sure all of our partners, vendors, and clients are made aware, too, and ask them to bear with us," instructs Nick.

"Already did." Rick's leg is shaking wildly again.

"Has there been any breach of the company's computer files or bank accounts?"

"Checked that, too. Nothing."

"Any idea who did this?" asks Johann.

"No way of knowing. Anyone mad at us, Mr. Rohr?"

Nick jumps in. "Rick, please keep the three of us regularly posted on your progress. In the meantime, do whatever's needed to make *absolutely* sure that *all* the company's security systems are airtight."

Rick nods. "There's something else, too."

"What is it?"

"I needed—not needed, but *had* to—call the Feds about this. It's required by law."

"What's required by law?"

"Informing the FBI about the D.D.O.S."

"And?"

"And the agent who called me back sounded particularly interested in the case. He said he wanted to speak with the president of the company. Not sure why, but that's what he said."

"Okay," Nick says. "Did you give him my number?"

"No. I said you'd call him. I wanted to have a chance to speak to all of you first."

"Good," says Nick.

Rick reaches into his front right pant pocket and pulls out a stick of gum, two quarters, a paperclip, an old ticket stub to a Death Cab for Cutie concert, and a crumbled yellow Post-it note with the FBI agent's phone number. He hands Nick the note and re-pockets the rest.

"Thanks, Rick," says Johann.

Rick bounces out of the room in much the same manner as he arrived.

After Rick leaves, Sally steps through the office door, silently catches Johann's attention, and taps her watch with her index finger.

"Sorry, gentlemen, but I need to get to a meeting," says Johann. "It looks like this Web site issue is well in hand, at least for the moment. Yes?"

Nick and Jim both nod.

"Nick, if you learn anything more from the FBI, be sure to let us know. As for our earlier conversation, I'd like for us to continue that later. I'm flying to New York this afternoon, and I'll be back on Thursday. Let's regroup then. In the meantime, I'm sure you caught the drift of my message to both of you." Nick and Jim exchange uncomfortable glances. Johann gives them both another smile and then ushers them out of his office.

# Chapter 19

Nick races back to his office, sits behind his desk, picks up the receiver on his phone, and taps in the number on the crumpled piece of paper Rick gave him. He struggles to read the scribbled name: *Special Agent Clay Salter.* The phone rings just once.

"Salter." The voice at the other end of the phone is all business.

"Hello. This is Nick Steele, I'm the president of Rohr. Rick Hastings said you wanted to speak with me."

"Yeah, Mr. Steele. Thanks for calling. Just had a quick question for you. Got a minute?"

"Sure."

"The D.D.O.S. you got zapped with this morning ... it has the markings of an organization I have some familiarity with. So I'm curious: does the name Vladimir Yurovsky mean anything to you?"

Nick's throat constricts.

"I take it from your silence that it's a name, is it safe to say, you're not unfamiliar with?"

Nick still struggles to find the right response, concerned that he may complicate matters by confiding in the agent, yet anxious to elicit some help that might bring a swift end to his predicament. He now also has the security of the company to protect.

"Mr. Steele? The more I know, the more I can help."

Nick takes a moment to respond. "Can I speak confidentially?"

"I don't see why not," Salter clears his throat, "unless you're going to confess to involvement or complicity in the crime."

"Of course not."

"Well, then, I don't see a problem. Tell me what you know, Mr. Steele."

"I *have* heard of Vladimir Yurovsky."

"Yes?"

"And, I may be involved with him—indirectly—on a personal matter. I'm not certain yet."

"Go on."

"It's complicated."

Salter says, "Mr. Steele, perhaps it would be easier to talk in person. How about late this morning or early afternoon? Our offices are right downtown, not far from yours."

"Can't. I've got wall-to-wall meetings until 4:30. I could do it at 5:00."

"'Fraid not. My son has a soccer game at 6:00 tonight in Sherman. I promised him I'd be there."

*How times have changed*, Nick thinks. Not long ago, people tended to put business first. If there were pressing business matters, conflicting family demands or commitments often lost out. No longer. Now family is *the* priority. It's the new working norm, accepted and understood by everyone, although still not always appreciated by co-workers left in the lurch.

"I live just two towns over," says Nick. "Maybe we could meet after the game somewhere."

"That could work. Or we could meet *at* the game. And talk there."

*This guy is really pushing it*, Nick thinks. "Okay. What time?"

"Meet me at Sherman elementary school at 6:30. I'll be wearing a Michael Jordan basketball shirt."

"You'll recognize me by ... ?"

"I know what you look like, Mr. Steele. Did a little homework after your IT person called me. Don't take it personally. It's my job."

Nick hangs up the phone and sits for a moment in silence, staring at nothing, steadying his nerves. He sinks back into the swivel desk chair, trying to make sense of what's going on.

*"His name is Vladimir Yurovsky. He's Russian mafia. The real deal. He runs his own syndicate out here in Denver. He's rich, well-connected politically, and very well armed. Do some homework. You don't have to dig too deep."*

Mina's words from yesterday crash land into his head, a reminder that he needs to take a closer look at his adversary. He boots up his computer and Googles "Vladimir Yurovsky." Fifty-six results pop up on the screen.

An extract from a recent book on the Russian mafia in the United States:

> *Vladimir "The Genuflector" Yurovsky left Russia as part of a mass Jewish migration of persecuted Soviet Jews in the early years of détente. At that time, the American Jewish Establishment lobbied Congress to bring Soviet Jews to the West. Under pressure from lobbyists, Congress threatened to limit trade with the Soviets if they continued to restrict Jewish immigration. The Russians responded by releasing tens of thousands of Jews to the United States. The KGB was only too happy to use it as an opportunity to purge its gulags of hardened, professional murderers, hooligans, and thieves, who, some falsely, claimed to have Jewish roots. Yurovsky was one of its happy beneficiaries.*
>
> *He arrived in Brighton Beach, New York, Little Odessa, the capital of Russian immigrants in the United States, with an assortment of prominent tattoos displaying his elite criminal pedigree: an eagle with sharp talons across his chest, proud symbol of the vor, Cyrillic letters on each finger, identifying him as a made man,*

*and snarling wolf heads covering both knees, signifying that he bowed to no one.*

*Yurovsky tried to find himself a position of prominence in the Russian criminal ranks in Brighton Beach but was unable to break into the over-crowded, well-entrenched Russian mob establishment, unable to move beyond a meager foot soldier's livelihood of petty theft, hooliganism, and contract killings. So he decided to do what many immigrants before him had done seeking new horizons and better opportunities: he headed west. After bouncing around a few cities for a year plying his illicit trade, he ended up in Denver, with a small but thriving Russian émigré community and a burgeoning independent group of Russian mobsters.*

*In Denver, Vladimir, moved quickly to establish himself as a local kingpin, eventually forming his own small syndicate consisting of strip clubs, prostitution, narcotics, embezzlement, weapons trafficking, extortion, truck kidnappings, auto theft, robberies, and contract killings. But over the years Yurovsky has evolved his business to a much higher and more lucrative tier of criminal activity as well. Relying on rogue Russian PhDs in encryption and computer sciences, he has created complex and untraceable online financial hacking systems for propagating insurance, medical, stock, and bank account fraud and theft, making him a very rich man indeed.*

A news clip from the online edition of the *Rocky Mountain News,* with today's date:

> *A local businessman, Misha Rabaev, was found stabbed to death in his home this morning. Police believe Mr. Rabaev may have been the victim of a gangland slaying. Mr. Rabaev is the owner of an import/export business long associated with local crime boss Vladimir Yurovsky*
>
> *…*

A year-old article from the *Denver Post*:

> *The case against Denver mob boss Vladimir Yurovsky, accused of orchestrating two gangland killings last year, was dismissed today by circuit court Judge Morris Philips. The two lead witnesses for the prosecution, who had earlier confessed to the murders, have now rescinded their confessions and refused to testify at the trial, according to a spokesperson for the DA.*

A news clip from the local ABC TV station:

> *Over the last fifteen years the Russian mafia has spread across all corners of the United States. Unfortunately, Denver is no exception. Local police and federal authorities believe that our city now has a thriving underworld—one that is dominated by Russian mobsters, and in particular, by this man …*

There's footage of Vladimir entering a nightclub, large and imposing in a close-fitting European style black suit, thin black tie, silk white shirt, his long, jet black, hair molded to his head. A slender, attractive young woman is at his side in an elegant yellow, floral summer dress. Nick recognizes her. Mina.

> *…Vladimir Yurovsky, whom local officials believe heads a crime syndicate in Denver…*

A broadcast from ESPN:

> *The governing body of the National Hockey League is investigating a report that Russian mobsters may have fixed the second round Stanley Cup playoff between the New York Rangers and the Colorado Avalanche. The*

*Avalanche were seen as clear favorites, but suffered a stunning 0-4 series loss. The report alleges that a large sum of money was paid to Colorado's goalie, Nikolay Ivankov, to throw the series. Reputed Denver mob boss Vladimir Yurovsky is a suspect in the case ...*

A photomontage of Vladimir flashes on screen, each picture showing him neatly dressed in expensive suit and tie, looking more like a Wall Street executive than a brutal mobster.

Then something from *60 Minutes*:

*The FBI has warned that increased criminal activity from the Russian mafia has resulted in the worse year ever of cyber-crime. Hundreds of companies have reported major security breaches, thousands of personal bank accounts have been broken into, and millions of credit card numbers have been stolen.*

*Tell me about it*, thinks Nick.

A slide show of the country's reputed Russian crime bosses scrolls across the screen, their names at the bottom of the screen. One of them is Yurovsky.

After a few more minutes of searching, Nick discovers that there's more to his rival than murder, extortion, and cyber-crime. He learns that he's also the chairman of the Russian Historical Society of Denver; founding partner of The Russian Cultural Society of Denver; and that he has a private foundation called Russian-to-Russian, a charity to help newly arriving Russian immigrants settle financially and socially in Denver. Nick chuckles. *Hell of a guy.*

He also learns, eerily, that Vladimir shares the last name of the revolutionary commandant who was responsible for guarding the Romanov family, when they were under house arrest in Siberia. The residence was called the House of Special Purpose—the same name, he remembers Mina telling him, as the apartment she's in. He learns, too, that Commandant Yurovsky led the execution team that slaughtered the Romanov family in 1918.

*Quite a role model.*

How has this guy managed to stay out of jail? How has he avoided conviction, after so many years, in so many ways, of blatant disregard for the law? It can't just be luck. And it's not that he's smarter than everyone else. Sooner or later, people like him get caught. "Professional mobster" is not a long-term employment prospect. Too many unsavory accomplices. Too many soldiers cutting deals with DAs to save their own hides. Too many scene-of-the-crime witnesses to suppress. Too many law enforcement officials shadowing their every move who'd like to make a name for themselves. He then remembers what Mina said: *he's well connected politically.*

Finished reading, Nick feels sick to his stomach; it's the same nauseated feeling he got when, as a teenage boxer, he stood across the ring from a new opponent he knew was stronger than himself. Until now, Nick viewed Vladimir as an abstraction, devoid of meaningful substance, a mono-dimensional, cartoon-like figure, lacking depth and complexity. He now sees a man of substance, a mighty opponent, sweat-drenched muscles glistening on the other side of the ring, armed with a full repertoire of potent jabs, crosses, hooks, counterpunches, sucker punches, and head butts—all capable, if Nick is not careful and smart, of a decisive knockout.

Nick pinches the bridge of his nose between his index finger and thumb, eyes closed tightly, then rubs his forehead as if trying to chase away some internal pain.

"Welcome back," says Alicia Johnson, Nick's executive assistant, as she enters his office.

"Morning, Alicia." Nick tries to pick himself up.

"Had a good trip?"

"Yeah, it was. How's everything back here?"

"Quiet without you around." She drops a pile of documents, letters, and faxes onto his desk. "I went through everything that came in while you were gone and handled what I could. The rest, I'm afraid, you'll have to look through."

"Thanks."

"On the top is a fax that came in this morning. Strange. Looks like spam, but I wasn't sure."

"No problem, I'll take a look."

When Alicia leaves his office, he reaches for the pile, grabs the fax sitting on the top, and starts reading.

*To: Nick Steele*
*From: Me*
*Re: Time Is Running Out*

*Nick,*

*As per our conversation yesterday, it's imperative that you act now. The offer I made is only good for a limited time. In a few days it will be too late, for you and for me!*

Nick's mind explodes, a ticking time bomb that finally reaches the last second of containment and ignites. *My God. This is crazy. Out of control. Enough's enough. It's got to stop. Now!*

He calls Alicia back into his office, his voice louder and more strident than he'd like.

"Alicia, I need to make an unexpected visit to my brother-in-law in Denver tomorrow. It's a personal trip. Shouldn't be gone more than a few days. Book two round-trip tickets, departing tomorrow morning, one for me, one for Daniel Stevens. Leave the return open. Put it on my personal credit card. Cancel all my meetings tomorrow and let Johann know that I'll be back for our meeting on Thursday."

Alicia looks at him with concern. "Is there anything I can help with, Nick?"

"No, thanks, it's nothing. Just a minor family matter," he says. There it is, those two magic words, *family matter*, that earn you an automatic pass from work associates, no questions asked. He feels guilty using it, but has no alternative.

Seeming to have difficulty hiding her concern, but respectful of Nick's obvious desire for privacy, Alicia leaves his office. Nick calls Daniel at home, where, as a freelance PR professional, he works most days.

"Danny. You still interested in going to Denver with me?'

"Yeah, course."

"We'll be flying out tomorrow morning. Should be back on Wednesday. I'll take care of all the arrangements on my end."

"What should I bring?"

"What do you mean?"

"I don't know. Black clothes, a nylon stocking to put over my head, black shoe polish to rub on my face, brass knuckles?"

"Knock it off."

Daniel asks, "You know what you're doing, right?"

"No."

"Good. For a minute there I thought you had a plan."

"We're meeting with an FBI agent tonight at 6:30."

"What?"

"Don't ask. I'll explain later. I'll pick you up around 6:00 at your house."

"The plot thickens."

"More than you know. See you later."

# Chapter 20

It is nearly 5:30 in the afternoon as Nick parks his car in his home garage and heads into the kitchen where his two daughters, both in their summer team soccer uniforms, are making sandwiches, layering on thick slabs of sliced meat and American cheese, famished after three hours of soccer practice and games.

"Is bologna bad for you, Dad?" asks his youngest daughter, Sarah, as she adds a third slice of bologna to a piece of white bread smothered in mayonnaise. "Charlotte says it is, and that I shouldn't eat it."

"A little bit is fine, sweetheart. I'm not sure I'd make it a staple of your diet, though. "

"See, I told you." She turns to her older sister and sticks out her tongue in victory.

"By the way, aren't you having dinner soon?"

"Mom told us that this would be dinner," answers Charlotte.

*Unusual.* "Where's your mother, girls?"

"She's in the den," says Sarah, trying to fit the two-fisted sandwich into her mouth.

"Save some of that bad stuff for me, honey bee." Nick walks across the hallway and turns into the den. It's a warm, cozy room with floor-to-ceiling knotted pine paneling and well-stocked built-in bookshelves lining the walls. A brown dhurrie rug covers the entire floor. Family pictures adorn the walls. As he enters the room, Denise is sitting on the leather sofa, leafing through a large photo album on her lap. Other photo albums are strewn about on the leather footrest in front of her. He recognizes the open pages from a vacation they took rafting down the Grand Canyon ten years ago. He also notes the music playing in the background. Joni Mitchell's "Blue." He needs to tread carefully.

"Hey, babe," he says.

Denise looks up and smiles with her lips, but not her eyes. Her mind is lost in the photos.

"Be nice to take that trip again, wouldn't it?" Nick tries to get her attention.

"Yeah." Denise answers without emotion, her head still drawn downward, fixed on the photo album in her lap. Seconds pass before she speaks again. "I did some research online today. I'm trying to understand this whole thing—you know, your motivation for calling that prostitute. Did you know that twenty-five percent of men claim to have had extramarital affairs?"

"Nope." Whatever's on her mind is well beyond his control. He's known her for too long—far too long not to understand that she needs to intellectualize issues before resolving them. Denise's intelligence is one of the qualities Nick has always been attracted to, especially in combination with her natural physical beauty and feminine charms. He also knows that being on the receiving end of her analytical reasoning can be exhausting. The best thing to do, he's learned, is to let it come out; let her express her thinking, uncontested. In this state of mind, even when she asks questions in the course of conversation, he knows she's not really looking for answers. She's simply projecting her thoughts on a human sounding board, the better to hear herself think.

Denise finally looks up at Nick, engaging him directly for the first time since he walked in the room. "Of course, researchers think this number is actually understated."

"No doubt."

"Do you know all the different reasons people cheat?"

"No. But I have a feeling you do."

"Well, there's the exit-affair. That's when someone has already decided to leave a relationship but doesn't know how to tell the other person. Ring a bell?"

"Nope," Nick says. "Wild horses couldn't drag me away."

"How about the split-self affair. That's when an overly rational, overly responsible person finally caves into his more repressed emotional side. Could be you. Don't you think?"

"No shortness of emotion here."

"Hmmm. Intimacy-avoidance. Let's try that one. The desire to keep one's spouse at a distance."

"Nope. Fact is, I can't get enough of you."

"How about sex addiction?"

"Guilty as charged. But then again, you'd have to charge most of mankind."

"Well, what do you think it is then?"

Nick ponders her question for a moment before answering. "IMR: Isolated-Masturbation-Replacement. The desire to substitute one's hand—just once—one isolated time, after sixteen years of marriage. After eight lonely days on the road."

"Mmm. I don't think I read about that one."

"Funny, my guess is it's the most common reason of all."

Denise regroups her thoughts. "They say some people feel like war victims, or survivors of a major disaster, after being cheated on."

"Good thing I didn't cheat on you, then."

"You did, Nick. Or at least you tried to." Denise's tone is more serious now, bordering on anger.

"True. That was a stupid thing to say," Nick says.

The room is quiet. In the distance, the faint sound of the girls' voices can be heard from the kitchen, as they chat, giggle, and argue over dinner.

"Maybe you should start coming to church with us," Denise says.

"Huh?"

"Amy told me going to church together has made her and Jack's marriage stronger." Amy is Denise's best friend from childhood. Although she lives in California, they remain extremely close, regularly sharing unguarded confidences for mutual support in their marriages and in raising their children. They share a deep feminine empathy, offering each other reassurances that lubricate their everyday emotional engines. Amy, on her third marriage, is all-too-often the source of Denise's new ideas about their relationship.

Nick is silent.

"Well, I also read that people who go to church have more self-control. They're less likely to act on impulses. When temptation strikes, they're better able to chase it away. Apparently people who go to church are less likely to cheat."

Nick wants to remind her of Jimmy Swaggart, Jim Bakker, and other well-known preachers, highly religious men, all regular churchgoers, who apparently were not made aware of this fact. "You've been reading a lot, haven't you?"

"Um-hum." Denise looks like a wounded child. "Nick?"

"Yeah, baby?"

"What if the tables were turned? What if I did this to you?"

"I'd kill you," Nick jokes.

"I know. It's not fair. Men have such a double standard."

"Or maybe I'd just forgive you. As long as you were traveling alone for eight days, true to me for sixteen years, and as long as you promised to never, ever do something idiotic like that again. Then I'm pretty sure I'd spare your life."

"I haven't entirely figured this out," Denise says.

"I know. And I really am sorry. And I almost wish there was more to what I did than a stupid, impulsive act. But it *really* is ridiculously uncomplicated. And it *really* doesn't have anything to do with our marriage. All I can promise you is that it'll never happen again."

"I know. I believe you. I just wish I could shake it off. But I can't. It's going to take some time."

"I know."

Denise's gaze falls back into the pages of the photo album on her lap. "In my heart, I know that what you've told me is true. That there's nothing complicated about it, and that it won't happen again. But, still … I can't chase away the sadness I feel— that you wanted someone else. That you needed to go to someone else—even if it was only once." She shakes her head. "It'll take time."

Nick reaches out and strokes her shoulder.

She stiffens her back. "I also don't like the idea of playing the accommodating, jilted wife—just another dutiful spouse casually accepting her husband's infidelity, or attempted infidelity, as if it were a natural insignificant occurrence—a non-event. I don't want to *have to* forgive you, Nick. Why should I make it too easy for you? Especially after the trouble you've brought upon our family? It's bad enough that you tried to fool around. Now we've got people robbing our bank account. And who knows what else they have in mind? I can't forgive you, at least not yet."

"Nor should you. Not until you're ready." He pauses briefly. "Nise?"

She looks up from the photo album.

"I know this may not be a great time to ask, but I need you to do something for me."

Denise gives him a stern look, leaving no doubt that he's treading on thin ice and in no position to be asking for a favor.

He decides to plow ahead anyway. "I'd like you and the girls to go up to the cabin for a few days."

The "cabin" is their rustic vacation home in a remote, northern part of the state, along Lake Michigan. "I need to go to Denver tomorrow, to sort this thing out. I'd feel better knowing you and the girls were —"

Denise bolts upright. Her eyes widen. "Nick, you're scaring me!"

"It's just a precaution. I'm sure there's nothing to worry about."

"Nothing to worry about? Don't patronize me. You're not equipped to deal with this—at least not on your own."

"That's true, but I'll have Daniel with me," Nick immediately wishes that he'd stop trying to make light of the issue. The last thing he wants to do is to insult his wife's intelligence or get her back up. Never a good thing.

"Enough! You need to get the police or the FBI involved," she says. "It's not something you can fix. There are people, professionals, who deal with this sort of thing."

"I know. But we don't have time. It'll take them weeks, even months, to dig into this, let alone solve it, if at all. I *am* meeting with an FBI agent tonight, at 6:30. I'm meeting him in Sherman. But honestly, I doubt there's much he can do—quickly, that is. I just don't think we have time to wait."

Denise's eye's narrow as she shakes her head. "I'm not with you on this."

"Nise … I need to go."

"Like hell you do. This is insane. You're insane."

"You need to trust me."

"Trust you? Trust you to go back to Denver as if you were some kind of cop or sleuth? Trust you to go back to Denver to see a woman you tried to sleep with?" Her eyes turn cold. "Maybe there's more to your relationship with her than you told me."

"You know me better than that."

"Right now, I'm not sure I know you at all."

"You know I'd never do anything to jeopardize the safety of you and the girls."

"You mean never do anything *again*."

Nick feels like a knife has been stuck in the side of his ribs. "I'm sorry, Nise. But I need to go. I understand your concern … and anger. But …"

"You're in way over your head. You know that, *don't you*? Do you even have a plan?"

"Not exactly. But I'll figure it out. I always do, right? I have some ideas. Of course, I'm not going to do anything stupid or dangerous."

"You already are."

Nick hangs his head, at a loss for words that will make a convincing counter-argument.

Denise's voice softens. "You handle most things better than anyone I know, Nick. But this is different. These are dangerous people. You can't just wing it."

"I won't. I promise. I'll be back on Wednesday. While I'm gone, I just want to be sure that you and the girls are safe. It's just a precaution. Promise me you'll head up to the cabin tomorrow. I'll call you when I get back. And this whole thing will be over."

Nick hesitantly decides not to tell Denise about Vladimir's absurd vendetta, about his grandfather's letter validating the shooting almost a century ago, the cyber attack on Rohr's Web site this morning or Mina's foreboding fax, partly because he doesn't want to upset her anymore than he already has, partly because if she knows all the facts he'd never make it out of the house, and partly because he can still hardly believe it himself. He hates lying to her, he's done far too much of that lately, but is convinced it's essential to bringing a rapid end to this fiasco. "Will you do that, please?"

She takes a deep breath and nods her head in defiant surrender. "We'll go. But I don't like it. Not one bit. And I don't agree with how you're handling it. I know you've been self-reliant all of your life, but if there was ever a time to let go a bit, it's now. You need to let others take charge. People who know what they're doing."

"I hear you. But first I need to go and scope things out. If the situation looks beyond my control, or in any way dangerous, I'll head home, and we'll do as you say—get others involved." He looks at her. "Okay?"

Denise is silent

"I'll call you every few hours, to let you know what's going on, and that I'm all right."

Still no response.

"Okay?" pleads Nick.

She slowly closes her eyes and almost imperceptibly nods her head.

"I'll take that as a yes." Looking at his watch, Nick realizes that he's running short of time. He needs to head out, pick up Daniel, and meet with Clay Salter. He shifts the conversation to one final pressing issue that requires Denise's involvement. "There's something else I need you to help with."

Denise looks at him in disbelief.

"Our credit card companies need to be alerted to what's going on. You know, about the fact that someone is stealing from us. They'll probably want to issue us new cards. Also, please call our brokers at Vanguard and Merrill Lynch. They'll know what to do to protect our accounts. You should also call our mortgage company, just in case."

"Oh, man, you're really pushing it."

"Sorry. I know. But it's going to be over soon." As Nick bends over to kiss her on the forehead, she turns her head away from him.

"I love you," he says.

Silence.

Nick turns and heads upstairs to their bedroom to pack.

# Chapter 21

"Come on, Ref! Open your eyes!"

Nick hears Clay Salter's distinct, booming voice rise above the small crowd, as he and Daniel approach the soccer pitch from the elementary school parking lot. Nick watches the parents lining the field, engrossed in the game, each intently focused on their own child's every move, concentrating hard, willing them to do something marvelous, something extraordinary, something that will help promote their one-of-a-kind progeny, for all to see, above the pack. Sometimes Nick harbors similar feelings, watching his own daughters compete.

"Get a move on, Ref!"

Clay is standing on the sideline, screaming at the overweight referee officiating his nine-year-old son's soccer match as he waddles up and down the pitch, barely able to keep pace with the scurrying children, sealed in his skin-tight, black-and-white polyester shirt. Clay, too, is short and stocky but seemingly fit. Nick guesses he shaves his head to hide his baldness. He projects an uncontrollable intensity.

Nick and Daniel approach Clay from behind. As promised, he's wearing a sleeveless red Chicago Bulls jersey with Michael Jordan's name and retired number on the back. Long baggy cargo shorts hang just below his knees, and untied high-top sneakers adorn his oversized feet. *A boy-man*, thinks Nick. That's what

Denise would call Salter. It's a phrase she often uses to describe adolescent American men, coined by one of her literary idols, Norman Mailer.

Standing directly behind Clay, Nick taps him on his right shoulder. "Clay?"

Clay looks back, annoyed by the interruption. He reaches sideways to shake Nick's extended hand, his eyes darting back and forth between Nick and the field, anxious not to miss any of the game. Nick watches with surprise as Clay eventually turns his full attention back to the field, leaving Nick and Daniel staring at his broad, unwelcoming backside.

Nick taps him on the shoulder again, harder this time, raising his voice, trying to sound friendly. "This is my friend, Daniel."

Just as he had done with Nick, Clay looks back, rigidly extending his arm. "Nice to meet you," he grumbles. He shakes Daniel's hand and then promptly returns his focus to the field.

"Shoot, Jimmy, shoot!" Clay yells, digging the toe of his right shoe into the ground in disgust. Half the crowd releases a collective moan at his son's missed shot on goal. Clay bows his head toward the ground, as if trying to bury his disappointment in his son and perhaps in himself. Nick knows the feeling. Every move his daughters make on the field feels like his own.

Nick interrupts again. "Clay, can we get a few minutes of your time?"

"Yeah, yeah, just give me a minute. The half ends in forty-five seconds." Clay points to the electronic score board and timer on the right side of the field. Still watching the game, he asks Daniel, "What's with your face? Looks like a squirrel tried to nest on it."

"Yard accident."

"Ah ha," responds Clay, in a flat voice that suggests he knows there's more to it but doesn't really care.

Nick and Daniel wait patiently for the clock to run down.

"Out of bounds. *Out of bounds!* Come on. Come on! Get some glasses, Ref!" Nick marvels at the veins bursting from the back of Clay's neck. He envisions rivers of blue blood flooding his constricted muscles with much-needed oxygen.

The referee's whistle blows, signaling the half's end. Clay turns around, his face puce and sweaty from the hot, humid summer sun and, Nick suspects, the strain of the match. Clay gestures for Nick and Daniel to walk with him around the perimeter of the playing field, far enough away from the crowd so as not to be overheard. He makes no attempt at small talk, anxious to be back on the sideline the second the referee's whistle signals the start of the second half. "Glad you could make it, Mr. Steele."

"Nick."

"Okay. Nick. Tell me what you got." Nick and Daniel are walking on opposite sides of Clay, each standing a full six inches taller than he. From a distance, one might think they were adults escorting a degenerate youth off the grounds. Clay's head is hanging downward, making him look every bit the guilty adolescent. Nick guesses he's still thinking about his son's missed shot. He decides he needs to get his full attention.

"Vladimir Yurovsky," says Nick.

Clay looks up at Nick. "Yeah. Right. I'm all ears."

"I have reason to believe he's after me." Nick is getting pretty good now at telling his story, having confided in both Daniel and Denise. He recounts it calmly and completely, taking care not to omit any detail that might have relevance for his newest confidant, who as a professional law enforcement officer, he assumes, is used to hearing sagas far worse than his own. For the first time, Nick chronicles his predicament unapologetically, without embarrassment or shame. He is pleased to find himself liberated from the emotions that have hampered his ability to act until now. His focus is no longer on bemoaning his misfortune, but resolving it.

"My last posting was in Denver—was there for five years, so I know enough to tell you that what you're dealing with here is *very* serious. This guy Vladimir Yurovsky is what they call a *vor v zakone*—a thief-in-power. He's one of the top dogs in the

Russian mob in Denver. If there's a way to make money illegally, he's doing it. His special talent is cyber crime. Sounds like you've already discovered that. He has Russian exiles working for him, some with more advanced degrees than you can count. Still, he surrounds himself with plenty of mindless thugs." Clay hesitates and glances from side to side, appearing to double-check that no one is within hearing distance. He continues in a hushed tone, like a basketball coach kneeling before his huddled players during a time-out during the final minutes of a close game. "You need to know: Yurovsky and his kind are extremely dangerous. The Italian mob will kill you if you cross them. The Russian mob will kill you *and* your whole family *and* anyone else they fucking feel like. Cops, politicians, journalists, businessmen—all fair game. They don't follow the unwritten rules of the underworld. They have no parameters, no limits. Probably a result of too many years living under a totalitarian regime. Messed with their heads."

While Clay shares this information, Nick ponders the surreal juxtaposition of his, now, two disparate yet interwoven realities: the world of feudal, cold-blooded Russian mobsters intent on destroying him—strange, foreign, and dangerous—and the quiet suburban landscape of innocuous, law-abiding fathers and mothers, those standing before him on the sidelines—comfortable, predictable, and safe.

"My advice, Nick, is to meet with someone at the bureau. I can give you the name of a top guy in the organized crime division down in Washington. But *don't* try and deal with this on your own. You don't have just yourself and your family to worry about, there's your company too. What you got this morning was just a taste of the damage these guys are capable of."

"What can he—your guy in Washington—do for me?"

Clay answers without hesitation. "Probably nothing. Not immediately, at least; not unless you have some proof or evidence of what you're saying that will allow them to go after this guy. They'll need something to work with, something beyond your story."

"What about the money stolen from my bank account, or the credit card fraud, or the attack on Rohr's Web site?"

"There's no evidence yet on who committed those crimes, right? And it's unlikely there's going to be. These Ruskies are real smart. Smarter than the Colombian cartels, the Japanese Yakuzas, even the Chinese Triad. They don't leave many traces. They're professional hiders. You get pretty good at it, I guess, when you come from a nation where you never know who to trust. You won't find a stealthier group of criminals than the Russians. Hell, they stole the H Bomb from right under our noses. Thieving's part of their national character."

"I don't have time to waste," Nick says. "I'm beginning to believe—truly believe—that this guy, this Vladimir Yurovsky, is out to wipe me out financially. Maybe even kill me. I'm even more concerned that my family may be in danger. And I believe I have days, not weeks or months." Nick stops for a moment. "Would the FBI be able to protect me and my family if I went to them now for help?"

"Unlikely. Again, the bureau doesn't make a practice of that unless they know for certain that a contract is out on someone. Even then, they'd be hesitant if it meant jeopardizing an inside or undercover source."

"Clay, with all due respect, you're not exactly making a case for me to waste my time going to your organized crime unit."

"All I can tell you is that it's better than dealing with this on your own," says Clay. "You're a businessman. What do you know about how to deal with people like this? This is way beyond anything you're capable of handling."

Nick pushes further. "If it's true what Mina says, about having recordings of Vladimir's business dealings—if I were able to get them to the FBI, would they be able to help me then?"

"Yeah, of course," concedes Clay, ready to be finished with the conversation. "Now you've got something they can work with. You'd be giving them hard evidence to help put this guy away. They've been trying to nail him for years, with no success. They want him. Make no mistake. I just don't think you're the guy to deliver him to them."

Nick's head is spinning. He feels like he's been thrown from a tornado into the Land of Oz. If he brings back the witch's broom, he'll be granted his wish to go home again, to return to his peaceful former life. If not, he'll never secure safe passage from the strange, hostile, foreign land he's crashed into.

They arrive back where they started, having come full circle around the playing field. The referee blows his whistle, signifying the end of their discussion. Before Clay takes his place back on the sideline, he turns to Nick and offers one last piece of advice. "Do not fuck with these people. You'll be making a big mistake." He turns to Daniel. "Talk to your pal, Danny." Salter turns his back to both Nick and Daniel, takes his position alongside the other parents on the sideline, and starts clapping his hands, encouraging the players who are taking the field again.

Clay stops in mid-clap and turns back toward Nick. "By the way, if you're stupid enough to do what you're talking about—and I hope you're not—call me as soon as you get back, assuming you're still with us. I'll handle everything from there." Clay's face is emotionless as he turns back to the field.

Nick and Daniel walk back toward the parking lot. "I guess that wasn't too helpful," says Daniel.

"No, it was. It's strengthened my resolve. I know now, more than ever, that I need to get out to Denver fast and figure this thing out on my own."

"Not entirely on your own. I'm coming with you. Remember?"

As they approach Nick's car, they can't avoid hearing one loud, severe voice rising above the din of the crowd. "Come on, Ref! Wake up!"

# Chapter 22

Steam rises from the simmering pot of homemade stew, clouding the kitchen with the wholesome, earthy aroma of potatoes, onions, carrots, leeks, cabbage, and pork, spiced with liberal pinches of fresh basil, fennel, fenugreek, salt, and pepper. The recipe is from Vladimir's mother. Every Monday night he insists Mina recreate this remembrance of home. It took her months to cook it exactly the way he likes it, exactly the way his mother makes it. He refused to eat the stew until it was perfect, spitting it out on his plate week after week, instructing her to cook it longer, cook it shorter, add more of this, or less of that, until finally, she achieved perfection. Ever since that momentous Monday, Mina watches him enter the apartment with a broad, excited grin, his nose tilted upward, inhaling the savory sent of his favorite stew.

"I am here, my princess," Vladimir calls from the entrance hallway as he steps into the apartment. He's dressed in an expensive, custom-tailored black Armani suit, a white shirt made from Egyptian cotton, bejeweled with studs and cufflinks encrusted with diamonds, and black handmade Russian Calf shoes. While other Russian mobsters in Denver dress down so as not to draw attention to themselves—*they are all peasants*, he tells Mina—Vladimir Yurovsky dresses in the manner of the master-of-the-universe he proudly purports to be.

"I am smelling something beautiful," he calls into the kitchen. Unlike so many of his Russian contemporaries who have worked hard to polish their American syntax and neutralize their accents, Vladimir has never wanted to sound like an American. Although living in the country for more than thirty years, his strong accent and clipped phrasing, stems, he told Mina one day, from a desire to avoid blending in with the *Amerskozty*, a derogatory Russian term he often uses for Americans. It also serves Vladimir's purposes that others, particularly his enemies, sometimes wrongly interpret his diminished linguistic capabilities as a sign of a diminished intellect. Those who know him well, including Mina, know better.

So it came as no surprise to Mina to learn that his sense of Russian nationalism is as strong as the day he left his home country, perhaps stronger. Amongst fellow émigrés, a shot of vodka in hand, Mina has watched him on many occasions recite with passion a speech from Gogol's heroic Cossack, Taras Bulba—one that Vladimir told her all Russian school children were required, in his day, to memorize from an early age. She has heard it so many times that she too can now recite it word for word. *"No brothers, to love as the Russian soul loves is to love not with the mind or anything else, but with all that God has given, all that is within you."*

As he strolls into the kitchen, Vladimir smiles at Mina and raises his arms in surprise. "All this for me. You should not have."

"Very funny."

"That's me, my angel, Mr. Funny. How much you miss me today? We have fun last night, yes?"

"Oh, yeah, a barrel of laughs." Mina's voice is flat, lifeless.

"Oh, look, my princess is pouty." He pauses for a moment as if pondering the last word to leave his mouth, both fascinated and amused by it, looking like a child in a bath enchanted by a large, floating soap bubble. "I like this word *pouty. Pouty ... pouty ... pouty ...*" He plays with the word, exploring its elasticity, tossing it around, louder then softer, infusing it with excitement then tedium, anger then affection, stretching it then contracting it, alternating pitch and tone, seeming to enjoy its diverse resonances. He smiles, pleased with a new toy. "What you call this word that sound like what it is?"

"Onomatopoeia."

"On-oh-mon-oh-pee-ya."

"Close enough."

"Fuck is om-no-mon-oh-pee-ya. Yes? Fuck, and suck, and cock, and pussy."

"Clever man," she says.

"And I like when you are pouty. Go on, give Vlad your most pouty look."

Mina stirs the pot of stew, trying to ignore him, and then decides to play along. She contorts her face into a grotesque, sulking pantomime, sticks her tongue out, and then returns to a flat, expressionless countenance and the chore of stirring the stew. "There, happy now?"

Vladimir bursts out laughing. "Oh, you even more beautiful when you make ugly face. It make me hungry for you, more than for stew."

"Take it easy." Mina holds up the cooking spoon as if a sword, warning him off.

"Okay, I take it easy—until after my super. I am in good mood. Pour me vodka."

Mina reaches into a kitchen cabinet where the liquor is stored and pulls out a half-empty bottle of Putinka vodka, a top-selling brand in Russia named after Vladimir Putin and imported by Vladimir for his own private consumption. She grabs a shot glass and pours it to the brim. With haste, Vladimir wraps a large, fleshy index finger and thumb around the tiny glass, raises it to Mina, and makes a brief, traditional toast. "*Buden zdorovy.*" Let's be healthy. He throws his head back, downs the clear liquid, and then pounds the glass on the blue, ceramic-tiled kitchen counter, as if trying to get the bartender's attention, appearing in immediate need of a refill. "More Satan's blood."

Mina looks up from the pot and frowns at him.

Vladimir puts on his best imitation of polite boy. "Pah-leeeze."

"It's Monday night. Maybe you ought to slow down a bit." Mina is anxious to keep Vladimir from getting drunk, knowing all too well that a drunken Vladimir is an unpredictable and often hostile Vladimir.

"I am in good mood. We have good month. Business is good. I celebrate. You celebrate with me. Pour two glasses."

"I'll pass."

"You know, not drink is sign of *stukatch*." A snitch.

"Well, I must be a stukatch then, whatever that is."

"*Stuckach* is on-oh-mon-o-pee-ya," Vladimir says. "*Stuckach* sound like rat; *stuckach* is rat."

"Oh, thanks. Now I'm a rat. You sure know how to charm a girl."

"I hope you not rat. That not be good for me—or you." His eyes narrow, emphasizing the risk she, or anyone else, would be taking if they were to double-cross him.

Mina shrugs off his threatening look, one she's all too familiar with, and refills his glass, three-quarters full this time. Again, he reaches for it, and holds up the glass for his next toast. "To the dead." He downs the glass in one swig and eases it back onto the kitchen countertop, which Mina interprets as a downshift in the pace of his commitment to getting drunk.

"Anyone in particular you referring to?" Mina asks, mostly out of self-preservation, knowing full well that Russian toasts are really a way to get a point across.

"Right now, I think most about my murdered grandfather. I also think about the soon to be dead, Mr. Nick Steele. He must pay for his grandfather's sin. And I must avenge my family's loss."

"That's crazy. That was almost a century ago!"

"You do not understand. Family is everything. My father tell me before I come to America that his father's killer in U.S. That the family name is Steelovich. That I am to avenge my grandfather's death. I must honor my father."

"Vlad, this is the twenty-first century. You're talking like someone from ancient times."

"Is true. I am connected to ancient world. My family direct descendant of the last Khan of the Golden Horde. I have royal, ancient blood."

"How anyone can be proud of being related to a murderous Mongol is beyond me," Mina mumbles, speaking half to herself. The words barely out of her mouth, it dawns on her that perhaps this rogue ancestry explains Vladimir's penchant for stealing, raping, and killing. Maybe he's carrying some vicious, aberrant twelfth-century Mongol gene. She chases the absurd thought from her head, not wanting to forgive Vladimir his sins by legitimizing the idea that he might be a victim of a pre-programmed genetic disposition toward cruelty.

She wants to change the conversation before Vladimir has a chance to react to her insult about his Mongol roots. "Nick Steele has done nothing to you. His grandfather ... *his grandfather,* who lived in Russia, committed the act. And he's long gone. You can't blame subsequent generations for the crimes their parents and grandparents commit."

"Oh no? How about Stalin deciding to use family history to decide if you comrade or not? If your grandfather bourgeois, then you bourgeois too, and off to Siberia with you."

"I don't think it helps your point to use a mass murderer as an example—although I'm not entirely surprised at your choice for a role model."

"Okay. How about God punishing Pharaoh by killing all Egyptian firstborn sons? And how you explain the Israelis and Palestinians? English and Irish? Indians and Pakistanis? They kill for crimes against their fathers and grandfathers. No?"

"And you think that's a good idea? You think all that mindless killing has served any purpose, has improved the situation in those countries, or made anyone's lives better off?"

"I not care. I not care about how world should be. Just how is. I must respect my father's wishes."

"A very enlightened philosophy."

"Come. I not want talk about this anymore. I am in good mood. Pour me more vodka." Vladimir puts on a sickly sweet smile. "Pah-leeze."

Mina pours Vlad another shot, which he downs after making a toast to vengeance. She asks him to take his seat at the kitchen table. The stew is ready to be served.

# Chapter 23

"You know, Vlad, I don't really understand why I have to have a bodyguard follow me wherever I go." Mina is feigning sweetness, adorableness, congeniality, and whatever other feminine charms she can muster to soften Vladimir. She purposely waited until after he finished his meal before raising the issue of her captivity. From experience, she knows it's not a good idea to interrupt him when he eats Monday dinner. His attention is singularly focused on the food. Like a starved man, he shovels the stew down his throat, barely coming up for air until his plate is wiped clean with a thick piece of pumpernickel bread coated with thick slabs of butter.

Vladimir presses a cloth napkin across his lips and tosses it onto his plate. "You know, my princess. It is for your safety. If anything ever happen to you, I never forgive myself."

"Nothing's going to happen to me."

"Not true. Lots of bad men out there."

"I can handle myself."

"No, you safe here in apartment. And when you go out, Alexander with you. You not like Alexander? Is that what this about? You want new bodyguard?"

"No, no—he's fine, for an illiterate thug. I just don't want to spend all my time alone in this apartment and to be chaperoned when I go out anymore. I feel like a prisoner."

"You can go wherever you like, but Alexander be with you. I'm sorry you feel bad. But for your own good." He reaches out to her lovingly, appearing to be an adoring, wise father comforting his confused daughter, who is bound to appreciate the wisdom of his decision in time.

"Of course, my *Tsaritsa*, you not be happy, or sad, or anything else, if you not alive. There are some people who not like me. Maybe they want to hurt me. Maybe they want to hurt me by hurting those I love."

"What about your wife and kids?" Mina asks.

"They protected too," answers Vladimir, in a tone that suggests this is of no concern to her. "Just pretend you President of United States. Or first lady. She can go nowhere without many bodyguards. She is not sad. She is happy to be safe."

"So when does it end? I can't live like this forever."

"I do not know," he growls.

Mina can tell by the tone of his voice that Vladimir is starting to lose patience with her.

"You will have to be patient," he continues. "And be happy. Many girls happy to be mistress of Vladimir Yurovsky… and happy to be protected."

"What if I just sneak away and never come back?" she says.

"Do not talk like that." Vladimir's voice turns cold and threatening.

Mina continues to challenge him, seeing how far she can venture before it becomes dangerous, carefully tempering her tone with a breezy air so as not to appear aggressive. "Why not, Vlad? I think I might just do that. I'm getting tired of living like a prisoner. You don't own me. Your Mongol ancestors may have owned people, but you can't … not in this day and age."

Vladimir's brow furrows, his jaw tightens. "I have told you before, and I will tell you again, but only this one last time, if you try to leave, I will find you. And then—you will not need bodyguard ever again."

Mina's cell phone rings. The ringtone is a 1970 recording of Eddie Holman's "Hey There Lonely Girl," which Mina initially downloaded from her computer as a joke but decided to keep because after a while it seemed more apropos than parody. She pulls it from her front jeans pocket.

"Who is that?"

"No one. Just one of my girlfriends."

Vladimir grabs the phone from her hand. "Let me answer."

"No, it's just a friend. It's none of your business." She tries to pry the phone from his grip, but his fingers are wrapped tight as it's pulled away, beyond her reach.

"Everything about you is my business." He looks at the number displayed in the lighted panel on the phone. "Look, a Chicago area code. You have girlfriend in Chicago?"

Vladimir presses the Send button, lifts the phone to his ear, and listens, saying nothing, waiting for the caller to speak first.

"Hello? Hello? Mina?"

Vladimir presses the End button and hands the phone back to Mina, satisfied with his discovery. "Your girlfriend has very deep voice. Sound like your girlfriend has to shave in morning."

"I know some men, too. I know that may surprise you. And I know you don't like it. But that's just the way it is. I can't be told who I can speak to and who I can't."

Vladimir's face is expressionless, his inkblot eyes black and lifeless. "Did you fuck him?"

"Fuck who?"

"Him," pointing to the cell phone still in Mina's hand.

"I don't even know who called. You answered the phone, remember?"

"Did you fuck him?"

"Give me a break."

"You took long time. Longer than usual. I remember thinking, *Why Mina taking so long in hotel room on Thursday night?*"

"What are you talking about?"

"Did you fuck Steele?"

"No."

"You lie. Why he calling you?"

"I don't know."

"You lie again. What have you told him?"

"Nothing."

"You lie. You lie. And you lie. Stinking whore!" Vladimir swipes the backside of his left arm across the surface of the kitchen table, sending everything, the dishes, the glasses, the silverware, the salt and pepper, the bread and butter, all of it, crashing onto the hard wood floor, launching shattered fragments of china and glass across the room. With both hands he picks up the end of the table, lifts it above his head, and flips it over, front to back, its large, flat surface thwacking loudly against the floor.

He turns his attention to Mina, who remains seated, wide-eyed and frozen with fear. Standing above her, Vladimir slaps the left side of her face, a full-force, open-handed whack. He strikes her again, harder, again and again. Before she can recover, he grabs a large clump of her hair and wrestles her to her knees. He unzips his pants and forces himself into her mouth. She knows better than to resist.

He forces her to her hands and knees, lifts her skirt, steps behind, and claws her panties to her knees. He sees the stick of butter on the floor next to him, and with one hand scoops a lump on his index and middle fingers, smears it on her ass, and rams himself into her. She screams in agony. He grips the hair on the back of her head like horse reins, riding hard and furious.

When he finishes, he stands before her collapsed body, fallen to the ground in pain and exhaustion. All is quiet for a moment, Mina hoping, praying, eyes closed, tears streaming down her cheeks, that it's over. Then she hears a hissing sound and feels the warm, wet spray of urine showering upon her back.

When he finishes, Vladimir pulls up his pants and his zipper, tucks in his shirt, and notches his belt buckle. He pulls the comb from his back pocket and slicks back his hair, top first, then the sides, in his usual ritualistic fashion. "Good for nothing piece of shit. Clean this up. I be back on Wednesday. You not leave apartment till then. I tell Alexander. Your Chicago *girlfriend* be gone by then. Then I figure out what to do with you."

He sees her cell phone on the floor and stomps his left shoe heel into it, over and over, until it's reduced to bits and pieces of scattered metal and plastic. *Smash it. Go ahead and smash it, you pig*, thinks Mina. She has a back-up cell phone, on the same number, hidden in the apartment. He steps over the broken shards and heads toward the front hallway.

Before he exits the apartment door he calls back to her, "Thank you for delicious dinner … and especially for dessert."

Although she tries, Mina is unable to stand, her backside throbbing with pain. Cautiously, so as not to cut herself on the broken plates and glass, she crawls across the kitchen floor until she reaches a nearby floor cabinet. She stretches underneath and grabs hold of her digital recorder. She looks at it to make sure it was running properly. Relieved, she presses the off button.

# Chapter 24

## TUESDAY

Nick and Daniel land in Denver at 2:03 Tuesday afternoon. In the taxi from the airport to the hotel they speak little. Nick rolls down the window on his side and marvels at the expansive, blue sky. The smell of surrounding flatlands penetrates his nostrils with the dense aroma of late summer, tall dry grass, sweeping across the golden prairie sea from the east. The Rockies loom before him like mounds of dripping wax under the burning flame of the midday sun. He savors the peaceful ride and hopes Daniel does too, suspecting it'll be their last moment of calm for the next twenty-four hours.

When they arrive at the hotel, they walk through the lobby and present themselves to the attendant at the front desk.

"Good afternoon, gentlemen. Do you have reservations?" The attendant is a young man in his early twenties with close, neatly cropped hair, a white, freshly shaven face still at battle with ill-tempered adolescent acne blemishes, and an excessive propensity to smile subserviently and bow formally, a byproduct, Nick suspects, of taking his customer training a bit too seriously.

"Yes. Nick Steele. I reserved two rooms."

The attendant taps some keys on his computer, staring into the monitor. "Ah, yes, here you are, Mr. Steele. I have you here for one night. Is that correct?"

"That's correct."

"And how will you be paying, sir?"

"American Express." Nick hands over his platinum card.

"And for our records, sir, may I have please have your name?" The attendant looks up at Daniel.

"Dick Cochran." Daniel is expressionless except for the twinkle in his eyes, which he shares with Nick, who raises his eyebrows. The two of them are ten years old again.

"Very good, Mr. Cochran," says the attendant, as he types Daniel's assumed name into the computer. "I trust you had a good trip here?" he adds, presenting them each with their room cards.

"Uneventful. Thanks." Nick answers for both of them.

"Oh, I almost forgot. Mr. Steele. You have a package, sir." The attendant reaches under the front desk and pulls out a shoebox-sized parcel wrapped in brown paper, sealed with adhesive tape. Nick reaches out, takes hold, and places it under his arm.

"Thanks," says Nick.

"You're welcome, sir. Enjoy your stay, gentlemen. If there's anything else I can help you with, please don't hesitate to let me know." The front desk attendant sends them off to bed with a square, gummy smile.

In the elevator up to the fourth floor, Daniel is fixated on the parcel in Nick's hands, wondering what's inside, curious to know if and how it's related to their mission. Perhaps Nick has more of a plan than he'd led him to believe. "What you got in there?"

"I'll show you in a minute. Put your stuff in your room, then come by mine." Nick looks at his magnetic room card. "Room forty-two."

Daniel in turn looks at his room card. "I'm just down the hall. Room forty-eight."

After dropping his bag in his bedroom, Daniel heads back towards Nick's room. He silently steps along the empty, dimly lit corridor, taps on Nick's bedroom door, and slips inside undetected.

This arcane meeting vaguely reminds Nick of the times he and Daniel, in their early teens, would sneak out of their homes, late at night during the summer, and meet on the middle of the high school football field. They'd talk, stare at the stars, drink beer if they could get their hands on some, and fall asleep till the first hint of dawn, when they'd return home, their midnight adventure unbeknownst to anyone but themselves.

Inside Nick's hotel room they huddle around the small wooden desk as Nick rips open the parcel. The first thing he pulls out of the box is a roll of duct tape. The second is a pair of tightly fitting athletic gloves, the kind used by football wide receivers, which he pulls on to both hands. The third and fourth items, which he draws from the box with special care, as if he were a doctor delivering a newborn, are a black, 9mm, SIG Sauer semi-automatic pistol, and a fresh box of twenty-four bullets with soft-nose heads.

"Whoa! Nick. What the hell's going on?" Daniel appears to be in shock, as if he's for the first time coming to grips with the danger that may lie ahead. "This is getting serious."

Nick tries to reassure him, maintaining a calm, steady voice. "It's just for show—in case we need to intimidate anyone."

"You know how to use it?" Daniel asks, eyes wide open, looking disconcerted and in disbelief.

"Yeah. But I won't."

Nick takes command of the gun, jettisoning the empty clip from the handle, slipping off the safety catch, cocking the bullet chamber, taking a calculated look down the open barrel to ensure it's empty, then aiming it at the bedroom doorknob, his right eye peering expertly through the sight: all this, within a matter of seconds.

"Where did you learn how to do that?" asks Daniel in awe. "I never knew there were things about you I didn't know—especially things like proficiency with lethal weapons."

"Denise's brother, Tom. He's ex-Navy Seal. An Iraq vet. The first war. Whenever we come to Denver on a family visit, usually once a year, Tom takes me to the shooting range. He has a Colt forty-five, a twenty-two pistol, and a nine-millimeter SIG Sauer. That's how I learned how to handle this thing."

Nick remembers the first time he held a pistol. It was in Tom's kitchen, being prepped prior to going to the shooting range. Seeing the gun up close, then holding it, produced a surprisingly profound impression, much akin to the first time he saw the Grand Canyon; it was so much wider and deeper and inspiring than he'd imagined from photographs. Gun in hand, intensely strange and foreign, he felt an immediate force emanating from the weapon's deadly and unapologetic power, generating feelings of both excitement and fear. It was so much more imposing than he'd imagined: so light, so compact, so smooth, so easy to hold, and yet so lethal. The space around him, too, all that was within sight, came rushing into hyper-focus. Everything seemed at risk, in harm's way. The gun's authority became a magnet, a center of gravity, commanding all things in close proximity to take notice, to beware, to be on guard.

When he got to the shooting range a few hours later, these unnerving feelings had disappeared, replaced by a sense of mastery and control. In no time he'd been loading, aiming, and firing the gun as if it were second nature. After shooting for a half hour, it dawned on him, in a frightening way—indeed, it was a thought he tried to chase away—how easy it would be to pull the trigger on someone, if need be. The gun, once familiar, almost beckoned one to turn it on humans, like letting a dog off its leash and allowing it to run free—allowing it to be true to itself, to pursue its *raison d'être*, as its creator intended. Nick knows he must temper this impulse at all costs, no matter how threatening or dangerous things may become.

"Tom's the one who sent all this." Nick points to the package with his head. "I spoke with him yesterday. I wanted to get his advice. Of course, he offered to come along. But I couldn't let him. Denise would never forgive me if she knew her kid brother was involved. Especially since she's against the whole thing in the first place. Still, he insisted on sending all this." Nick turns the gun on its side. "Check this out." He points to the spot on the gun where the serial number is supposed to be. "Look. Burned away with acid. So it's untraceable. That's a felony." Nick shakes his head, suddenly feeling a heightened awareness of the illegality and inherent danger of their venture. "We're getting into some serious shit here, Danny." He looks at Daniel, who still appears dumbfounded. "You still with me?"

Daniel takes a moment to respond. "Yeah. I guess so. Hell, John Henry. This is getting a little scary."

Nick flashes him a nod and a smile, as if to say, *yeah, it is a little scary, but it needs to be done.* Inside, though, he's feeling much the same. His sweat glands seem to be working overtime. His heart is pounding.

"Dan, if you're not comfortable with this, that's fine. I can handle it on my own."

Daniel shakes his head. "No. It's all right. I'm all right."

"You sure?"

Daniel closes his eyes as if searching for limited reserves of bravery. "No. Not at all. But you need my help. You're hopeless without me."

Nick sees the resolve returning to Daniel's face and appreciates his friend's humor and loyalty. He considers sharing his own insecurities but decides it'll serve no good purpose. They both need to minimize doubt. Satisfied that no further discussion is required, Nick places the gun back in the box, takes off the tightly fitting gloves, lays them on the side of the desk, and reaches for his cell phone in his right pant pocket. He looks up at Daniel. "We need to call Mina." He puts the phone on speaker, taps out her number, firmly committed to memory, and waits for an answer.

"Hello, Nick." Mina's voice is cool and composed, as usual, but Nick can hear through her calm that she's pleased to hear from him. "You here?"

"We're here."

"We?"

"Yeah. Me and Daniel."

"Oh, yeah. Daniel. The PR guy. Your secret weapon."

"That's right." Nick holds his right index finger up to his lips, and blows against it lightly, signaling for Daniel to remain silent, to let him do the talking. He keeps going. "We've come a long way, and we want to get this thing over with as quickly as possible. Where are you?"

"The Rosemont Tower, one sixty-five Fourth Avenue. The penthouse. The elevator will take you to a private landing on the fifty-fourth floor. Come tonight at seven o'clock. Vladimir's out of town. You'll need to get past the doorman on the ground floor," she continues. "I'll call and tell him I'm expecting you. Have cash. You'll need to grease his palms. He's not supposed to let anyone up after 6:00 pm. Vlad's instructions. The hard part's the guard sitting outside the apartment door."

"Any advice on how to get past him?"

"I thought that's why you had Daniel along. Maybe he can neutralize him with some PR spin," Mina says.

Nick decides to deny her the pleasure of a response.

"Okay," she continues. "Here's what you do. Right before you step into the elevator, call my cell. While you're on the way up, I'll stick my head out the apartment door and ask Alexander— Alexander, that's the guard's name—I'll ask him for help. I'll say there's a flood in the bathroom. A fire in the kitchen. Something like that. When he gets close, I'll spray him with Mace. Remember how much fun that is, Nick?" Silence. "Anyway, by that time, you'll be landing on the fifty-fourth floor. You then wrestle Alexander to the ground, and tie him up, or whatever you like. He just needs to be—incapacitated. Think you can handle that?"

"Is he armed?" asks Nick.

"Of course. A small pistol under his pants, strapped to his right calf. But he won't be expecting anyone. Remember, his job is to keep me from leaving. He won't be expecting visitors."

Nick processes her instructions, concentrating on the timing. There's very little margin for error.

"Nick?" asks Mina, sounding softer, even vulnerable.

"Yeah."

"What are you going to do with me once you get me out of here?"

"We're going to get a flight back to Chicago tomorrow. Then we're going to hand you over to the FBI. We know someone at the bureau. Make sure you don't forget those recordings."

"I won't."

"Okay. We'll be at your building at seven o'clock. Be ready."

"I will. I have been—for months."

Nick disconnects the call. He looks intently into Daniel's eyes. "Get some rest. We'll leave here at six-thirty. I'll arrange a taxi."

"Rest? I'll need a horse tranquilizer for that. What are we going to do when we get there?"

"Exactly what she said." Nick reaches for the duct tape and tosses it to Daniel. "This is to tie the guard up. I'll pin him down. You wrap this around his arms first, then his legs, then his head so he can't speak."

Daniel laughs nervously, eyeing the roll of tape in his hands as if it were an object he had never seen before. "Hello, is anyone home? This is me, your buddy, Daniel here. I was the kid everyone loved to pin in wrestling class in junior high school. 'The Amoeba.' Remember?"

"You know how to wrap duct tape around a pole. Right?"

Daniel nods.

"Same thing."

"You sound like someone who's done this a thousand times before. Is there something else you're not telling me? First I learn about your mastery of guns. What's next? Maybe you're a secret agent or something."

"Look, Danny, I'm figuring this out as we go along," Nick says. "Just like you. But I won't be intimidated. These people are messing with my life, my family, my future." He leans forward across the desk. "I'm tired of being afraid. I made a mistake. That went from bad to worse. Now I need to find the courage to make things right again." He looks aside, chasing a thought, before returning his gaze to Daniel. "I'm prepared to do whatever it takes."

Nick leans back, stretches out his right hand to Daniel, palm facing upward. "You with me?"

Daniel brushes his hand over his friend's, affirming their pact.

When Daniel leaves, Nick calls home.

"Nick?" Denise sounds groggy, woken from a deep sleep.

"Hey, babe. Sorry to wake you. You napping?" Nick is checking in, as promised. More than that, he wants—no, *needs*—to know she and the girls are safe.

"What time is it?" asks Denise.

"About five o'clock your time."

"Yeah, musta nodded off."

Nick has never known Denise to nap in the afternoon. "Everything okay, sweetheart?"

"Yeah … yeah. Everything okay with you?"

"Everything's fine. I just wanted to let you know we got here safely. Girls good?"

"Yeah, we're all fine." Nick can hear the rustling of sheets, a pillow being fluffed to prop up her head, a sip from a glass of water that she keeps by the side of her bed—at home.

"Denise, where are you?" Nick tries to suppress the panic in his voice.

"Home."

"Home? I thought we agreed you were going to go up to the cabin today." His panic turns to anger.

"I know. I know," she says. "It's Amber's birthday party tonight. I completely forgot. Charlotte would be crushed if she missed it."

"Christ almighty. What could be the harm in missing one birthday party?" Nick can feel his anger getting away from him. "With all the friends she has, seems like they take place once a week."

"But your *best friend's* birthday party happens just once a year," Denise says.

Nick takes a deep breath. He hopes Denise isn't doing this just to get back at him for going to Denver. "Okay … okay. But promise me—*promise me*, please—you'll leave first thing tomorrow morning."

"Promise."

"And double check that all the doors and windows are locked tonight. "

"Promise."

Having a casual attitude about locking the house at night when he's traveling is something that Nick repeatedly reprimands Denise about. Despite the upscale neighborhood, burglaries, though rare, are not unheard of. In fact, someone broke into their house last fall and stole all of Denise's jewelry. Of course, tonight his concern lies elsewhere, beyond a random break-in. As an extra precaution, Nick makes a mental note to call Ralph Garasio, the chief of Oakwood's police force, and ask him to have a patrol car drive by the house every few hours throughout the night. Ralph won't ask any questions. He owes Nick a favor, a big one, having, as chairman of the local Policeman's Benevolent Association last year, raised over $1,000,000 for the town's retired police officers.

"I'll call you first thing tomorrow morning. Bright and early. I expect to hear that you're on your way. Okay?"

"Okay."

"Excellent."

"Nick."

"Yeah?"

"Your mother called."

"What about?"

"She wanted to know what you're up to. She knows you, Nick. She knows you're interested in more than just family history."

"What did you tell her?"

"That I knew nothing about it. I knew you wouldn't want to worry her."

"Thanks."

She pauses. "Nick?"

"Yeah."

Nick can hear her take another sip from the glass of water, then a shallow, worried breath.

"What are you doing right now?"

"Nothing. Gonna get some rest and head out this evening."

"Do you have a plan?"

Nick grimaces and rubs his furrowed brow with his left index finger and thumb. "Yeah." Nick would like to give her more, but he can't. He doesn't want to frighten her more than she already is.

"Please be careful," she says.

"I will. I promise."

"Despite the fact that I disagree with your approach to this whole thing, you know I still love you, right?"

"Me too. Ten times back.

He disconnects the call and immediately begins to concentrate on the task at hand.

# Chapter 25

The early evening air is warm and dry as Nick and Daniel pull up in front of the Rosemont Tower building. The taxi ride from the hotel was silent, each man contending with his own nervous thoughts.

Nick gives the driver a hundred-dollar bill and points to a parking space across the street. "Wait there. We'll be back in half an hour. There's another hundred for you when we get back."

The driver turns on a console light above his head, holds the bill up between both hands, and snaps it two times, looking though the illuminated greenback for evidence of counterfeit.

"It's real," says Nick.

"Never can tell, mate. Only been in this country two months and already had two punters try to pass bogus Ben Franklins on me." Satisfied with his visual analysis, the driver pockets the money.

Nick and Daniel step out of the car. Standing side-by-side on the sidewalk, in unison, their heads, as if connected to the same internal crankshaft, slowly and evenly tilt back as they follow upward the steel and glass skyscraper's smooth ascending contours, glistening in the setting sunlight like liquid metal. As they both gaze upon the summit, Daniel says, "I feel like we're about to rescue a damsel in distress from the top of a castle."

Nick nods, eyes still fixed on the top floor. "We are," he says, adding after a moment's thought. "Difference is, a damsel is usually a noblewoman. Not sure noble's how I'd describe this one."

The uniformed doorman, middle-aged, tall, thin, and balding, with a prominent noodle protruding from his throat—the throttle for his deep, husky voice—greets them with distant regard as they enter the lobby. "Evening."

Nick steps forward and announces that they're here to see Mina on the fifty-fourth floor, that she's expecting them, that she would have called down earlier in the day to authorize their passage upstairs.

"Sorry, don't know anything about that." The doorman is being transparently insincere as he shrugs his narrow shoulders, shakes his pointy head, and elevates his eyebrows, all as if playing the spurious villain in a pantomime, thinly disguising a solicitation for bribery.

Not missing a beat, with no time to lose, Nick reaches into his front left pants pocket, pulls out five crisp $100 bills, and discreetly places them in the doorman's right hand hanging at his side. "Are you sure you don't remember her calling down earlier?" asks Nick.

After a quick glance at his newfound wealth, and a darting smirk at Nick, the doorman slips the money in his front right trouser pocket. His noodle bobs as he swallows contentedly. *The bird gulping down the worm*, Nick thinks. "You know, on second thought, I think she might have," says the doorman. "Yeah. Now I remember." He shakes his head and grins as if he were merely suffering from a temporary bout of forgetfulness. "Fifty-fourth floor, gentlemen."

As the doorman steps aside, Nick and Daniel walk across the lobby toward the elevators. Standing in front of the two lobby elevator banks, Nick pulls out his cell phone and taps in Mina's number, struggling to direct his restless right index finger, which suddenly seems to have a mind of its own.

"You in the lobby?" asks Mina. For the first time since Nick's spoken with her, she sounds nervous.

"Yeah. We're about to get on the elevator."

"Give me a minute before you come up." Silence. "You do know what you're doing, right?" she asks.

"That seems to be the question everyone wants to know. I guess we'll all find out soon enough." Tired of being second-guessed, he decides to take charge. "You have one minute before we get on the elevator. Starting now." Nick disconnects the phone and looks at Daniel. "Here we go." He then presses the up button with concentrated purpose, feeling like a gambler seeking good fortune at a slot machine, praying that pushing this button—this one time—will be a winner.

The elevator door opens thirty seconds later. After they step inside, Nick holds the doors open for another thirty seconds, time enough to put on his gloves. He then presses the top button on the illuminated floor selection panel. As the elevator rockets skyward, it leaves his stomach behind on the lobby floor.

"Just stick with the plan we talked about at the hotel." Nick's voice is rational, calm, focused. He's talking to himself more than to Daniel, psyching himself up, adrenaline-induced concentration, back in the ring. His eyes are fixed straight ahead on the elevator doors.

"Ah huh." Daniel's lips refuse to move.

"Duct tape?" Nick asks.

"Ah huh."

The elevator slows and pulls to stop. "Let's do this."

The doors slide apart like stage curtains as the opening scene unfolds before him. Nick sees Alexander, the guard, doubled over in pain, grinding the palms of his hands into his eyes. Moans of agony are interspersed with screams of anger. "You bitch! You fucking bitch!"

Mina, languid and expressionless, looking as if nothing unusual were happening, stands in the apartment doorway, a few feet from her victim: the temptress, adorned in a short, slinky, silky white nightgown—part of the enticement to capture her prey—with a can of pepper spray held in her right hand as if it were a cocktail. She gives Nick a plaintive what-are-you-waiting-for look.

Nick, as if he'd spent days training for this moment, sprints from the elevator, careens across the landing, and pile drives Alexander to the ground. The combined weight of the two men creates a loud thud as they slam onto the hard floor. He headlocks the guard, flips him over onto his stomach, pulls both hands together behind his back, and drives his left knee into the man's lower spin. The guard grunts in pain as air is forced from his body.

"Danny!" Nick turns to look for Daniel. He sees his friend standing frozen with fear just outside the elevator.

"Danny! The tape!"

Daniel, face blanched, stares at Nick with glossy, blank eyes. He scans right, following the beckoning of an unfamiliar, loud, threatening voice emanating from the apartment door—Mina. "Help your friend, you idiot!"

Daniel, at last, shaken from his stupor, runs to Nick's side, duct tape in hand, an army medic with vital supplies to tend the wounded. He kneels beside his friend. At first he struggles to unwind the tape, his fingers fat and clumsy with fear.

"Take it easy. He's not going anywhere." Nick's voice is firm but reassuring enough to settle Daniel. Daniel nods to his friend. A balloon full of oxygen escapes from his lungs. He'd been holding his breath since the elevator door opened. Eventually, he manages to pull a strip of tape from the wheel and wrap it around the guard's wrists four times.

"Now his legs," instructs Nick.

Daniel moves back toward the guards feet, and tries to force his ankles together. But his legs are flaying about wildly. "I can't do it. He won't stop kicking."

Nick rams his knee into Alexander's spine with twice the intensity of before, then slips his left forearm underneath his throat and pulls back hard, cutting off his breathing. "You can make this easy or not. Put your legs together now."

Alexander relaxes his legs, placing them together on the floor.

"Danny, grab his gun. It's strapped to his right calf," says Nick.

Daniel lifts up the guard's right pant leg and removes the gun from the small leather holster with his right thumb and index finger, keeping it at arm's length as if it were a contaminated object.

"Slide it across the floor to the other side of the hallway."

Daniel places the pistol on the floor, like a time bomb that if not handled carefully might explode, and then gives it a soft, careful push, sending it sliding eight feet along the limestone tiled floor.

"Okay. Now his ankles," says Nick.

Daniel draws Alexander's ankles together and winds the tape around four times, extra tight. Without having to be instructed again, appearing to gain confidence, Daniel crawls toward Alexander's head and wraps the tape around his mouth. The guard's face is grimacing in pain from the pepper spray, eyes reduced to scarlet slits, tears smearing his cheeks.

Nick pulls a plastic hotel laundry bag from his back pant pockets and puts it over Alexander's head, protection from being seen.

"I'm not sure he can see anything anyway," says Daniel.

"Just to be safe."

Before getting up, Nick leans close and whispers into the bag. "We're not here to hurt you. Stay still. We'll be gone shortly. Nod once if you understand." Alexander nods once, then rolls wincing to his side, as Nick rises from the floor.

Nick looks toward Mina. "Get a wet towel and rub that shit from his eyes."

Mina, still expressionless, nods and signals with her hand for them to come inside the apartment, then hurries out of sight.

# Chapter 26

Stepping through the apartment door, Nick and Daniel find themselves in an opulent entrance hall. White marble tiles cover the floor. A rare, one-of-a kind piece of antique furniture—a large, rectangular glass-top table supported by a baluster-shaped shaft resting on four serpentine legs—sits in the middle of the room. On the glass top are two finely crafted, miniature bronze statues: one of an American eagle, the other a Russian bear. They sit facing each other, looking poised for attack. An imperial crystal chandelier sparkles directly overhead. On the wall to the left of the entrance hangs a large, rare Russian icon painting of the Madonna. Next to it, equal in size, is a contemporary photo of the pop singer Madonna baring all. On the opposite wall, there's a similarly large Russian icon portrait of John the Baptist. Next to it is a fanciful, life-sized self-portrait of John Lennon sketched in pencil.

"East meets west," says Daniel, speaking mostly to himself. "There's certainly nothing subtle about this guy."

Mina returns from the kitchen with a dishtowel and small cooking pan filled with water. She stops near Nick and Daniel, who are looking at the paintings. "Like those? That one," she points to the icon of the Madonna, "was painted in 1840. And that one," she turns and points to the icon of John the Baptist, "dates from 1450. Vlad had them smuggled out of Russia," she adds with a hint of danger in her voice, as if wanting to remind them whom they're dealing with. "Take a look around." She nods toward the entrance to the living room, as if inviting dinner guests to make themselves at home. She then steps outside the apartment door to tend to Alexander's eyes.

Passing through a garish triumphal archway that looks like a miniature Arc de Triomphe, Nick and Daniel enter the living room. Floor-to-ceiling glass windows wrap around two sides of the room, offering unobstructed panoramas of the city below and the Rockies far off on the horizon. Two large Persian rugs sit atop a dark, oak-paneled floor; the refinished wood is handsomely pocked and striated, bearing scars from centuries of foot traffic from another place, another world. Above the walk-in sized hearth, supported by marble Corinthian columns, is a sepia-toned photo of the famous early-twentieth century Russian ballerina Anna Pavlova, her small, narrow, delicate body posed in pirouette. Next to it is a black-and-white painting of a young Alvin Ailey, spread-eagled, soaring through the air like Peter Pan. On the right side of the fireplace hangs an original Rodchenko and on the left, a Picasso. The room is replete with European-style antique tables, commodes, chairs, and sofas, interspersed with Asian vases and lamps.

"Vlad says —" Both men, mesmerized by the grandeur of the room, jump when Mina returns. She grants them a moment to regain their composure. "Vlad says most of this furniture was seized from aristocrats' homes during the Russian revolution." She sounds like a dutiful tour guide, her script committed to memory.

"Smuggled here, no doubt," says Daniel under his breath.

"Nope. He bought most of it at a Sotheby's auction. Or his designer did, that is. Ever heard of her? Carrie McCarthy. Her stuff's in *Architectural Digest*. Mostly designs homes for rich and famous types."

"And mob-types."

"Yeah, and mob-types," concedes Mina, giving Daniel an unmistakable look: *don't get too smart with me, pal.*

"First *designer* prison I've ever seen," says Daniel.

"It may not look like a prison, Daniel, but I assure you it is."

"If I knew what crime you had to commit to get locked up in a place like this, I'd do it today."

Before Mina has a chance to respond, Nick jumps in. "Okay, you two. That's enough. Mina, grab your stuff, time to get out of here."

"I'm going to need some help. It's in my bedroom." Without waiting for a response, she turns and heads out of the room.

Nick and Daniel look at each other with shared concern. "What's she bringing?" asks Daniel. Nick shrugs. They follow behind.

Once inside the master bedroom, they see three enormous fluorescent blue suitcases standing upright on the wall-to-wall white carpet at the foot of the king-sized bed, over which hangs a gigantic mirror. Nick can see that Daniel is distracted by the mirror, and knowing his friend as he does, guesses where his thoughts are taking him.

"Danny!" barks Nick.

Daniel shakes his head and turns his attention to the suitcases. He tries to lift one of them, barely able to get it two inches off the floor. He turns to Nick. "No way."

"This isn't going to work," says Nick to Mina. "Just one. Pull out what you need and throw it into one suitcase."

"Are you crazy? This is all I have."

"It'll slow us down. One bag. That's it." The tone of his voice makes it clear that this is not open to discussion.

Mina turns to Daniel for support. He shakes his head.

"Okay," says Mina, turning back toward Nick. "But you're buying me all new clothes."

"No problem. There's a Salvation Army store one town over from ours."

Mina's eyes blaze with anger.

"Come on, hurry up," says Nick.

Mina topples her suitcases onto the floor, unzips each one, and starts sorting through her clothes. Nick can't help but take pleasure in seeing her sulk.

As Mina applies triage to her clothing, Nick and Daniel poke around the bedroom. More than the magnificent bedroom furnishings—a continuation of the none too subtle East meets West motif—more than the bedside view of the mountains, more than the bathroom that looks more like a spa, complete with Jacuzzi, steam bath, massage table, and glass shower with four nozzles the size of sunflowers lined from head to toe—more than all this, what intrigues them most are the framed photographs of Vladimir with famous people.

Vladimir with Tony Bennett, standing backstage after a concert. Vladimir with Dustin Hoffman, on the set of a movie being shot in Denver. Vladimir with Donald Trump, shaking hands in front of a newly constructed Trump commercial high-rise. Vladimir with two past governors of Colorado. Vladimir with Bono. Vladimir with Bill Clinton. Most of the pictures appear to have been taken some time ago. Vladimir looks thinner and younger than Nick remembers from the photos he saw online a few hours earlier. *Probably all taken before he became a public enemy and a less than desirable photo partner,* he guesses.

"This guy is something else," says Daniel.

"No shit. Come on. Let's get out of here."

They each turn back toward Mina to see if she's finished.

"Okay. Happy now?" Mina is pouting, her clothes strewn about the floor. She's sitting on top of her one allotted full suitcase, over-stuffed with clothes, trying to use her body weight to press the sides of the suitcase lid down close enough to the base so the zipper can go all the way around. Daniel kneels down to help her, managing to negotiate the zipper from one side of the suitcase to the other as she moves with him, shifting her body weight along the lid.

"Thanks," she says.

Daniel half smiles back. Nick can see that his friend is pleased, perhaps even a tad enchanted, to be on the receiving end of even a modicum of Mina's sweetness.

Daniel stands the suitcase upright, pulls out the retractable handle, and tilts the suitcase onto its rollers. "All set to go," he says to Nick. Back straight, stomach sucked in, Daniel looks like he's standing at attention, ready to salute. In a matter of minutes, Daniel has transformed into Mina's humble servant.

*Not again*, Nick thinks. He turns to Mina. "Recorder?"

"Here." She grabs her purse sitting on the back edge of the bed, opens it, and points inside.

Nick recognizes the device with mixed feelings: disgust, for having been on the receiving end of it, and relief, his ticket out of this mess. He looks down. "Is our hotel room conversation on there?"

"Don't worry, Nick. I erased it," she says.

"Good."

"Does your friend Daniel here know what a dirty mouth you have?" Mina asks.

"Knock it off," says Nick with a threatening look.

"Course I do," says Daniel. "I'm the one who taught him everything he knows."

"Well, I guess there's more to you than I thought," says Mina, giving Daniel an exaggerated flirtatious grin.

Daniel's knees seem to weaken.

"I want to hear what's on there." Nick points to the recorder inside Mina's purse.

"You don't trust me?" Mina's eyes compress to slivers. "You come all this way. And you still don't trust me?"

"No."

"Well, fuck you, too." Mina reaches inside her purse, pulls out the recorder, and holds it in her right hand. She raises it up to the side of her face, like a pitch woman on QVC featuring a new item. "What's your preference? Murder, extortion, theft?"

Nick shakes his head. "Just play me a few samples. Get on with it. We need to get moving."

"I know, Nick. You're the one holding us up," Mina says.

"Just do it."

Mina looks down at the recorder in her hand, presses fast-forward, and after a few seconds, presses play. Nick overhears one of Vladimir's henchmen reporting that he'd successfully planted toxic mercury pellets in the car of a Denver reporter who had been investigating Russian mob activity. The lackey reported that the victim's health would soon begin deteriorating. Nick can hear a few chuckles in the background.

He shakes his head in disgust and twirls his right index finger, indicating to Mina that she should move to the next sample. She fast-forwards the recorder once again, stopping at random, and pressing play. This time Nick hears Vladimir discussing a high-level FBI agent who has agreed to provide protection for his local drug dealing operation in exchange for cash. Vladimir chortles as he says that that poor bastard's wife has MS and can't cover her experimental medical expenses on his salary, even with his generous government health plan.

Nick signals for her stop the recording. "All right, one more."

"We can do this all day."

"One more will be fine."

Once again Mina advances the recording, stops, and plays it where it lands. This time Nick can hear Vladimir clicking through an electronic file and commenting on lists of stolen customer credit card numbers from a major retailer. Relaxed and professional, he sounds like he could be an executive running a meeting at a software company.

"Enough. Let's go," says Nick.

"Don't you want to know for sure if what I told you about Vladimir coming after you is true?"

"I wouldn't be here if I didn't."

"Still, you might want to hear this. Just in case there's any lingering doubt that I'm the one saving your ass here, not vice versa. I recorded this last night." Mina fast-forwards the recorder to a spot she earmarked earlier. "Vladimir made a toast in Russian, and I asked him what it meant." She presses Play.

*To the dead.*
*Anyone in particular you referring to?*
*Right now, I think most about my murdered grandfather. I also think about the soon to be dead Mr. Nick Steele. He must pay for his grandfather's sin. And I must avenge my family's loss.*

Mina flicks off the recorder with her thumb and throws it back in her purse.

Nick is stunned. He knew he was in trouble, that he was facing a dangerous man, but hearing it now, for the first time, Vladimir's cold, life-threatening voice brings it all much closer to home. There's no time to waste. He needs to get back to Chicago, to his family, immediately.

"Nick—there's one other thing," says Mina.

"What?" he snaps.

"Remember I told you Vladimir is out of town?"

"Yeah."

"Well … I think he's gone to Chicago to find you."

Nick's eyes flare with anger. "What?!"

"Last night, he said that when he gets back on Wednesday you'd be taken care of, and that he'd deal with me then."

Nick's cheeks turn a blotchy crimson. Veins pop from his neck. "Why the hell didn't you tell me earlier?"

"Because you would have gone right back to Chicago."

"You fucking bitch." Nick has to contain a sudden urge to strike her.

"Hold on … hold on, take it easy. He's not interested in your family. He wants you."

"Bullshit. You know damn well he'll go after anyone he chooses."

"Not your wife and children."

"How do you know?"

Mina scratches her head and looks down at the floor looking less than convincing. "Just do."

Nick looks at his watch. *Damn.* Too late to catch a commercial flight.

He pulls his phone from his pocket and calls his assistant.

"Hello?" He hears a sleepy voice.

"Alicia, sorry to wake you."

"No—no—not at all. It's not even that late. I just fell asleep in front of the TV. What's up, Nick?"

"I need you to book a private jet from Denver to Chicago. As soon as possible. Within an hour."

"What's going on?"

"I'll explain when I get back."

"Okay, let me see what I can do. I'll call you right back."

He pockets his phone and turns to Mina. "You better be right about Yurovsky having no interest in my family, or I'll kill you myself."

Disgusted, angry, and beyond worry for his wife and daughters, Nick turns and heads for the bedroom door. Mina follows closely behind, with Daniel bringing up the rear, rolling the heavy suitcase.

When they reach the entrance hall, Nick turns to Daniel. "We need to drag the guard inside the apartment."

Stepping outside the apartment onto the landing hall, Nick reaches down and takes hold of Alexander's right arm. "Grab his other arm," he tells Daniel. They drag the exhausted, withering man inside the apartment and prop him up against the wall to the right of the door.

"Check his eyes before we go," Nick instructs Mina.

"Hey, stop telling me what to do."

Nick looks at her blankly, with cold, hard, hateful eyes. "Fuck you. Just do it."

After Nick and Daniel step outside the apartment, out of sight of Alexander so they can't be identified, Mina leans over and pulls the plastic laundry bag off of the bodyguard's head. His eyes are red and teary, still not fully opened, but improving.

Mina speaks softly to Alexander. "The maid will be here in the morning. You'll make it till then. Then you should make yourself scarce."

Alexander tries to speak to her through the duct tape. She can't hear his words but she knows exactly what he's saying. It's in his fearful, terrified eyes. He's begging her to let him go. He knows that when Vladimir finds him, as surely he will, today, tomorrow, a week or year from now, he's as good as dead, compensation for his incompetence.

"Sorry, Alexander. We need time."

She steps outside the apartment and closes the door quietly, leaving Alexander, firmly bound in duct tape, squirming and squealing.

"He's okay," Mina says to Nick.

"Okay. Let's go."

Nick's phone rings.

"What do you have, Alicia?"

"Bad news, I'm afraid. No private services are flying out of Denver tonight. Apparently there's a line of severe thunderstorms along the entire route. Not expected to clear till morning."

"Dammit."

"Sorry, Nick."

He sighs. "Not your fault. Please keep on eye on the flight status. If anything changes, let me know."

"You got it."

"Thanks."

"Bye."

Nick presses the down elevator button, the only button on the wall. The doors slide open immediately, the car having never left the floor. He signals for all to board. Once inside, he presses the L button. The door closes, creating pressure on their ears. They descend in silence as Nick burns an imaginary hole in Mina's forehead.

A swoosh of air rushes back into the elevator as the doors open onto the lobby floor. They each walk straight ahead with haste toward the glass doors at the front of the building. Nick can see the taxi still parked, much to his relief, across the street. Watching the three of them exit the elevator from behind his security station, the night doorman rushes toward them, perplexed and angry, a cop's truncheon in his right hand. As he approaches, his face is compressed, checks and jaw muscles drawn taut. "She stays. This wasn't the agreement," he says.

Nick reaches behind his back and pulls the 9mm pistol tucked underneath the backside of his jeans. He points the gun at the doorman's forehead. "We never had an agreement." Nick's voice is threatening, uncompromising, his gun hand steady.

"Whoa. Whoa. Take it easy." The doorman backs off a step, wide-eyed, creating some distance between him and the gun.

"Go back into your cubbyhole, watch TV, go to sleep, jerk off, or do whatever it is you do back there," says Nick, waving his gun toward the security station behind the doorman. "And forget we were ever here."

The doorman raises his hands. "I never saw you come, and I never saw you go."

Nick continues to hold the gun on the retreating doorman as they hurry toward the glass doors and exit the building.

Crossing the empty street toward the parked taxi, Nick calls under his breath to the taxi driver through his open window, "Pop the trunk."

Nick helps Daniel lift the heavy suitcase and drop it into the trunk. They slam the hood, and then quickly jump into the taxi from the curb, Nick in the front, Daniel slipping in beside Mina in the back.

"Back to the Marriott," instructs Nick, slightly out of breath, pulse racing.

"Ay mate, I don't want no trouble," says the driver, with a barely contained look of fear.

"Just get going and you won't have any." Nick tries to sound reassuring, but the adrenaline surging though his body adds an unintended edge of menace to his voice.

"Don't be getting agro with me, mate. If I knew you was planning a burg up there, ya think I would a been your dill?" The driver's voice sounds both insolent and submissive.

"What the hell are you talking about?" asks Nick, his face festooned with frustration.

Mina jumps in. "He asked you not to be so aggressive—that if he knew you were a criminal he wouldn't have been stupid enough to wait for you."

"How did you know that?" asks Daniel.

"Had an Australian boyfriend," Mina says.

"Look, *mate*, I'm not a criminal." Nick tries to sound less threatening, tempering his voice as best he can, endeavoring to calm the driver down. "Just drive. Okay? And you'll be on your way home in ten minutes. Simple." Nick reaches into his pants pocket, pulls out another hundred-dollar bill, and places it in the driver's right hand.

"You got your lucky dip, driver, now get us the fuck out of here," says Mina.

The driver looks back at Mina with languishing eyes, then at Nick, and shakes his head. He pockets the cash, starts the car, puts it into gear, and hits the gas, tires skidding.

# Chapter 27

As the taxi pulls up to the front of the hotel, Nick hands over another hundred-dollar bill to the driver. "We cool?"

The driver looks offended as he pockets the money. "I mind my own. Ain't no stickybeak. And I ain't no dobber."

Remembering Mina's proficiency as a linguist in Australian slang, Nick turns to her in the backseat for help with a translation. As she's about to offer an interpretation, Nick shakes his head, signaling for her to stop. With a little imagination, he can interpret it well enough on his own, mostly from the driver's indignant tone, which indicates, in any language, that he has no intention of remembering them to anyone, and what's more, how dare Nick assume he might.

"Use some of that money to learn how to speak American. Maybe take some lessons," Nick says.

"Right, mate. Don't want to sound like a blow-in."

Halfway out the car door, Nick turns back again toward Mina for help.

"Newcomer," she says. "He doesn't want to sound like he just arrived in the country."

Nick turns to the driver and nods. "Ah. Good idea."

"No need to waste your money learning how to speak American," says Daniel, still sitting in the back seat next to Mina. "We have our own brand of unintelligible slang. Just turn on the

TV. You'll learn it in no time. Then *your* gibberish will be the same as *our* gibberish."

The driver is silent, mulling over Daniel's comment, looking unsure whether he's been extended the hand of helpful advice or slapped with an insult. He scratches his head as he drives away.

After stepping from the taxi, Nick, Daniel, and Mina stand for a long moment in front of the hotel entrance as Nick lays out the next step of his plan—such as it is, still largely improvised.

Nick looks at his watch. "It's nine fifteen now," he says, thinking how slowly time seems to be moving. "Too late to get a flight back tonight. Courtesy of *her*." He sneers at Mina. "There's an American Airlines flight at six forty-five am. I checked it out earlier. If we're going to be on it, we need to leave the hotel by five o'clock am. Let's meet back down here in the lobby then. Mina, you stay in Daniel's room until then. Daniel, you can stay in mine."

"I don't want to be alone," says Mina.

"Why not?"

"Cause I don't." Mina's voice is defiant.

"Okay, you can stay with Daniel in his room."

Daniel's eyes bulge.

"I'd rather stay with you, Nick," says Mina, with a look of having smelled something unpleasant. "You've got the gun."

"We've spent time together in a hotel room once before," says Nick, stone-faced. "That's *not* going to happen again."

"Jesus, Nick, what do you think's going to happen?"

"Nothing." Nick's voice is calm, determined. "When this is over, I don't want to have to explain to my wife why you and I ended up in a hotel room together again—regardless of the circumstances."

"That's ridiculous," she says.

"Yeah, it is. But that's the way it's going to be. And besides, after that stunt you pulled—not telling me about Yurovsky going to Chicago to find me—I can barely stand the sight of you."

Mina turns to Daniel, who seems barely able to contain his excitement. "Don't get any ideas, pal."

"Don't worry. There are two double beds," says Daniel, unable to entirely disguise his glee. "I won't bother you."

"Okay, let's stop squabbling," says Nick. "Get whatever sleep you can. I'll make the plane reservations and order the taxi for the morning. Ideally with a driver we can understand. See you at five."

They walk into the hotel lobby, Daniel dragging Mina's suitcase, past the desk clerk standing at attention, smiling broadly, ever dutiful, welcoming them back to the hotel.

# Chapter 28

Once inside Daniel's room, Mina heads to the bed closest to the window, throws back the covers, and fully clothed, hops in, pulling the covers—like a protective shield—up to her neck. Wide-eyed, still, and silent, her head resting on a large, fluffy pillow, she stares at the ceiling as if in a trance, shutting out the rest of the room, including Daniel.

Trying to respect the solitude and distance she unmistakably desires, Daniel sits in the armchair before the window, a few feet from the foot of Mina's bed. He opens the book he brought along for the plane ride and begins to read—or at least tries to read, fighting the impulse to slip into bed beside her.

A half hour passes in silence.

"I suppose you're wondering how I ended up like this. I mean, in this situation." Mina is staring at the ceiling, eyes unblinking, sounding bored and lonely and full of self-pity.

"Not really," replies Daniel, head still buried in his book.

"Yes, you are."

"No, I'm *not*."

"Come on. You're not even just a little interested?" she prods him.

Daniel looks up from his book and places it on his lap. "Okay. Maybe just *a little* curious."

"Knew it." She flashes a victorious grin. "So what are you most interested in knowing about?" she asks, looking like a cat with a mouse in its mouth.

"I don't know. I guess about the life you've chosen."

"The life I've chosen?" Mina asks, with an air of mockery. "Does anyone really *choose* their lives?"

Daniel thinks for a moment. "Suppose not. Some do. Most don't. I certainly haven't been a model of successful life planning."

"I didn't choose this life, Daniel. It chose me," she says.

"Maybe so."

"*Maybe* so? Definitely so!"

"Whatever you say."

"My life was preordained. It's been told a thousand times, a thousand different ways—throughout history, in books, on TV, in movies. Go on, Daniel, use your imagination, tell me my story. Use some of that PR spin of yours. Tell me about the life that was chosen for me."

"This is stupid."

"No it's not. I know you think you've got me figured out. You know my *type*, Daniel. Don't you. You know *exactly* who I am."

"No, I don't."

"Yes you do. Go ahead, tell me my life story."

"No."

"Yes."

"Why?"

"Because I'm asking you to."

"Don't you know it?" Daniel feels like he's in a schoolyard engaged in a childish verbal duel.

She looks at him as if his question is so utterly lame it doesn't merit response. "Course I know it, Daniel," she says, as if speaking to a simple person. "All too well. But I want to hear you tell it," she says, overly enunciating each word.

He looks into her eyes to ascertain whether to proceed, uncertain as to her motives—uncertain as to *his* own motives.

"Come on, Danny, what's the harm?" she says in a soothing, singsong voice. She's turning on the charm, and he's going to have trouble resisting it.

Daniel looks out the window for a moment before turning back toward Mina. "Okay," he says. He gathers his thoughts. "Of course, I'm just speculating, but here goes." He takes a deep breath before starting. "Your parents are first generation immigrants. Korea, right?"

Mina nods.

"They arrived speaking no English." He looks to her again for confirmation, which she provides with the blink of her eyes.

"They struggled to fit into their new country. It was hard to get good-paying jobs, hard to find a decent place to live, hard to raise a family, hard just to fit in. That was the worst part. Fitting in. Accepting, and being accepted by, this strange, crass, new culture. Like many other first-generation immigrants, they couldn't really offer you much help in navigating this strange, new world. You were on you own. Had to figure things out for yourself."

Daniel looks at Mina to see if he's on track.

"I'm guessing, purely guessing, mind you, that you had a contentious relationship with your father. When you were a teenager, he was angry about the way you talked, the way you dressed, your liberal ideas about life that were alien and abhorrent to his modest, understated old world sensibilities. You were a foreigner living under his roof, someone he couldn't understand or accept. Not the daughter he'd hoped for. I suspect he may have even hit you from time to time out of frustration. Disappointed with his own life, as much as yours."

"Hitting me is putting it mildly." There's a slight tremor in Mina's voice. "Go on," she says.

"You were attractive as a teenager, and you knew it. You knew it because you couldn't help but notice all the attention you were getting from the boys at school. Lots of them tried to sleep with you. You probably went along with some of them. Not so much for the sex, but more for the feeling of intimacy, warmth, and kindness—all those things your father never provided."

"Wow. Now you're getting Freudian on me."

"Well …"

"I'm not disagreeing. Keep going."

"I don't know how you got into—prostitution. Maybe some guy handed you fifty bucks after you slept with him, and you realized that this was a lot easier way to make money than a real job. Whatever it was, you needed the money. Needed it to get away—away from home."

"It was a friend." Mina jumps in. "I was sitting in a diner one night. She raced in and asked, 'How'd you like to make seventy-five dollars in twenty minutes?' Without thinking, without even knowing what I was in for, I followed her. It was so easy. That's how it all started. I was sixteen."

"Did you like it? I mean, sleeping with men for money?"

"You know the answer to that. You got everything else pretty well figured out. So don't start playing dumb with me now. Of course I didn't like it. No one really *likes it*. But it's not all bad. Sometimes I felt more like a shrink than a hooker. Sometimes, I actually felt that I was doing some good, you know, helping people.

"I've been with all kinds of men, Daniel. And not all of them pay for sex. Some pay for companionship. Some want to act out bizarre fantasies while I watch—personal fantasies that they'd never, ever expose to their wives or girlfriends, too afraid that they'd repulse them and be rejected. Some pay just to talk or to have someone nonjudgmental listen to them."

Daniel is transfixed, thoroughly absorbed in what Mina is telling him, and increasingly aroused.

"Maybe, too, without prostitutes society would be a lot worse off than it is. Vladimir told me Napoleon once said that 'prostitutes are necessary—without them men would attack respectable women on the streets.'"

"That may have been true back in the eighteen hundreds, but don't you think times have changed since then?"

"Have they?" She raises her right eyebrow.

Daniel ponders her response. Before he has a chance to respond, Mina continues.

"What else? Tell me more," begs Mina. "You're pretty good at this."

"I don't know. I think that's about it," say Daniel.

"Come on, Daniel. I'm enjoying this. And you're doing so well," she pleads.

He looks out the window again, at the unnatural yellow-orange night sky, a glowing polluted blanket covering the city, seeking inspiration, before turning back toward Mina. "You've probably had lots of names. I'm guessing mostly Waspy names—like Laura, Suzy, Wendy, Janie, Amy, Emma. That sort of name. They sounded a bit more upscale."

Mina snorts, amused by the embarrassing truth.

"By the way, is your real name Mina?" he asks.

"No, it's Ae Sook. It means love and purity. Ironic, huh?"

"No, not ironic. It's a pretty name. You should go back to it."

"Thanks, Daniel," she says. "Do you have any idea how many Johns have told me that? After you have a regular customer for a while, they always want to know what your real name is. When I tell them, they always go, *Ooo and ahhh, isn't that a pretty name.* For that reason alone, I'll never use it again. Also, a couple of assholes refused to pronounce my name properly—kept calling me 'I Suck.' Clever, huh? That didn't help either."

"Well, maybe they were telling you the truth. I mean, those men who told you it's a pretty name."

"Daniel, in my line of business, there is no truth," she says. "But I'm sure you already know that from first-hand experience."

Daniel averts his eyes to the floor, scratches his head, raises his eyebrows, and half smiles on the right side of his mouth in surrender. He has no case to argue.

"Go on. Tell me more," she says.

Daniel looks back up at Mina. "You haven't had enough?"

"Nope. I told you how easy this was going to be for you. How my life is nothing more than one big cliché, told a thousand times before. Pretty boring, huh?"

"Not at all. You can reduce everyone's life down to a stereotype. There aren't that many of them. We all fit into one or another. What matters is who you are—your attitudes, beliefs, and values—not just what you've done."

"Oh, Daniel," she says, pretending she's going to cry.

He gives her a *mea culpa* look, realizing he's beginning to sound like a self-improvement video. "Anyway, the point is, we can all be reduced to a cliché. That's what I do in my business: put people into generalized buckets. It's easy to do, great for selling stuff efficiently, but not very accurate, or respectful, of people's true, individual, and often very complex natures."

"You don't need to try and make me feel better, Daniel. I'm well aware of who and what I am. No matter what you say, my life is still a script that's been acted many times before. Remember? It's out of my control. Chosen for me."

"That's nonsense. If it were out of your control, we wouldn't be here now. You wouldn't have decided to contact Nick. You wouldn't have decided to leave Vladimir. You wouldn't have decided to do something better with your life."

"Who said anything about that—about doing something better with my life?"

"Just guessing, right?"

"You give me way too much credit, Daniel. This is no more complicated than saving my ass from that crazy fucker."

"Whatever you say." Daniel raises his eyebrows.

Mina looks back up at the ceiling for a moment and takes a deep breath through her nose. "Tell me what else you know about me," she says, wanting to reset the course of the conversation.

"No. That's enough."

"Come on. Let's keep going."

"Mina, this is getting —"

"Please." She softens the contours of her cheeks and brow and lowers the lids over her soft, brown eyes.

"I don't know," says Daniel, weakening, once again.

"Pretty please?" She leans over on her right side, lowers the sheets, and rests her chin in the palm of her right hand. *My God, she looks cute*, thinks Daniel.

"Okay. You win," he says. "If we follow your *stereotype*—which I don't want to do, but if you insist —" Mina nods. "Then I'd say you probably got involved with drugs at some point. Cocaine, maybe heroin. Partly to dull the pain, partly to escape. You may have become an addict. That would have kept you working your trade, probably more than you wanted, just to cover the expense of the drugs."

Mina bolts upright in the bed. "Well, the good news is that that chapter of my life is over," she says.

"I'm glad to hear it."

"More. What next?"

Daniel sighs, growing tired of this game.

"Come on. Use your imagination. What's the biggest cliché you can think of about someone running away from home?"

"You got me." Daniel shrugs. "Let's see. I bet you ran away with the circus," he says.

"*Yes!*"

"Come on. I was joking."

"No, it's true. Can you believe it?"

"No." Daniel's voice is awash with skepticism.

"I swear." Mina holds up her left hand as if she were taking an oath in court. "There was a small traveling circus that came through our town every couple of years—the Cohen Brothers Circus. Been around for a hundred years, maybe more. One of the last of its kind, maybe *the* last. There were only eight performers—a Mexican juggler, a clown from Austria who was mute or something—never spoke a word—three acrobats from

Russia, two motorcycle riders who went in the Globe of Death, and a Hungarian knife thrower. His name was Ferenc."

Daniel shakes his head in disbelief.

She ignores him and continues. "I was hanging around after a performance one day, outside the tent, watching Ferenc pack his knives. By the way, did you know that knife throwing is referred to as 'the impalement arts'? Isn't that gruesome? Anyway, we got to talking and I told him I wanted to get out of town. I was sixteen. He asked how old I was. I said eighteen. He told me he wasn't happy with his current assistant—you know, the woman who gets strapped to a large rotating wooden wheel and spun round and round while knives are thrown around her legs, arm, stomach, and head. I guess she complained too much. Anyway, he took me on. I left with the circus that night."

"As the assistant to a knife thrower?" Daniel's still not buying her story.

"That's right, Daniel. I'm not making this up," she says. "I did it for six months. Ferenc would dress up as Buffalo Bill, and I'd dress up as an Indian squaw."

"A sexy Indian squaw?" he says.

"The sexiest." She winks at him. "Ferenc ordered my outfit from an online adult costume store. It had a low-cut suede corset top"—she sweeps her hands down across her chest in a V culminating at her sternum—"and a matching tasseled suede mini-skirt. I was the sexiest squaw you ever saw." Mina chuckles. "Ferenc said that if the fathers in the audience were happy, their families would be happy too." She seems lost for a moment in memories. "It was fun. And I was never really afraid. Not really. Not until I found out that Ferenc liked to drink. Even before performances. After that, I bolted."

"Smart girl," says Daniel.

"Smarter than you think. Ferenc also taught me how to throw knives. I bet you never met an impalement artist before."

"No, can't say I have," Daniel says.

"Of course, unless you're in the circus it's a totally worthless skill to have."

"You never know."

"That was a long time ago. Seems like forever." Mina appears to be truly enjoying herself. "Tell me more, Daniel. Tell me about how and why I ended up with Vladimir, oh great soothsayer," she says.

"Well. That's the easiest part of the story. You were attracted to his power—the ultimate aphrodisiac. Especially for a wounded young woman in search of a strong father figure."

"Wounded young woman?" says Mina, grimacing.

"Stop me whenever you like."

"No, no. That's okay. You're right. By the way, I'd only let a wounded old man tell me that," she says. "Is it really just coincidence that we both have bruises on our faces, Daniel?" She points to the scabbed scratches on Daniel's face.

He shakes his head uncomfortably and shifts in his chair.

"I'll take over from here," says Mina. "This is where it gets a bit complicated." She takes a deep breath. "I fell in love with him. Deeply. Madly. Crazily in love. I know that's hard for you to imagine. Is for me, too, now, but back then, when I first met him, he was *so* charming. Yes. That's right. Charming. He treated me like I was his princess. Called me his *tsaritsa*. Still does. I would have done anything for him. And I did. I gave him all of me: mind and body, however and whatever he wanted. You know, Daniel, I left home at sixteen. Been on my own ever since. Till I met Vlad, no one's ever really cared for me. Not *really*. He loved me. Truly. Still does."

She tries to steady her quivering upper lip.

"You got me figured out pretty good, Daniel. Pretty good. I needed his love. Just like I needed my father's. Just like you said. Even if it meant being abused. Putting up with his sickness, his perversions. But I would have done anything to keep him. His love. And I did. Anything and everything."

She stops and looks at him. "Truth is, I liked it, too. The abuse, the cruelty. Sometimes, at least. Does that shock you?"

Surprised to see that she actually cares what he thinks, Daniel finds himself unable to respond.

"It's very liberating, Daniel. Very liberating, abandoning yourself to someone else—to get sucked into their needs and desires, to feed them, no matter how perverse or sick they are. It wasn't really sexual pleasure, not for me. More emotional. You got that right, too. The pleasure came from pleasing him, in whatever way he wanted, even when it involved cruelty or masochism. And it often did. By enduring the physical pain, I felt closer to him, more essential to him, more assured of his commitment to me."

She looks into his eyes, as if trying to gauge his reaction.

"Sick, right? Sounds like the *Story of O*, doesn't it? You familiar with that book?" she asks, seeming to want to extricate the hazardous emotion from her story, to return, like a deep sea diver swimming upward from a risky depth, to a level of logic and reason, where oxygen is safely replenished in the blood.

Daniel shakes his head.

"Not important," she continues. "A friend gave it to me. Said it was about me. Anyway, I let myself be his sex slave. Same as the woman in the book. My friend was right. I was just like her. Willing to put up with any abuse and perversion, as long as he loved me in return. I guess I was also testing how much I loved him." She sucks her upper lip. "But here's the difference. I woke up. I snapped out of it. Unlike the stupid woman in the book."

"Why?" asks Daniel.

"Because it all went too far when he took my freedom away. When he said he owned me. When I wasn't free to do as I pleased. I didn't mind sacrificing myself to him. Not really. Not as long as I was free to come and go. But nobody owns me. Nobody. I come and go as I please. Period. I see who I want, when I want." A dark shadow casts over her eyes. "He also started to really scare me. If you knew what he did to me over the last two nights —" She gasps. "He wants to kill me, Daniel."

Daniel is perplexed. A sympathetic look comes over her face.

"I'm not sure where my story goes next," she says. "No place good, I'm sure."

He shakes his head, returning his attention to her. "That's easy."

"Where?"

"Redemption."

"Redemption? You mean like in the movies?"

"Yeah. Like in the movies." Daniel says.

"You mean redemption like where I reconcile with my parents, get a real, honest to goodness job, fall in love with a decent, law-abiding man, maybe even help others less fortunate than me … maybe even girls like me who have lost their way?" Mina's voice is caustic but not harsh, as if what she's saying is far-fetched but not entirely implausible.

"That's right. It happens in real life, too. Every once in a while."

"Redemption, huh? I'd half like to believe it." After a few moments, all remnants of sarcasm have dissipated from the corners of her mouth. "Redemption. At first I thought you were joking. But the way you just said it … it was so sincere, so kind, it sounded like a gift." She looks at Daniel and smiles—a smile the likes of which Daniel never expected to receive from her—unguarded, honest-to-goodness, straight-from-the-heart.

Mina says to him, "Daniel, would you lie next to me?" This invitation sounds to Daniel like the beckoning of a child seeking the comfort of a parent to help her get to sleep, to keep the hobgoblins and demons that lurk in her bedroom closet at bay; a lost girl, in need of a protective, loving embrace, until light and hope returns with the morning.

Hesitantly at first, but then with more confidence, Daniel rises from his chair and steps over to the side of Mina's bed. He lifts the covers and slips in next to her, sitting with his back straight against the headboard, trying not to read too much into her invitation, other than that she might like the comfort of another human being. After a moment, she leans over and rests her head against his stomach and strokes his side, nestling in, wrapping her left leg gently around his lower waist.

Daniel's pulse races. This is no child in need of parental comfort. This is a woman desiring the warm, loving touch of a man. The uncertainty, the fear, and the anxiety of his last twenty-four hours sink into oblivion. He's now aware only of the beautiful, vulnerable woman lying next to him. He lifts the jet-black hair from her porcelain white neck, leans over, and lightly kisses it, luxuriating in the fresh, sweet scent of her youth. She purrs. He unbuttons her silk shirt, slowly, savoring the discovery of her small, white, perfectly shaped breasts. He kisses them, lovingly, sweetly, as if they were a delicacy, things to be adored and honored and revered; works of art. Her nipples harden, arousing him further, a sign of mutual participation, shared feelings.

She unbuttons her jeans and slips them off. He pulls off her pink silk underwear and explores her body with his hands, tantalized by the touch of her skin, the soft, smooth, roundness of her buttocks, the slight, feminine indent of her bellybutton, the hairless wonder of her Mount of Venus. He can't help but marvel at the sheer physical beauty, the absolute perfection, of this earthly goddess. He sheds his clothes—clumsily, fearful that if he's too slow she might disappear. He's throbbing like a teenage boy. He gasps as she wraps her gentle, delicate fingers around him. He kisses her breasts, her stomach, her hips, her thighs, her calves, her feet, her toes, and works his way back up again, stopping mid-way. She tastes of something beyond words, beyond description, beyond comparison. He wants to drink all of her. He listens as her breathing deepens, sensing, hoping, this is not just for him, that she, too, finds pleasure in their intimacy.

He rises above her, parts her legs, and slowly, carefully, enters her, slipping into a warm, dark cavern of fine, handmade silk. He thrusts gently at first, delighting in the rare, warm, damp delicacy, then increases his pace, pushing harder, deeper, surrendering entirely now to his baser animal instinct, compelled by a thoughtless compulsion he has no control over. She whispers in his ear, "Yes. Yes," driving him into a frenzy of excitement until, unable to contain himself further, he climaxes, with an intensity so powerful it borders on pain. His body quivers and shakes and stiffens, then turns limp, all bones and muscles rendered useless. He falls to her side in exhaustion, wonderfully lost in a state of bliss, a bliss such as he's not known for a long, long time.

Daniel and Mina lie together, their bodies warm and radiant. No words are spoken. The silence feels natural, comfortable, coupled. They look into each other's eyes, lending themselves a brief passage to the other's soul—an unexpected, precious moment of tenderness for both of them.

Exhaustion and tranquility fuse into one as they drift to sleep in each other's arms.

# Chapter 29

Desperate to hear her voice, to know that she and the girls are safe, the first thing Nick does when he gets back to his hotel room is to call Denise. He's relieved to hear her answer after just two rings.

"Hi, babe. Everything okay?" He tries to hide his worry.

"Yeah—yeah, fine, we're just packing. Charlotte got home from the party about a half hour ago. Had a great time. I'm glad we let her go."

Nick silently questions her presumption of complicity, feeling he never really had a say in the matter.

"We're planning to be in bed shortly, so we can get an early start in the morning." Denise's voice is flat, lacking its usual effervescence. It sounds perfunctory to Nick, as if she's merely following orders, telling him what he wants to hear.

"Good," says Nick without reacting to the tone of her voice. "Everything locked up?"

"Yes, sir." Denise now sounds like a private responding to a drill sergeant.

Refusing to be baited, Nick continues. "Not so hard, was it?

"Nick, *we're* fine. What about you? What's going on out there?"

"Good news. I think we have a solution to the problem."

"What is it?" Denise's voice reanimates.

"I'll give you the full rundown when I get back tomorrow. But everything's going to be okay."

"No way. Don't try and pull that one on me. Keep going."

Nick realizes he needs to give her something more than a blind promise. "Okay, we got hold of a secret recording of the Russian guy I told you about, you know the one who robbed our bank account. It's evidence—hard evidence that can be used to have him arrested. I'll be handing it over to the FBI when I get back tomorrow."

"Nick, how in the world did you get hold of that?" Denise asks.

"*That* will have to wait to tomorrow." Nick would like to tell her more, but it's best she only knows the half of it.

"Nick, you're a businessman. What the hell are you doing out there?"

"I'll tell you everything tomorrow, I promise."

Silence.

"Nise, I'm going to go now," says Nick.

Silence.

"Okay?" Still searching for a response.

Silence.

"Nick, I spoke with Amy today."

*Oh, no.*

"I told her about what you did."

"What do you mean, *what I did*?" He's upset that Denise has confided in her friend, though not at all surprised.

"You know, inviting that woman to your room in Denver."

"Anything else?"

"No, that's all. Just that part."

Relieved, Nick adds, "And?"

"And she says I should forgive and forget."

"Smart friend."

"Maybe," Denise says. "She says you're a good man. A good husband. A good father. Not easy to find these qualities nowadays."

"An even smarter friend than I realized."

"She says what you did was stupid —"

"Um hum."

"— but forgivable."

"Ahhh."

"She says she has some girlfriends on the West Coast with husbands with advanced degrees in lying and cheating, and that they'd welcome my kind of *minor* marital problem."

"There you go."

"She asked me if I love you."

"Um hum?"

"I said yes. She also asked me if I wanted to spend the rest of my life with you."

Nick's silence begs a response.

"I said yes. *And* she asked if I thought you had—you know—a problem chasing other women."

"And?"

"I said no."

"So?"

"*So* ... she said I need to get over it."

"And?"

"*And* ... I'm working on it."

"Nise, you already know this, but I'm going to say it anyway. You and the girls are everything to me—*everything*. I'd never do anything again to jeopardize what we have. We both just need to get this behind us."

"I know. I'm trying."

"Sleep tight, my angel."

"You, too. And Nick, please be careful. This is all so surreal. Attacks on our bank account, running up to the cabin to hide, finding secret recordings. My God. It's insane."

"I know. We're not in Kansas any more. But everything's going to be back to normal. Real soon. Give the girls a kiss goodnight for me."

"I will."

"Love you."

"Me too."

"Night."

"Night."

Nick ends the call, temporarily relieved, but with a dull, gnawing queasiness in his gut that he knows isn't going to disappear until he's reunited with his family and Yurovsky is in the hands of the Feds.

# Chapter 30

## WEDNESDAY

"Mommy! Mommy!"

Charlotte's terrified voice shakes Denise from her restless sleep. As a child Charlotte suffered recurring nightmares and would sometimes cry out in the middle of the night. But that was a long time ago.

And this sounds different to Denise: fraught with desperation and panic. What's more, "Mommy," sadly, isn't a name Denise has heard either one of her daughters call her in years. *Is she sick?*

"Coming, Charlie." She rises from bed and hurries across the hall to Charlotte's bedroom.

As she opens her eldest daughter's bedroom door, Charlotte and Sarah are the first things that come into her sight. They're sitting next to each other on the side of Charlotte's bed, tightly gripping each other's hands, furled into a ball. They appear agitated and confused.

Denise scans the room. Nothing looks amiss. The lamp next to Charlotte's bed casts a warm golden glow across the room. The digital clock reads 4:30 am. It wouldn't be the first time the girls stayed up all night talking. Next to the clock is a well-worn paperback copy of Dickens' *Tale of Two Cities*, Charlotte's summer reading assignment.

The family cat, Archie, a plump calico, looking characteristically uninterested, is curled up at the foot of the bed, his usual sleeping place. Denise registers all of this in less than a second. But all is clearly not well. The girls are frightened, their fully dilated pupils darting wildly back and forth between Denise and the darkened corner of the room to their right.

Denise pushes the door open wider to see what lies behind it. She gasps. Sitting in Charlotte's armchair, usually reserved for her many childhood stuffed animals, is a man, an intruder: large, early fifties, slicked jet-black hair, and with strange symbols, no letters—Cyrillic letters—tattooed on each of his fingers. His right leg is flung over the right armrest as if he were right at home, a stuffed panda bear resting on his protruding stomach.

"Hello, Denise."

"Who are you? What do you want?" Denise yells at the man, a she-wolf guarding her pups.

"Relax. No one going to get hurt." He looks down at the stuffed animal. "Are they, Mr. Panda?" He holds it up to Denise and turns it side-to-side. "See, even Mr. Panda say no." Denise sees the barrel of a handgun in his lap.

"What do you want?" she asks again, trying to overcome her mounting fear.

"I come to see your husband. Where is he?"

"Out of town. On business."

"Where out of town."

"I don't know. He travels a lot. I lose track of where he is sometimes."

"You lie. Wife not *ever* forget where husband is." The man chuckles, looking pleased with his incisive observation.

"Please leave my home, now."

"Tell me where your husband is and maybe I go."

Refusing to be intimidated, Denise turns to her daughters and ushers them toward her with the wave of her hand. "Girls, come with me."

The man jumps in, less friendly. "*Girls*, do not move. I will tell you when to move and when not to move."

They look to Denise for guidance. She nods for them to stay put.

Denise looks back toward the man, jaw clenched, angry. "You're him, aren't you?"

"Him? Who is him?"

"The man who's been stealing from our bank account and credit cards."

"I know nothing of this." The man sounds dismissive, bored.

"Then who are you? And what do you want with my husband?"

"He and I have common destiny. That is why I am here."

"What are you talking about?"

"It is between your husband and me. I ask you again. Where he is?"

"And I'll tell you again. I don't remember."

"You will find I can be very impatient, Denise. I suggest you stop pretending and tell me what I want to know." He picks up the gun and points it at the panda's head. "Otherwise I will have to kill panda." The man laughs out loud. He then puts on a high, squeaky voice, imitating the panda. "Don't shoot me, Mister. I am endangered species." He laughs again, enjoying himself.

"Look, this isn't funny. You need to go now," says Denise.

The man's expression hardens instantly as he points the gun directly at Charlotte. "I will not ask you again. Where is your husband?" His voice is cold, threatening.

Left no choice, Denise answers. "Denver. He's in Denver."

"Good."

"Now, please put the gun down."

Ignoring her, the man continues. "When he is going to be home?"

"I don't know. He didn't say."

"Again you lie." He extends his arm with the gun toward Charlotte's head.

Denise responds instantly. "Today. I think. He said today. But I don't know what time. He didn't know exactly when his business was going to be done. I promise. That's all I know."

"Then we wait."

"Wait?"

"That's right. Until he gets home. We wait." He puts the gun down on his lap, and pats the stuffed animal's head. "Is that okay with you, Mr. Panda?" He chuckles.

Denise walks to the bed. As she does, she glances through the side of the closed bedroom window shade—a small sliver of visibility to the street below—and sees a police car driving slowly by. She contemplates rushing to the window, lifting the shade, pounding and screaming, but the car has already moved too far down the road by the time she finds the courage to make a commitment. Deflated, she sits between her two daughters who open a space for her and wraps them in her arms.

"You go back to sleep. I wake you when is time," Vladimir says, sounding avuncular, as he sinks back into the armchair, making himself comfortable.

Too exhausted to argue, too confused to know what to do next that might in some way improve their situation, Denise decides to comply, at least for the moment. At her direction, Charlotte and Sarah crawl into the bed together. Denise slips between them and pulls the covers up underneath their necks. They embrace each other tightly. They feel like a protective egg to Denise, able to absorb any outside force and transmit it in all directions away from the direct point of contact, preventing harm to anyone.

Denise strokes their hair and whispers, "It's going to be fine." She wishes she believed it was true.

# Chapter 31

"Who is hungry? Breakfast time!" Vladimir is standing directly over Charlotte's bed. His voice booms as if it were 7:00 at night, as opposed to 7:00 in the morning.

Denise looks out from underneath the light summer quilt covering Charlotte's queen-size bed. She and the girls are still curled up together—have been for the last two and a half hours—wrapped in each other's mutually protective embrace. No one has slept; fear has blocked exhaustion from following its natural path to slumber.

Denise peers into the wide, maniacal, pockmarked face that looms directly overhead. She hears a distant voice, as if in a dream. "Eggs, bacon, toast." The voice belongs to *him*—the stranger who broke into their house—now leering down upon her. He addresses her as if placing a breakfast order with a diner waitress. "Denise, you get up. Make me some breakfast. Now!"

She remains motionless, staring skyward into the man's dark, vacant eyes. She tries to process his instructions—tries to make sense of anything. Lying under the covers with Charlotte and Sarah over the last few hours has, in their quiet, protective nest, dulled her senses. Did he just say *breakfast time?*—this interloper … this threatening intruder—as if he were master of the house?

Coming to her senses, fueled by outrage, Denise's first reaction is to take offense. *How dare he!* She clenches her jaw, narrows her eyes, and gnashes her teeth.

Vladimir promptly presents a broad, toothy, conciliatory schoolboy grin. "Pah-leeze."

Denise bolts upright, back against the wooden headboard. She breathes deeply through her nose, twice, the lung-deep oxygen penetrating and cooling the capillaries of boiling blood careening through her body, before responding. Despite her best efforts to take control of her emotions, there's a thinly disguised tint of sarcasm in her voice. She knows she's walking a fine line. But she's unable, perhaps unwilling, to fully contain her contempt.

"Sure. How do you like 'em? Fried? Over easy? Medium? Hard? Scrambled? Poached? Or maybe you'd like to hear about our special this morning."

"Scrambled will do." Vladimir squints his eyes and rubs his pursed lips with his right index finger, appearing not sure, and not at all pleased, that she may be mocking him.

Before he has a chance to consider this further, taking a clue from the intensified, increasingly dangerous expression on his face, Denise jumps from bed and rallies her daughters to do the same. "Up and at 'em, girls," she says.

After tending to their personal duties in the bathroom and changing into simple slacks and button-down shirts, Denise, Charlotte, and Sarah march down stairs behind Vladimir and enter the kitchen where Denise intends, despite her personal and principled objections, to prepare breakfast. At Vladimir's instruction, offered with a strange, almost charming, blend of kindness and harsh insistence, the girls sit quietly at the round pine kitchen table. He pulls up a chair next to them, sits down, tugging at his crotch like a grocer sorting fruit, while Denise tends to the breakfast duties at hand.

"You have attractive daughters. Just like their mother."

"Keep your hands off them," Denise snaps.

"Whoa. What kind of man you think I am?"

"I *know* what kind of man you are," she says.

"Well, then you know I prefer mature woman … someone more like—you." He grins.

"Don't even think about it." Every muscle in Denise's body tightens.

"Oh, no, no, no. You do not understand. I *think* whatever I like, and you will do for me whatever I say." He pauses. "Lucky for you, *right now*, I want eggs."

Denise exhales a silent sigh of relief. She knows, though, that she's been given only a momentary reprieve. She changes the subject. "What's your name? You know mine. What's yours?" Denise tries to hide the fear she feels as she cracks the first egg with a fork, pulls it apart, and drops the egg white and yolk into a glass mixing bowl. Her hands are shaking.

"It is no concern of yours," he says.

Denise cracks another egg, more firmly this time. "You break into my house. You hold me, my children hostage. You threaten us with a gun. The least you can do is to tell me who you are, let alone what you want."

"I told you before, I am someone who shares a common destiny with your husband. That is all you need to know."

"Common destiny?"

"*Da*. We share common history."

"When? Where?"

"It is not important for you to know this."

Denise whips the eggs in the bowl with a fork. "If it involves my husband, it's *very* important to me. What are you going to do when he gets here?"

"Again, that is between me and him."

"Do you want to hurt him?" Denise is gambling but figures she has nothing to lose posing this direct line of questioning. She pours the bowl of mixed eggs into a frying pan of sizzling butter

Vladimir stares at her in silence.

She inquires again, stirring the eggs in the frying pan with a spatula: "Do you want to hurt him?"

"You talk too much. Did not your husband ever teach you how to shut up? You be quiet." Vladimir places his gun on the table.

As the eggs begin to harden from the heat of the stove's gas flame, Denise looks over to Charlotte and Sarah, trying to reassure them that nothing bad is going to happen, that this bad man will go away, eventually, and for now, at least, to try and remain calm. Inside, though, her heart is racing as she tries to contain the fear that's competing with her desire to present a calm and controlled exterior to her children.

"Are you going to hurt my dad?" Charlotte looks at Vladimir, appearing to have drawn inner strength and courage from her mother.

"Oh my God. Not you, too. The little one now is just like the mother." Vladimir holds his head in his hands.

"I'm not *the little one*." Charlotte looks at him squarely, unafraid. "Do you know what you're doing? You've come into our house. Threatened us." She looks at the gun on the table. "And refused to answer any questions."

"Everyone be quiet. No more talking. My head hurt. Where my eggs?" He barks at Denise.

Charlotte continues, ignoring him. "What do you want with us? What do you want with my father?"

"You be quiet now. You learn soon enough."

"Learn what?"

Vladimir grimaces at Denise. "You must instruct your daughter to stop now. Because I am soon losing my patience." He reaches out and grabs the handle of his gun resting on the kitchen table.

Denise continues to stir the eggs, proud of her daughter's fearlessness, drawing her own strength from it.

Getting no response, he turns his head back toward Charlotte "You need to learn your place, young lady. Be quiet now. This not your concern."

"I love my father. If you're here to hurt him, I won't let that happen. None of us will."

He looks toward Denise. "Control of your daughter. Now!"

Denise hears the threat in his voice turned up a notch. "Charlotte, quiet now, sweetheart." There is both love and respect in her voice.

Everyone is silent as Denise serves Vladimir his eggs, bacon, and toast.

His face lights up as the food is placed before him.

Denise watches in disgust as his face hovers directly over the plate and he shovels the scrambled eggs, toast, and bacon into his mouth, almost all at once, looking like a chipmunk stuffing his cheeks with nuts for winter storage, barely pausing for air.

When he finishes, he wipes the back of his left hand across his mouth. "Ah … that is exactly what I need."

Denise senses a peacefulness pervading his mood as he finishes his meal. She decides to take advantage of the opening. "I'm not asking much. Just please tell me what you're doing here. Please."

Vladimir looks at her in anger, but then relaxes, calmed by the warm, home-cooked food settling in his stomach. "You would not understand."

"Try me. I'm fairly intelligent."

"You would not understand," he insists, once again.

"What wouldn't I understand?"

He looks out the kitchen window directly behind Denise. "Honor. Tradition. Revenge."

Denise conjures her best empathetic look. "I know about these things. They're things we all feel. But how do they involve my husband?"

He pulls a pack of cigarettes and a gold-plated lighter from his breast shirt pocket and places the cigarette between his lips. Before lighting up, he pauses. "Do you mind that I smoke?" he asks. Denise shakes her head.

"Good. I would smoke anyway, but my girlfriend tell me it is polite to ask first."

He lights the cigarette and takes a deep breath, savoring the rush of smoke into his lungs. He releases a long, thin stream of white vapor from his mouth toward the ceiling.

Denise's cell phone vibrates on the tiled island countertop directly in front of her, making a loud buzzing sound. She reaches for it.

"Do not answer," commands Vladimir. He rises from his chair, steps to the counter, and looks down at the quivering piece of metal. He picks up the phone, looks at the incoming number on the display, turns it to Denise, and holds it up to her face. "Whose number this?"

She hesitates.

"Tell me!" His tone of voice leaves no doubt he's losing patience.

"I'm not sure."

Before the last word is out of her mouth, Vladimir lunges for her throat. His large, gaping right hand throttles her slender neck as effortlessly as if it were a vodka bottle. Her fingers claw at his hand as she struggles for air, face reddening, tears streaming down her cheeks.

Charlotte and Sarah jump from their seats at the kitchen table and step to their mother's defense. Eyes still focused on Denise's pained and deteriorating face, Vladimir points the gun held in his left hand at the approaching daughters behind him. "Sit down, young ladies, or this going to be bad ending for everyone."

The girls look to Denise for guidance. Unable to move her neck, she bats her watery eyes, instructing them—begging them—to do what he says.

The girls return to their chairs.

The cell phone stops vibrating.

"Who was that?" Vladimir keeps a suffocating grip on Denise's throat.

She shakes her head with limited mobility.

Vladimir squeezes tighter. Denise's bloodshot eyes bulge from their sockets.

The girls, scared and confused, stir in their seats.

The cell phone explodes into song—a loud, techno riff, indicating a voice message.

Vladimir releases his grip on Denise's neck and hands her the phone as she gasps for air. "Play message."

She hesitates. He tightens his grip again, her windpipe almost completely cut off. "Denise. You must understand. I will break your neck if you do not do as I ask."

Unable to breathe, feeling faint, panicked now, staring into the black, bottomless pit of his soul, she tries to nod.

He loosens his grip. She buckles over, holding her neck in agony, coughing, spitting, gasping, struggling to return a steady flow of oxygen to her lungs.

"You bastard," she says under her thin breath as she begins to regain her composure.

He strikes her with the back of his left hand. "Watch your mouth."

Her cheeks, chin, and lips bright red and drenched in tears and saliva, Denise reaches for the cell phone through her blurred vision and types in her password: NICHSA, the first two letters of her husband's and two daughters' names.

Vladimir grabs the phone from her and holds it to his right ear so that only he can hear.


*Hi, Sweetheart. I hope you're on your way to the cabin. Just wanted to let you know everything's good here. No worries. We're on a 6:45 flight this morning back to Chicago. In fact, we're on the plane right now. I'm going to go home first—to take care of some things—then try and join you up north. Everything's going to be fine. Anyway, I'll call you when I get home. Should be just after 11:00 or so. Give the girls a big kiss for me. Love you.*

Vladimir gives Denise a wry smile as he presses the End button. "It is strange that you do not even know your husband's phone number—maybe you have bad marriage." He chuckles.

Denise pulls a dry cotton dishtowel from the drawer underneath the sink and rubs it across her face with both hands. "He's the best man I know. And for your information, we have a *great* marriage," she says from behind the towel. She immediately regrets having legitimized his comment with such an impetuous, defensive, overzealous response. She doesn't want to be baited by him—this man who knows nothing of her life or her relationship with her husband and who certainly has no right to know any of it.

"Oh, he is? Then how you explain your *best man* visit prostitute in Denver." Vladimir says.

Denise throws the towel into the sink and looks him in the eye, a face of stone. "Oh, that? I know about that. It's nothing," she says.

"Oh, I see, you are liberal woman." Vladimir tries to hide his disappointment.

"We all make mistakes."

"Yes, but this mistake—your husband mistake—it is big one."

"Why?"

"Because, now …" he seems to decide whether to continue or not "… his destiny, my destiny, the same. It is fate."

"I don't understand."

"It is beyond something a woman can understand."

"Try me."

"I know that sound *sexist*, that some things woman cannot understand," Vladimir concedes, struggling with the word "sexist" as if it were bitter tasting. "But true, is it not?"

Denise looks at him without responding, hoping her silence will serve as a vacuum he'll fill.

"My family come from city in Russia, same as your husband."

"How do you know that?"

"I know," he says.

"But how?"

"I spend many years studying my ancestry. You know, I am direct descendant of Genghis Khan," says Vladimir.

"Congratulations. You and a quarter of the planet."

"What you mean by this?" he asks, taking offense.

"Well, it's pretty well documented that Genghis Khan impregnated most of the women in the towns and cities he conquered in Central Asia and Russia. For all I know, I may be related to him."

"It not matter," he says, seeming to brush aside her comment as pure nonsense. "I study my ancestors going back long time."

"So how does that affect my husband?"

"Because I know—that he—his grandfather, and my grandfather —" Vladimir cuts himself off.

"And—?"

"And that enough. End of conversation."

Vladimir pockets Denise's cell phone. "You stay here while I go take pee. Main phone disconnected. If try to leave kitchen, I will kill you all. I have ears of wolf. You understand?" He looks into each of their eyes, one by one, waiting for them to signify confirmation. They each nod stiffly.

Vladimir turns, with gun in hand, and enters the bathroom just to the side of the kitchen, leaving the door open. Denise, Charlotte, and Sarah rush to each other and embrace.

"Mom, what are we going to do?" asks Charlotte.

"I'm scared," says Sarah.

"I know, baby." Denise strokes the top of Sarah's head. "Let's just stay calm, okay? Everything's going to be fine. We just need to be patient."

Both girls nod.

"What about Dad? What's going to happen to him?"

"I don't know yet, sweetheart. Nothing, I'm sure. He's going to be fine. We all are. This is all going to be over soon."

"What did he mean about Dad and a *prostitute*, Mom?" asks Charlotte.

"Nothing, sweetheart. The man is confused. He has no idea what he's talking about."

From the bathroom, their conversation is interrupted by three long, slow, deep snorts as Vladimir recharges his batteries.

# Chapter 32

Nick's seat—5A—on the early-morning CRJ90 regional jet flight from Denver to Chicago, with two small passenger seats on each side of a thin, barely navigable aisle, was not designed with a six-foot-one, 185-pound male in mind. Nick's knees are jammed into the back of the seat in front of him, and the narrow width of his own seat restricts any movement side-to-side. He imagines himself Gulliver imprisoned by Lilliputians.

When the cabin door closes and the seat next to him remains unoccupied, Nick's spirits lift at the thought of being able to untangle his constricted body and stretch out; until, that is, the stewardess makes an unwelcome last-minute announcement.

"Ladies and gentlemen, the captain has informed us that the plane needs to be rebalanced before we can take off. Because of the smaller size of the plane, we need to reapportion some of the weight. This is unusual, but it does happen from time to time."

The stewardess continues. "We need to fill all of the seats in rows five through twelve. Could we please have some volunteers who are willing to move to the front of the plane?"

Resigned to the fact that his modicum of good fortune is about to disappear, Nick remembers a popular self-help book Denise once mentioned to him, *The Secret*. A how-to guide for getting everything you want in life. The basic idea, astonishingly simple in theory and practice, was that if you want something—

anything, a new car, a new house, a new boyfriend, a promotion, financial success, more regular bowel movements, even something as seemingly insignificant as a small person sitting next to you on a small plane—all you have to do is imagine it in your mind. It's as simple as closing your eyes, visualizing what you want, thinking very, very hard about it, wishing it to come true, and eventually, voila, it's yours. Of course, he didn't believe a word of it then, when Denise told him about it, and he doesn't believe a word of it now. *Ridiculous, really.*

But still … *What the hell? Nothing to lose. Desperate times demand desperate measures.* With no time to waste, he closes his eyes and conjures the image of a petite four-foot-ten, ninety-five-pound woman sitting next to him.

His eyes closed, his hands pressed together forming a temple in front of his tightened lips, his brow deeply furrowed, Nick resembles a young boy saying his nightly prayers. Approaching him from behind, loud, thumping footsteps interrupt his conjuring.

"Thank you, sir, for volunteering," says the stewardess. Nick opens his eyes, turns his head toward the aisle, and catches sight of his new traveling companion: a three-hundred pound man with an inch-wide, dark, hairy mole on the side of his face in a sleeveless T-shirt that says, *"Drunk Chicks Dig Me."*

Within minutes of struggling to shimmy, squirm, wiggle, and tuck his oversized bulk into the undersized seat and strapping himself in with a belt extender readily provided by the stewardess, the guy-drunk-chicks-dig promptly falls asleep, his immense mass overflowing across the arm rest well into Nick's limited seating area. Pressed firmly against the side of the plane, Nick decides to abandon any further attempts to manifest his desires. *Just my luck*, he thinks.

Shortly after takeoff, having read just a few pages of his book, Daniel nods off, the soothing, steady vibration of the fuselage no doubt lulling him into a deep slumber. Mina succumbs soon after, resting her head on a small, white airline pillow propped on Daniel's lap.

*I wish I could do that*, thinks Nick, glancing directly across the aisle at Daniel and Mina. Unfortunately, beyond his physical discomfort, courtesy of the airline designers and his super-sized seatmate, there's just too much on his mind to relax: too many concerns, too many worries, too many unknowns. The hmmm and wrrrr of the jet engines are a constant reminder of all that still needs to be done, all that still could go wrong if he's not careful and diligent. Like a boxer heading into the final round of a closely contested match, he needs to maintain his strength, energy, and focus to the very end.

Nick's primary concern is Denise and the girls. There was no answer when he called Denise before the plane took off. That is unusual, very unlike her not to answer her cell phone. Like so many other over-attentive, and perhaps over-indulgent, twenty-first-century parents ever ready to answer their children's calls, yearning for security in the knowledge that they have immediate access to them twenty-four hours a day, permanently wired into their whereabouts and activities, Denise carries her phone everywhere she goes. Nick tries not to worry about her and the girls. Of course, they're fine … well on their way to the family cabin in northern Michigan. Denise's cell phone probably ran out of battery power. That's it. Still, he would like to have heard her voice. Just to know—know for sure—that everything is fine.

Images of Vladimir Yurovsky flood his thoughts: the photos in his bedroom with celebrities and politicians all happily posing next to this illicit, dangerous, and deranged thug, the disturbing search results he found online, the threatening recording Mina played for him in the apartment. Where is he now? Stalking him in Chicago? Was he really hell bent on killing him? Could that truly be? Perhaps it's just an overblown fabrication? A posture? A threat? Not likely. Not after everything he's learned about the man from Mina, his Google search, and his conversation with Clay Salter on the soccer field. He suspects that forgiveness is not likely to be one of Vladimir's personality traits—nor is rational thought.

To neutralize Vladimir, Nick's going to need the help of Salter, to whom his attention now turns. Nick distinctly remembers his conversation with the FBI agent at his son's soccer match on Monday evening. Although not supportive of Nick's plan to get Mina and the recording, to say the least, Clay told him to call as soon as he got back—*if* he got back. *Nice.*

Salter said he'd handle everything. *He'd better.*

Nick tried repeatedly to reach Clay last night and this morning before leaving Denver. No answer. What if Clay isn't around or available to take Mina and the tape recording off his hands? What if his contacts at the FBI aren't able or willing to furnish protection for him and his family while they go about the business of arresting and incarcerating Vladimir based on the evidence of the digital recording?

He throws a few peanuts into his mouth. *New cut-rate airline breakfast food*, he muses.

His mind shifts to Johann Rohr, his boss and mentor. He needs to let him know what's going on. Another conversation he isn't looking forward to. He feels Johann would understand his indiscretion with Mina—his encounter—and most likely dismiss it as insignificant, no more than one man succumbing momentarily to mankind's greatest weakness. But still, he worries. It's likely things are different now that he's in contention to be chief executive. Certainly, the board isn't going to take such a lenient view, especially now that the company's security has been jeopardized.

If what Nick did becomes public, as it surely might given Vladimir's high profile, it could generate negative publicity for the Rohr Corporation and create an unwholesome impression among some of Rohr's more puritanical Bible-belt clients, business partners, and shareholders. Johann would probably understand and forgive Nick. He was fatherly toward Nick and generally liberal in his societal views, more European than American in his sensibilities. Besides, his own offspring aren't exactly poster children for clean living. No matter that Nick may have helped capture a notorious mob chieftain—one the FBI had been trying to nab for over a decade. His propositioning of a prostitute would not go down well outside the company. Once the story gets out, there's a good chance that his career at Rohr may be over, his dream of becoming the company's chief executive, so close within his grasp, gone up in smoke. He shudders at the thought.

Nick raises his window shade, against which his head has been resting, and looks out onto the break of dawn, which appears to be arriving like the pouring of orange juice along the distant horizon, slowly filling the glass of night's darkness. A song enters his thoughts: Paul Simon's "Slip, Sliding Away." Its catchy refrain keeps running through his head: *you know the nearer your destination, the more you're slip, sliding away.*

He thinks of Daniel. There was no mistaking the intimacy he and Mina showed toward each other on the ride to the airport, hand-in-hand in the backseat, and now snuggled up together on the plane. Daniel's last three girlfriends were bad enough. Now Mina? Her dysfunction puts all three of Daniel's past girlfriends to shame.

Nick feels guilty at having brought him along. The two of them would never have come in contact if he'd left Daniel at home. The last thing his friend needs right now in his mixed-up life is another mixed-up woman. He hopes Daniel has the good sense to avoid anything serious. Of course, he knows that's unlikely. Daniel has never been much for well-considered, rational decisions, especially in matters of the heart. No question about it, Mina would cause him more misery and pain than all three past girlfriends combined. She had, Nick guessed, the high maintenance of Candy the Corvette, the neediness of Sophie the VW Bug, and the rage, anger, and potential for explosive violence of Whitney the Pinto. Still, as much as he hated to admit it, there was a hint of sweetness about Mina, an appealing vulnerability, though he'd never want her to know he felt this way. And even he has to admit, she is quite beautiful. He shudders at his capacity to detest someone and still find her vaguely attractive.

*Poor Daniel.* Hopefully, the Feds will put her into a witness protection program as far away as possible. And fast.

How has it all come to this? Six days ago, Nick was a businessman on a simple business trip living a relatively straightforward, uncomplicated life. Just hours ago he had beaten up and bound a Russian hoodlum, abducted the girlfriend of an organized crime kingpin, and pulled a gun on a doorman. Two very different people separated by just a few days, hardly recognizable to one another. He feels like he's looking into a distorted mirror in a fun house, except the reflection he sees is disturbing, not amusing. All he knows for sure is that he wants his old self back, his old life back. And the sooner the better.

# Chapter 33

As soon as the plane touches down, Nick calls Denise's cell phone. Still no answer. Just a recording of the lovely voice he so desperately wants to hear in person. He tries the landline at the cabin. Again, no answer. He leaves a message on the answering machine asking her to call him the minute she arrives. He tries not to sound desperate. *Where is she?* His stomach aches.

On the drive back from O'Hare, Nick calls Clay Salter. He types the number on his phone, his knees steering the car as it careens eighty miles an hour down the wide, unwinding highway. He presses Send.

The phone rings twice before someone answers. "Yello?" It's Salter's unmistakable irascible voice.

"Clay?"

"Yeah, who's this?" He sounds pissed off. Just like on the soccer pitch.

"Nick Steele. Rohr Corporation. We spoke at your son's soccer game on Monday."

"Yeah, yeah. I remember. What's up?" he barks.

"I have Vladimir Yurovsky's girlfriend —"

Mina leans forward and raps Nick's shoulder with her fist. "I'm not his girlfriend anymore."

Nick corrects himself. "I have Vladimir Yurovsky's *ex*-girlfriend … and the recordings I told you about."

The other end of the line goes silent for a moment. "Christ," says Clay, half under his breath.

"What?" Nick is surprised by his response.

"I can't believe you went and did this." Clay sounds angry and confused.

"I told you I would."

"Yeah, but I didn't think you really would—and you shouldn't have."

"Why not?"

"'Cause you might've got yourself killed," Clay says. "You still might."

Nick tries to calm him. "That's why I'm calling you, Clay. To take you up on your offer to help." Nick wants to remind him that his responsibility as a federal agent, paid for at taxpayers' expense, is to catch bad guys and help protect the nation's citizenry, but he decides against it. Best not to antagonize the guy. "You told me to call you, remember? Said you'd handle things when I got back."

"Yeah … Yeah." Salter sounds hesitant, like he's struggling with inner thoughts. "Where are you now?"

"Driving back from O'Hare. I should be home in less than an hour. Can you come by my house then?" Nick holds up his left wrist and looks at his watch. "Around noon?"

"I'll be there, but it'll be closer to one o'clock. I'm at my office in the city." Nick can hear the rustling of a piece of paper. "What's your address?"

Nick gives it to him.

"You listen to the recording?"

"Parts of it."

"What's on it?"

"All that's needed to put this guy away, for a very long time. Hopefully forever."

"Anything else?"

"What do you mean?"

"Did you hear anything else? Anything—unusual? Anything—surprising?"

"It's all pretty fucking surprising to me, Clay." Nick is losing patience. "I'm not sure what you're asking."

"I don't know. I'm just trying to get a sense of what's on there."

"You'll find out soon enough."

"Is anyone else at your house?"

"No. My wife and kids are at our cabin up north." *Or on their way*, Nick hopes.

"Good."

"Why's that good?"

"Why?"

"Yeah, why?"

Clay stumbles over his words. "Oh, no reason, really. Just best to limit the number of people involved, that's all."

"You okay, Clay?"

"Yeah, why?"

"I don't know. You seem a bit—distracted."

"No, I'm fine. Just lots going on here. I'll see you at one."

"Please *don't* be late. I have reason to believe Yurovsky is in Chicago—looking for me."

"Christ almighty. How do you know that?"

"I'll explain everything when I see you at one." Nick is anxious to draw this difficult conversation to a close. "And Clay?"

"What?"

"Thanks for your help. I'm counting on you." Nick hopes a little positive reinforcement might help.

"Yeah." The line goes dead.

*Apparently not.*

Nick presses the End button on his phone and drops it into the empty sunken cup holder on the car's middle console. He turns to Daniel sitting next to him in the front passenger seat. "Charming guy," he says. "I hope he knows what he's doing. Something about him doesn't exactly instill confidence."

Daniel tries to reassure him. "He should know how to handle this."

"I hope so," says Nick. "We'll see."

Mina leans forward and speaks just inches from Nick's right ear. "You telling me you're not sure about this guy you're handing me over to?"

"No. I'm sure. I'm just being overly cautious." Nick puts on his best imitation of assurance. "He's fine, just like Daniel said. He's just a bit prickly, that's all." He looks over his shoulder, catching Mina's wary eyes, and gives her a cutting expression. "You should know something about that."

Before Mina has a chance to counter-attack, Daniel turns around, lifts his left index finger to his puckered lips, and blows—a silent shhh. Mina sinks back into her seat, folds her arms across her chest, and stares out the side window with blank eyes.

"Danny," says Nick, "I'm going to drop you two at your house. I think it's best to stay there for a while. Then come over to my house at one o'clock. That's when Clay says he's coming by. Okay?"

"Why don't we just come to your house now?"

"Because I want to be sure she"—Nick points back to Mina with his right hand, thumb set in a hitchhiker's position—"and the recordings are secure. You know, out of the way, until the minute we hand them over to Salter. It's just a precaution."

"Okay."

Nick looks at Mina in the rearview mirror, trying to gauge her reaction to his plan. She stares back, eyes ablaze, brows tightly knit together. "That's fine," she says, leaning forward, inches from Nick's face. "But stop talking about me as if I weren't here."

Nick gives her a brief side-glance, unwilling to cede his attention to her.

"Damn you. Look at me." Mina's voice is angry, insistent. She leans forward even further now, practically touching the dashboard, physically inserting herself into Nick's line of sight. She pinches a small area of flesh from her own thin, sullen cheek and shakes it back and forth. "Hath not I eyes? Hath not I hands, organs, dimensions, senses, affections, passions?"

Nick is surprised and, truth be told, more than a little impressed to hear her paraphrasing Shakespeare. *Where did she learn that?*

"It's me, Nick. Mina. I'm here. In the flesh. Right here. Right in front of you. Don't ignore me." Nick looks past her, pretending to concentrate on his driving. "Look, you bastard. You may hate me for getting you into this mess. But don't forget, you had a little something to do with it too. And don't forget, I'm the one who's going to save your ass."

Finally, responding to her demand for attention, Nick half-heartedly glances sideways to meet her eyes. "You fucking better," he says, his face devoid of expression, although his eyes can't hide his disdain. *I know who and what you are. The sooner we get this over with the better. The sooner you're in the hands of the Feds and out of my, and Daniel's life, the better for all of us.*

Seeming to surrender, at least for the time being, Mina collapses back into her seat and stares contemptuously at the back of Nick's head. "Don't worry, Nick. It'll be over soon enough."

# Chapter 34

Driving slowly down his street, ever watchful for darting children on bikes or skateboards or chasing after errant balls, Nick feels disoriented. Everything—the colonial homes, the freshly-mown lawns, the immaculately clipped hedges, the symmetrical stone walls, the clean foreign cars parked in the driveways, the basketball hoops hanging above garage doors, all of it—looks exactly the same as it did yesterday. But Nick doesn't feel the same. He has the distinct sensation of being a stranger, an intruder, an outsider, smuggling the harsh ugliness of the outside world into this peaceful, protected enclave.

Like Spanish explorers discovering South America, inadvertently carrying with them lethal germs, ultimately wiping out huge swaths of the native population, Nick feels he's unintentionally transporting something foreign, intrusive, and dangerous —something viral—that has no place here in the pleasant quietude of this sequestered suburban haven. He shakes his head.

Turning into his driveway, Nick is anxious to get inside his house as quickly as possible, anxious to bring an end to this nightmare—anxious most of all, to make contact with his wife and daughters. He reaches up and clicks the garage door opener clipped to the sun blinder above his head.

As the door automatically opens, revealing the contents of the garage, his stomach sinks. Denise's SUV is still there, parked in its usual space on the left side of the garage. *Why isn't she up north?* His breathing quickens. He steps on the gas, in a hurry now. After coming to an abrupt, lurching stop, tires squeaking against the smooth cement garage floor, he throttles the gear stick into park, heaves on the brake handle, snaps the door handle, kicks the door open, and jumps out of the car, all so fast it's one continuous motion.

After peering though the windows of Denise's SUV, scanning for contents—nothing there, no bags ready for departure, nothing unusual—he races through the garage door and into the mudroom, again searching for anything that might be out of place or unusual, anything that might offer a clue as to why his family hasn't left for the cabin yet. Nothing.

As he steps through the kitchen door, he calls out, louder than usual upon returning home. "Hello! Denise!"

Nick stops. Jammed against the hot, sweaty back of his head, he feels the cold, hard barrel of a pistol.

"Welcome home, Nick."

There's no mistaking who it is. The baritone voice. The Russian accent. Mina's dire warnings. It could only be one person.

He instinctively turns his head to address the intruder. The gun digs deeper into the back of his skull. He freezes.

"Raise hands." The voice is casual, matter-of-fact.

Nick does as he's told, raising his hands above his head. A large, hairy paw reaches around and pats him down. The frisking strikes Nick as unenthusiastic, more ritual than necessity. Habit, perhaps, after a lifetime of trusting no one.

"Where's my family?" Nick asks, still facing straight ahead. He notices Denise's cell phone on the kitchen counter. He feels nauseated.

"Everyone here. Everyone fine," says Vladimir, as if he were a warehouse clerk confirming the status of a misplaced item of inventory.

"Where are they?" insists Nick, trying to gain control of the adrenaline-induced fear surging through his body.

"In basement. You have nice basement, Nick."

"I want to see them."

"I have gun, Nick. Not you. I make demands. Not you." Vladimir presses the gun into his lower cranium.

"I just want to know they're all right." Nick pleads.

Vladimir shoves Nick forward. The gun still firmly against the back of Nick's head, they walk through the kitchen into the main hallway, stopping in front of the basement door. With no windows, Nick knows there's no way for Denise and the girls to escape other than through this door.

"You talk. Thirty seconds," instructs Vladimir.

Nick yells through the door, not wanting to waste a second, trying hard not to sound panicked or fearful. "Denise? You there?" Nick closes his eyes and prays for a response. *Please, baby, be there. Be all right—you and the girls.*

Nick hears footsteps racing up the basement stairs in response to his voice.

"Nick!" Denise screams. She bangs on the door. "Unlock the door. Get us out of here."

"I can't, baby. I'm not alone." Nick hears a deflated silence on the other side of the door. "Are you and the girls okay?"

"We're fine, Nick. No one's hurt." She pauses for a moment. "You?" Nick can hear Denise trying to force calm and reason through her constricted vocal cords.

"I'm okay, baby. Hang in there, everything is—"

Vladimir thwacks Nick on the side of the head with the butt of the pistol. "That enough."

Nick lurches over and grabs his head in agony. Specks of blood fall onto his shirt.

Denise yells through the door. "Nick! Nick! Are you okay? Leave him alone, you animal!" She kicks the door repeatedly.

Doubled over in pain, rubbing his head, Nick clenches his teeth and breathes deeply through his nose, trying to gather himself enough to disguise the pain in his voice. "It's okay, Nise. I'm fine. I'm okay. Everything's going to be fine."

Nick returns to a standing position. He removes his right hand from the point of impact on his head and examines the bloody Rorschach test in his opened palm. *Not too bad*, he reckons. *A few stitches, that's for sure. But I'll live.* He needs to get past the pain. His head aches like crazy, and his stomach feels like he just drank a cup of household cleaner. He can't let it be a diversion—the pain, the discomfort. He needs to have his wits about him, to find an opening, a moment of distraction—just a sliver—that he can exploit.

Before he has a chance to fully recover, Vladimir shoves Nick's left shoulder from behind and marches him straight ahead into the living room.

In the living room, no signs of violence appear. The room looks as it always does—comfortable and inviting, especially with the mid-day sun casting warm rays of light and shadows from the oaks outside the pane glass windows. He feels a sense of relief. But he knows it's a false emotion, an illusion. There's no security here. His thoughts instantly turn back to Vladimir—from whom, for the first time since entering the house, he detects a sweaty, putrid odor. His relief turns to rage. *If you so much as lay a finger on Denise or one of the girls …* He stops himself from continuing this line of thinking. He needs to stay cool-headed, his senses on high alert. An anxious, angry mind is a sloppy mind, prone to mistakes, he reminds himself.

Vladimir instructs Nick to sit on the right side of the large sofa facing the granite fireplace. He then places himself in the armchair directly to Nick's right, their knees practically touching. He sits back comfortably, crosses his left leg across his right knee, seeming to make himself at home, the gun pointed directly at Nick's gut.

Vladimir gazes around the room. The cacophony of books cluttered on the floor-to-ceiling shelves on both sides of the fireplace catch his attention. He eyes them up and down, as if studying a rare work of art.

"You like to read," Vladimir says, still inspecting the bookshelves.

"My wife," says Nick, stone-faced, eying Vladimir, glancing at the gun, trying to figure out how to wrestle it from him. His life is meaningless now. He needs to save his family and prevent Daniel from harm before he arrives with Mina. And he doesn't have much time.

"Ohhh, beautiful and smart." Vladimir raises his eyebrows, impressed. "My girlfriend beautiful and smart, too. She read Shakespeare."

Nick doesn't respond, though he remembers being surprised to hear Mina quote the great bard from *The Merchant of Venice* in the car back from the airport.

"You know my girlfriend?" Vladimir asks as if it were an innocent question, peering at Nick through the sight of his gun, twirling it with a limp wrist drawing an imaginary circle around his head, framing his target.

Nick stares defiantly past the gun directly into his eyes. "You know I do."

"Oh yes, of course," Vladimir says, pretending his memory was just jogged. "You try to fuck her in Denver. I remember, now. In hotel room. Maybe you *do* fuck her. Yes?"

"No. She took my money and left. You know that, too."

"My little princess, I not always know." Vladimir shakes his head at Nick, man to man, as if they had a common understanding of the sometimes unpredictable and conniving nature of women, as precious as they are. "Why you call her on her phone yesterday? In Chicago." Vladimir still sounds as if they were just having a friendly chat.

Nick decides it's best not to answer.

"You call her. I hear your voice." Vladimir answers for Nick. "Why? Why you call?"

Nick remains silent.

"Because you fuck her." Vladimir states this as an irrefutable fact, anger infusing his voice.

Nick decides he needs to keep Vladimir talking to buy time for an opening, a distraction, anything. *All I need is just one small crack*, he thinks. Just like his days in the ring. When his opponent got too comfortable or over-confident or weary from exhaustion—whatever the reason—he knew how to spot it, how to tell within a split second when his guard came down. That's when Nick would pounce.

"I didn't fuck her. Is this why you're here?" Nick asks with derision, as if there had to be more to it than that.

Vladimir grins wickedly. "No, no, that is not why I am here. But still, I want know…"

Nick interrupts him before he has a chance to continue, hoping he can steer the conversation away from Mina—the keeper of his family's salvation, she and her recordings. "Then why? Why are you here?" Nick presses the question hard. Of course, he knows the reason all too well but wants to keep Vladimir talking, hoping his thoughts will distract him and present Nick with an opportunity to strike.

Vladimir blinks his eyes twice, as if forcibly watering them. He then once again scans the room. A Norman Rockwell lithograph of a young Abraham Lincoln defending a chained black slave hanging on the wall behind Nick's head catches his attention. "Your Lincoln, he is a great man. Yes?"

Nick nods.

"He free slaves. Yes?"

Once again, Nick answers with a simple nod.

"Good for him," Vladimir says.

"Yes. Good for him. No one should be held captive or enslaved against his or her will." Nick immediately regrets the sanctimonious tone of his voice.

Vladimir looks closely at Nick, eyes narrowed to coin slots, and nods, looking as if a long-held suspicion had been confirmed. "I see. This is what Mina tell you. That she is slave?"

"I don't know what you're talking about," Nick says.

"*Da*. You do."

Nick shakes his head.

"No matter. I deal with her later. As you say, this not why I am here."

With his free hand, Vladimir pulls a pack of cigarettes from his shirt pocket and shakes one loose. He wraps his lips around the filter, pulls it from the pack. "You mind that I smoke?"

Nick shakes his head.

Vladimir lights the cigarette. He then settles back in his chair, as if he were in no hurry, and proceeds to explain why he's there. His voice is calm, slow, and steady, emotionally detached. He tells of their shared history. Of their grandfathers. How, when, and where Nick's grandfather killed his grandfather. Murdered him in cold blood. Unprovoked, he says. A brutal slaying. A bullet to the head. In the middle of the street. His grandfather had a wife and a newborn baby—Vladimir's father. It put great hardship on his family, and it was an affront to their honor—an affront to him, one that he intends to rectify. One he had hoped to rectify for some time. Now that time, at last, has come.

Nick remains silent. He knows the story already, although a vastly different version as explained in the letter written by his own grandfather. He examines Vladimir's facial features, searching for any hint of a family resemblance—probing for validation of his grandfather's suspicion that he may have killed his own half-brother. Thankfully, he finds nothing that suggests they might share a common bloodline.

Vladimir drops the butt of his lit cigarette onto the floor and grinds it into the white carpet with the toe of his shoe. Vladimir continues, explaining that he has come to seek revenge. He's here alone because it's a matter of personal honor—a matter upon which he has no choice, no free will—one that simply concerns the two of them. No one else is aware or involved. He's here to avenge a wrong and return honor to his grandfather and his family back in Russia. Nick, as the sole male survivor of the direct lineage to his grandfather, will have to be the one to pay. It was his destiny. He is sorry, Vladimir says, but there is nothing they can do about it. Nick probably wouldn't understand. Most soft-bellied Americans wouldn't. But it is a timeless old-world tradition that must be honored.

"You are familiar with the saying, '*Eye for an eye, tooth for a tooth*'? From Bible, no?

Nick nods his head, suddenly realizing who spray-painted those words on the floor of his building in Denver. *Of course.*

"Do you believe in Bible?" Vladimir asks.

Nick doesn't answer.

"Hmmm. Do you believe in God?"

Nick still doesn't answer.

"No? That is not good. Perhaps it is time you should reconsider." Vladimir chuckles.

"I find you one year ago," Vladimir continues. "Of course, I spend years looking. Since discovery, I decide to play with you. Why hurry? Fun for me. Maybe not fun for you. But that is point. No?"

"What are you talking about?"

"Why dispose of you right away? *So* boring. Better that you suffer first. Is that not reasonable? After all, my family suffer for long time after my grandfather murdered."

Nick's chest is pounding. He knows his time is short, and that trying to reason with this madman is unlikely to be productive. He needs to make a move. Fast.

Vladimir continues with a calm, even tone of voice, infused with a tinge of pride. "Perhaps you remember your house being robbed last January?" He offers a smug smile. "My girlfriend look very good in your wife's jewelry."

Nick is suddenly reminded of the surprising break-in—household robberies being very rare in Oakville—and of the all-too-familiar diamond necklace he saw dangling from Mina's neck back at Vladimir's apartment. *How stupid not to have seen through the coincidence.*

"Or perhaps you were surprised when your credit rating drop to zero? A minor inconvenience, I know, but still, these things take time to repair. No?"

Nick, who has never had less than a perfect credit rating, was astonished to have his bank reject an equity loan to pay for a new bedroom and kitchen at the family "cabin" up north. It took over a month to determine that his rating had been tampered with and to rectify the problem.

"And of course, you will remember your two dogs. I like dogs. I have dog myself. Laika. Russian hunting dog. Very beautiful. Adored by my children. How sad they would be if he should disappear. A father suffers most when his children feel pain. Is this not true?"

Nick shakes his head in disgust. Maggie and George, the family's two golden retrievers, were a Christmas present for his daughters three years ago. It took months for them to accept and mourn the inexplicable disappearance of their beloved pets.

"Ah, I see you are angry. That is good. For first time I can see hate in your eyes," says Vladimir with a smile.

Nick struggles to control a titanic impulse to strike out. Yes, he does feel hate. Vladimir is right about that—a gut-wrenching revulsion. But more than that, he feels a fool, obtuse, an imbecile for having failed to put these strange, foreboding events together, to connect the dots into a broader picture that might have allowed him to foresee, and ultimately forestall, future events, including his current predicament. He should have suspected that someone had him in his sights. In retrospect, the signs were there, including the things that Mina had mentioned: the increased levels of spam, the strange clicking sound on his cell phone, the unexplained credit card charges. He should have reflected on all of this, put it all together. It had indeed been an odd year, with far too many unusual incidences and signs of tampering, menace, and malice to ignore, though ignore them he did, with consummate stupidity. He was simply content to file it all under the category of "shit happens." *Idiot.*

"I save best for last. It is surprise." Vladimir continues, appearing to enjoy himself. "Your company very generous over past year. We invade computer system and steal bank account log-on information. We siphon off just enough each month to look like rounding error for big billion-dollar company like Rohr. No one notice. Maybe you need hire new accountants. Maybe we take one million dollars. Maybe more. Good for weekend spending. What is American expression? 'Is gift that keeps giving'?"

A muffled ring tone comes from Vladimir's lap. He leans back, stretches his legs out, reaches into his pants pocket, pulls out his cell phone, and looks down at the phone to identify the caller.

*There it is.* The opening. In a split second, Nick lunges. He knows the first strike is the only one he'll get.

He thrusts his left fist into Vladimir's throat. Vladimir reaches for his neck with both hands, dropping the gun into his lap, gasping widely for air through his now partially collapsed trachea.

Nick leaps to his feet, grabs the gun, steps back a few yards, and points it at Vladimir's chest.

"Get on the floor. Now! Face down."

Vladimir is still in too much pain, unable to breathe, to respond to Nick's command.

"I cannot … cannot." Vladimir's voice is thin and wheezy. His hands are still wrapped around his throat.

"I said, get on the fucking flo—" Nick is interrupted by three loud knocks at the front door. He glances at his watch—12:55. It's either Clay or Daniel. "Come in!" Nick yells, his attention still focused on Vladimir.

# Chapter 35

Nick's hears the front door open, shuffling footsteps, and then a loud slam as the door shuts behind someone. "Hello?"

Nick recognizes the voice. "Over here, Clay. In the living room," he yells.

Heavy footsteps pound the cherry-planked floor of the entrance hall, increasing in volume as they approach the living room.

Stepping through the square archway between the entrance hall and living room, Clay freezes in mid-stride, eyes wide open like windows without blinds. He stares in disbelief, struggling to make sense of the surreal scene revealed before him. Dressed in a dark blue suit, white shirt, and red tie, he draws his SIG Sauer P229 pistol—standard FBI issue—from a leather holster strapped around his shoulder underneath his jacket. He points the gun at Vladimir, arms fully extended, left palm cupping the gun hand, positioned to fire. "Nick. I'll take over from here," he says.

For the first time, Nick feels that Clay sounds and looks like an FBI agent assuming rightful responsibility and control of the situation. He breathes a sigh of relief.

Nick steps to the archway next to Clay and hands him Vladimir's gun, handle first. Clay opens his jacket and slips Vladimir's gun into his holster.

"Man, am I glad to see you," Nick says. He pats Clay on the shoulder and starts racing to the cellar door, anxious to reunite with his wife and two daughters.

"Hold on a minute." Clay's voice is stern, insistent.

Nick stops in mid-stride and looks back over his shoulder toward Clay, just a few feet behind him.

"Turn around, Nick. Toward me," says Clay, as he shifts the aim of the barrel of the gun from Vladimir to Nick. "Get back in here."

"What are you doing?" Nick looks at him in utter disbelief.

"Move. Now."

Nick steps back inside the living room a few feet from the federal agent.

Clay shakes his head in disgust. "Why the fuck did you have to go and do this?" Before Nick has a chance to respond, Clay turns his attention to Vladimir, who's slumped in the chair, panting, struggling to negotiate a steady flow of oxygen to his lungs.

"You stupid fuck. I can't fucking believe you're here," he says to Vladimir.

Vladimir looks up. Despite his labored breathing and the throbbing in his neck, he flashes Salter a welcoming, conspiratorial grin. "If it isn't Mr. FBI Man."

"You know each other?" Nick is shocked.

Clay ignores him and continues to address Vladimir.

"Yurovsky, you are way out of fucking line here. This is so fucked up. You're not going to drag me into this." There's mounting panic in Clay's voice.

Vladimir looks at him through red, watery eyes. "I am not your problem." He nods toward Nick. "He is."

Clay gives Nick a scolding look. "I told you not to get involved. I told you about him. That you didn't want to fuck with him. I told you. And you didn't listen. No, you wouldn't fucking listen to me. You had to stick your nose into it. And now this."

Clay shakes his head as if stopping at an intersection without any signs, uncertain which direction to turn. "Shit. Shit. This is bad. Real bad," he says, mostly to himself.

"You are such a fuckwit. How could you do this?" asks Clay, addressing Vladimir again, his body appearing taut with the nervous energy of a coyote pacing back and forth in captivity. "What am I going to do? What am I going to fucking do?"

"It is clear. We must dispose of him," Vladimir says, as if it required no thought at all, regaining his breathing and his composure.

"How about I just dispose of you?" Clay snaps back.

"That would be fine. Except you would not have very long life after that. Beside, remember, you and me, we were partners."

"Fuck you. We were never partners. You paid me to keep the Feds out of your hair. If I hadn't needed the money to pay for my wife's MS—Christ, watching her disintegrate, being reduced to nothing—I wouldn't have had anything to do with you. I needed the money, you scumbag. Plain and simple." He turns to Nick. "Everyone thinks federal employees have everything covered for them. Not experimental treatment, I can tell you. You have any idea how expensive experimental treatment is for MS? You know how expensive it is to care for someone who can't even wipe their own ass?" He turns back to Vladimir. "Course *you* do. That's how you pulled me in. I was easy prey." He stops for a moment and shakes his head. "Enough. That's not important. We need to get the recording."

"What recording?"

"Your girlfriend has been recording all of your conversations."

Vladimir looks bewildered. "When? Where?"

"She's been hiding a recorder in the apartment and taping everything. All of your meetings. She has *everything* on tape."

Vladimir's eyes bulge from his head.

"And he," nodding toward Nick, "he brought her and the recordings back here. To give to me. To hand over to the FBI.

Got it? See the irony? Chances are I'm on those recordings too. That's what I'm worried about. There's no way I'm going down with you. You have no idea what I'm talking about, do you? What a fucking mess."

"I understand. We must kill him," he points to Nick, "and destroy recording."

"Right about the second part, wrong about the first," Clay says. "You and me are going to leave here. Nobody gets hurt. I may have taken money from you, allowed myself to be bought, but I'm not like you. I don't go around killing innocent people. Especially not for some stupid-ass reason like you've got for wanting to kill him." He shakes his gun at Nick. "You're really going to kill this guy because his grandfather shot your grandfather—or something stupid like that—almost a hundred years ago in Russia? Are you fucking kidding? I always knew you were whacked-out, but this truly takes the cake." Clay stops, appearing to refocus his thoughts. "The only thing that matters now is the recording. Without that, there's no evidence. And your girlfriend's word is worthless."

Clay locks eyes with Nick, boring into them, as if saying, *Now comes the serious part.* "All you have to do is stay quiet. Got it? Not a word of this to anyone. None of it. The recordings. Him. Me. None of it. Can you do that?"

Nick doesn't move.

"Can you?" The volume of Clay's voice elevates, like a drill sergeant asking a new recruit if he understands that he's worthless and expecting to hear only one answer.

"Yeah. I can do that," Nick says, agreeing to play along, recognizing he has no reasonable alternative.

"Good. Now where's the recording?"

"I don't have it. I hid it away before I got here."

"Shit," says Clay, frustrated. "Where?"

"In a hotel room, nearby."

"Why?"

"Wanted it in a safe place until you came."

"Okay. All three of us are going to go get it. We'll take my car. Yurovsky, get your fat ass out of that chair."

# Chapter 36

Driving down Sunflower Lane, Daniel spots an unfamiliar car in Nick's driveway. *Clay?* he wonders. Unsure, he parks his car on the far side of the street as a precaution. He pushes the gear into park, pulls on the hand brake, and turns off the ignition. Suddenly, he's struck by the deafening silence of this sleepy suburban cul-de-sac. The children are off at school. The fathers are off to work. And the mothers—those who aren't working—are off shopping or running household chores around town.

"Here we go," says Daniel. "You okay?"

"Yeah." Mina conjures a half-hearted smile. "Let's get this over with."

"You know, whatever you need. I'm here."

Mina nods and blinks once, slowly, a simple gesture of appreciation.

He and Mina step from the dented, eleven-year-old BMW sedan, close their doors gently, so as not to be heard, and amble across the street with caution, scanning ahead for anything that might appear suspicious around the house. Nothing stands out, other than perhaps that everything appears extraordinarily ordinary. Mina slips her hand into Daniel's as they walk side-by-side along the slate rock pathway leading to Nick's front door. Standing on the doorstep, Daniel lifts the brass doorknocker. Before he brings the hammer down, he turns to Mina.

"Would you do me a favor?" he asks.

"Sure."

"See that tree over there?" Daniel points to a large oak on the right side of the house. "I'd like you to go over there. Hide behind that tree until I know the coast is clear."

"Danny, everything's fine. Nick said be here at one o'clock." She looks at her watch. It reads 1:07. She nods in the direction of the driveway to the left. "I'm sure that's the FBI guy's car. Who else's would it be?"

"I'm sure you're right. Just humor me. Please."

"Dan ..."

"Okay?"

"I don't know ..."

"It's gonna be fine, I'm sure," he says. "Just a precaution. Right?"

Mina looks at him for a moment with hesitation. "All right. But ..."

"No buts, okay?"

She stands on her toes and kisses him on the lips. "Okay. But I think you're being overly cautious."

"I'm sure I am, too."

She races to the side of the house and positions herself behind the designated tree.

Confident that Mina is safely out of sight, Daniel once again takes the brass doorknocker in his hand and raises it, ready to throttle downward, ready to get on with the task at hand. Suddenly, he's overcome with an unexplainable sensation: a discomfort, a disquiet that's purely visceral. He can't grab hold or define it. It's just there in his gut. Is it a warning?

Daniel lowers the doorknocker and surveys his surroundings. He scrutinizes the façade of the house—the top floor, the bottom floor, the windows, the shutters, the roof, the gutters—then turns his sights to the yard, looking for something, anything that might prove to be the source of his apprehension. There's nothing amiss, nothing tangibly suspect. Still, he can't chase away the feeling that something's wrong.

He needs to investigate further. He turns toward Mina, who's peering around the side of the tree. He signals to her, pointing to the ground floor windows on both sides of the house, indicating he wants to take a precautionary look before going inside.

She nods, appearing to grasp his crude sign language.

Squirreling through the thick, thorny laurel and holly bushes brushing against the side of the house, Daniel maneuvers his way to the side of the large, kitchen window on the far right side of the house, not far from Mina. He cautiously moves the right side of his head around the edge of the window, just enough to see inside the kitchen, without being detected by anyone inside. Empty. No one's there. He then moves left to the next window, once again stealthily peering in, this time into the dining room. Still no one. Moving further along, to the other side of the front door, hunched down like a cat burglar casing a job, he comes to the first of two living room pane glass windows. Sneaking a peek, what he sees this time defies logic. Clay is pointing a gun at Nick. A strange man, sitting in an armchair at the far end of the room, is holding his neck, struggling to breathe. No, that's not a *strange* man, he decides, not a strange man at all—it's a dangerous man. He recognizes him from the photographs he saw in the apartment in Denver. Vladimir Yurovsky. No mistaking him.

Daniel turns his attention back toward Clay. He can't hear what he's saying through the thick pane-glass window—it sounds garbled, thick like mud—but he looks angry, threatening: an enemy, not an ally. He ducks below the window. Hunched down, hugging the side of the house, he heads back to Mina, his left shoulder brushing against the white, wood clapboard siding, pawing his way through the thick bushes.

"You okay? What's wrong?" Mina asks.

Daniel shakes his head.

Out of breath, mostly from shock-induced adrenaline, he pulls his phone from his front pants pocket and dials 911. At a loss to explain what he's seen, he whispers under his short breath to the dispatcher that there's a robbery occurring at 764 Sunflower Lane—that one of the robbers has a gun, that it's an emergency, that people's lives are in danger, that they need to send a cop, no, lots of cops, immediately. Adhering to standard protocol, the dispatcher tries to ask Daniel a number of follow-up questions. "Just hurry!" he says, at a loss for patience and information, and ends the call.

"What's going on?" asks Mina, looking at the fear etched on Daniel's face.

"I don't get it." He shakes his head, still trying to make sense of what he just saw.

"What don't you get?"

"Clay Salter, the FBI agent, you know, the one we contacted? The guy who's supposed to help us? He has a gun pointed at Nick."

"Shit." She shakes her head. "He's working for Vlad."

"How do you know?"

"I don't. Not for sure. But what else could it be?"

Daniel stares at her in silence, trying to find other explanations. He can't.

"Somebody else is in there too," he says.

"Who?"

"Yurovsky."

"Oh my God." Mina gasps. "I told you guys. You don't know who you're dealing with here. Vladimir is protected in more ways than you can imagine. Even the feds."

"We can't wait for the cops to arrive. We need to do something."

"It's too dangerous, Daniel," she says, starting to sound panicked. "What are you going to do? He's got a gun. The cops will be here soon. This is a small town, right? How long can they take? Unless, of course, they're busy locking up a kid for selling lemonade on the side of the street without a permit."

Daniel frowns.

"Sorry."

"Okay. Here's the plan," Daniel says. "I'm going in through the back door. I have a key." Daniel pulls his car keys from his pocket and dangles them in front of Mina. Daniel and Nick have always had keys to each other's homes, mostly in case of an emergency. Of course, Daniel never could have imagined an emergency like this. "Just knock on the front door, good and loud, then run back here and hide. That'll give me time to get inside."

"What are you going to do then?" Mina says.

"When Clay answers the door, I'll come in through the back door, sneak through the dining room, then jump him from behind."

"Jump him from behind? Daniel. This is crazy. You're going to get yourself *and* your friend killed. You have no idea what you're doing," Mina pleads. "Please, just wait for the cops."

Daniel—fixated on helping his friend, and truth be told, newly empowered by his affection for Mina, whom he has a schoolboy compulsion to impress—barely hears her protest. "Don't forget: knock loudly, then run. Give me thirty seconds. Starting now."

Mina watches as he disappears around the backside of the house. She then steps from behind the oak, crouches to half her height, slides underneath the windows on the right side of the house—navigating between the firm, thorny bushes—and finds her way to the front door. Hesitantly, she reaches for the brass knocker, counts under her breath to ten … "one-one-thousand, two-one-thousand, three-one-thousand" … and hammers it three times, hard, as if she were cracking a large walnut. She then runs back along the side of the house, hiding behind the tree, well out of sight of anyone who might peer outside the front door or through any of the windows.

# Chapter 37

"Who's that?" Clay Salter says nervously, responding to the forceful knocks at the front door.

"Don't know," answers Nick, trying to hide his apprehension. Of course, he knows it's Daniel—exactly on time, just as planned. He wants to yell out, to warn his friend, *Run, Danny, run*. He takes a deep breath, filling his lungs with the extra oxygen required to launch his voice with the resonance it will need to carry across the entrance hall, cut through the front door, and burrow deep into Daniel's auditory canals where it will, he hopes, unmistakably resonate with warning.

"Don't say a word," says Clay, as if reading Nick's mind. He points his gun at Nick's head and then rubs his forehead with his left hand, straining to think. "Okay. Okay." He is speaking to himself. "I'm standing outside the front door. I see one car in the driveway, two in the garage. Three cars parked outside the house and nobody home? No way."

He suddenly grabs Nick's left arm, guides him into the entrance hall, and shoves him in front of the door. "Open it. Whoever it is, send them away. You give anything away, you're a dead man."

"I thought you didn't shoot innocent people, Clay."

"There's always a first for everything."

Clay moves behind the door and instructs Nick with the flick of his gun to open it. Nick turns the doorknob, pulls the door ajar, just a crack, uncertain as to what he's going to do if Daniel is standing there. But there's only one thing to do: tell him to run—run like hell—and get help. Then barricade the door to give him time to escape. High risk, he knew. Especially after Salter had threatened him. But what was his alternative? As long as Clay and Vladimir didn't have their hands on the recording, there was hope.

He takes a deep breath and holds it as he swings the door fully open and peers outside. No one's there. *Thank God.* He sticks his head out the door and glances on both sides of the house. Still no one. He releases the air locked in his lungs and turns back toward Clay, trying to hide his relief. "Whoever it was must have left."

Clay eyes him suspiciously.

"I mean it. No one's there. Look for yourself. Must have left before we got to the door. Probably a delivery of some kind."

Clay steps from behind the opened door, pushes Nick aside, and looks outside, straight ahead, then around each side of the house, one eye still holding Nick in his sights.

Suddenly, from the corner of his eye, Nick sees Daniel racing in from the dining room, clumsily, though with great force and conviction. He throws his body into the air and leaps on top of Clay, launching him off his feet, smashing him face down onto the hallway floor. Clay's pistol hits the hard wood floor and springs from his hand.

Daniel reaches for Clay's gun, scoops it into his hand, jumps back to his feet, and awkwardly, though with unmistakable resolve, aims the barrel of the pistol down at Clay. His chest is heaving, eyes blinking madly, a maniacal look cast across his face.

Nick stares in disbelief at the fallen FBI agent, and in amazement at his uncharacteristically courageous friend, gasping for air. Daniel was widely considered the weakest wrestler in high school gym class, cut from the freshman football team in the first round of tryouts, a virtual stranger to fitness centers, and a self-professed coward. Nick feels an uncontrollable tinge of pride.

"Get up," Daniel instructs Clay, sweat running down his forehead.

Clay rustles around on the floor as if in a stupor, still lying face down.

Daniel kicks the sole of one of Clay's shoes. "I said get up. Now!"

Clay is still for a moment, appearing not to respond. Then suddenly he rolls over on his back, slips his right hand underneath his jacket, and draws Vladimir's gun from the holster. He levels it at Daniel. Slowly, carefully, never taking his eyes or the gun off Daniel, he rises to his feet. The two men stand five feet apart, guns pointed directly at one another: a Mexican standoff.

"Daniel, drop the gun. You're way over your head. You don't even know how to use that thing," barks Clay.

"You drop yours." Daniel struggles to keep the gun steady.

"For Christ's sake, Daniel, put the gun down. I'm here to help." Clay sounds like a parent reasoning with a wayward son.

"Bullshit. I saw everything."

"Daniel, stay cool. Just hand it over and everyone will be fine."

Daniel's gun hand begins to shake harder.

"Danny, hold tight. *Do not* take your gun off him," instructs Nick, as if he were advising a friend with vertigo not to look down while standing on a high, narrow ledge. "He worked for Yurovsky in Denver."

"Don't listen to your pal, Daniel. You listened to him once. That's what got you into this mess. Don't listen again. No one's going to get hurt. You need to believe me. This is all …"

Clay stops in mid-sentence. His eyes pop from his head. He slowly looks down and sees the handle of a ten-inch stainless steel kitchen knife sticking out of his chest, just below his sternum. Everything suddenly seems to be moving in slow motion. He looks across the room toward the entrance to the dining room.

Standing there, right hand raised as if having just thrown something—not unlike a pitcher's pose after releasing a fastball— is an attractive, young, Asian woman. She looks familiar.

He peers back down at the knife lodged deep in his chest. He closes his eyes for a moment and then opens them again, hoping the image before him will disappear. It doesn't. He reaches for the knife, thinking that if he can just pull it out all will be fine. He has difficultly finding the handle. His arms are elephant trunks, heavy and slow. This sluggish feeling reminds him of a recurring dream where he tries to run—from what or to where, he can never remember—but can't, weighed down by some unexplainable supernatural gravitational force. Perhaps this is a dream, too. His sight blurs. His legs buckle. He collapses to the floor and lies motionless.

# Chapter 38

There are just a few things in life that Nick has struggled to believe, at least at first: the slayings of Martin Luther King, Robert Kennedy, John Lennon; the Challenger disaster; 9/11. All defied logic and reason. All were monumental. All related to death, sudden and violent.

Standing frozen underneath the archway between the living room and entrance hall, Nick has one more thing to add to the list, though this isn't some distant abstraction that he learned about on the news. It's here and now, directly within sight, lying still and lifeless at his feet. He stares in disbelief at Clay's frozen body, the large kitchen knife protruding from his chest as though it were a dwarfed third arm, the dark red, oxygen-starved blood oozing onto the floor, like a pool of dirty, spilled motor oil, the hollow, soulless eyes.

Mina moves to Daniel's side. They both appear to be in shock. Daniel wraps his left arm around her shoulder and nestles her into his chest. "I didn't know what else to do," she says, staring down at the body, wide-eyed, confused, and sad. He squeezes her shoulder.

Out of the corner of his eye, Nick catches sight of Vladimir dashing past him with a speed and agility that defies his physical bulk, like a three hundred-pound defensive tackle going after an exposed quarterback in search of receivers. Vladimir swoops over Clay's body and reaches for his gun.

"Stop or I'll shoot," Daniel yells.

Hovering over Clay's body like a vulture picking at a carcass, Vladimir pries the FBI agent's stiff, stubby fingers from the gun handle. He rises, turns toward Daniel, lifts the gun from his hips to his waist, like a gunslinger un-holstering his sidearm, and aims it directly at Daniel's chest, showing no sign of fear or alarm.

"You know, not all men capable of killing, especially in cold blood. Most cannot. I am guessing you cannot. This is interesting situation, no?" Vladimir says to Daniel with a smile that suggests he's enjoying himself.

Angry at himself not reacting sooner, a victim of his own shock-induced stupor, Nick is anxious to do something, anything, to regain the upper hand, to eliminate any further danger to his family, his friend, himself. He makes a sudden lurching move toward Vladimir.

"Ah, ah, ah," admonishes Vladimir, shaking his head, as if addressing an errant schoolboy. He turns his gun toward Nick who, back in control of his senses, freezes.

"Do not worry. As much as I would like to kill you, now is no longer good time. The situation has become ... too complex. Mr. FBI Man dead on floor. Too many people here. You can wait. Why not? I wait many years to find you. I can wait more."

Nick stares at him in disbelief.

"What? You think I leave seven dead bodies? I am not mass murderer. I come for one thing. You. But now I must leave. I am ghost. I fly here as somebody else, rent car as somebody else, use credit card as somebody else." He holds up his left hand showing off the hard, dried superglue thickly layered on each of his fingertips. "I am never here."

Vladimir pauses. "But there are two things I must have before I go," he says. "The recording ... and, of course, my *tsaritsa*."

Vladimir waves his gun, instructing Nick to move closer to Daniel and Mina.

Nick does as he's told.

With all three of them now lined up close together, side-by-side, Vladimir turns his attention to Mina. "My *tsaritsa*. You … amaze me." He nods his head back in the direction of the dead body on the floor behind him, and flashes her a smile. "But you make me sad that you are betrayer. How I ever trust you again?"

"There is no *again*," Mina says defiantly.

He glances down at the front right pocket of her jeans and sees the impression of the digital recorder.

"Perhaps not," he says. He turns his attention to Daniel. "I see you like my princess. You fuck her, too? Everybody fuck my princess. That what prostitute is for. *Da*?" He shifts the barrel of his gun to Mina. "It is time now for you to give me gun," Vladimir tells Daniel.

Daniel shakes his head.

"Do not be stupid." Vladimir stretches out his left hand, encouraging Daniel to hand over the gun.

Daniel shakes his head again.

"Enough! If you want she to live, you will give me gun."

Daniel turns to Nick now looking for guidance.

"Don't do it, Danny," Nick says.

Daniel turns to Mina, whose head is already wildly shaking back and forth. He looks back at Vladimir, who offers his own advice with a corrupt grin.

"You know what is right thing to do."

*What to do? What to do?* Daniel knows he needs to make the right decision, or there won't be any others to make. His chest is pounding. Beads of sweat condense on his furrowed brow. A surge of nausea challenges his ability to contain his bowels. He needs to concentrate. *The right thing—what's the right thing?* The words scream in his head. If he doesn't drop the gun, Mina dies. If he does, Nick, probably everyone, perishes anyway. This guy can't be trusted. But at least if he hands over the gun, it may buy more time. Maybe enough time for the cops to arrive. That's it.

That's the answer. Despite the urgings of Nick and Mina to hold his ground, he decides to surrender his weapon.

"Okay," he says to Vladimir.

"Danny, no!" both Nick and Mina cry.

"A gallant decision," Vladimir says. "Now, hand me gun. Slowly."

Daniel lowers the barrel of the gun to the floor and steps with caution toward Vladimir. As he hands over the gun, he's overcome by a sudden urge to act—a thoughtless, impulsive sense of obligation, devoid of any consideration for potential negative consequences to himself. Compelled to protect Mina and his closest friend, emboldened by his handling of Clay, he lunges for Vladimir's gun.

Nick watches in dismay. He hears a muted blast and sees a splash of blood pop like a firecracker onto the back of Daniel's light blue polo shirt. He watches in horror as his friend's body turns to rubber, as it collapses to the floor, as he smashes the back of his limp head on the hard wood floor, as he lies there motionless.

Mina screams and rushes to Daniel's side, kneeling beside him, grabbing his arms, shaking him, looking for signs of life. There's no response.

Hearing the gunshot followed by Mina's scream, Denise, Charlotte, and Sarah, until this moment quietly huddled closely together against the cellar door, begin to throw themselves against the door, screaming between loud gasping sobs. "Nick! Nick! Daddy! Daddy!"

"Tell them stop," Vladimir barks at Nick, raising his voice for the first time. His cheeks are crimson now, veins popping from his neck, his usual smug expression replaced by uncontainable rage. He reorients the barrel of his gun, now at Nick's head, directly between his eyes, reconsidering his earlier decision to postpone the slaying. Without looking down, eyes still fixed on Nick, he kicks Mina on the right side of her face with his brown, hand crafted Italian leather shoe. "Get up, prostitute."

The force of the kick knocks her over onto her side. She grimaces in pain. Blood drips from her head onto the floor. She looks alarmed, but also contemptuous. She steadies herself and leers at Vladimir.

*Bang.* The cellar door bursts open. Denise and the girls stumble out into the hallway. They look surprised to have succeeded in smashing through the locked door and alarmed by what they see before them: Two lifeless bodies on the floor—one of them Daniel's; Vladimir with a pistol leveled at Nick's head; a strange, young woman on the floor, next to Daniel's body, blood dripping from a deep gash on the side of her face. But they don't seem to stop to consider any of this. Being held captive in the basement, seeing the danger to Nick's life, appears to have emboldened them, fueled a determination to take action, whatever the consequences. Without speaking or looking at one another, as if uniformly of one mind, they race forward, looking like a pack of lionesses, heading straight for Vladimir, ready to attack with whatever force they can muster with fighting tools only nature has provided: their feet, hands, teeth, and nails.

Nick watches in disbelief as his precious wife and daughters charge blindly at Vladimir—and in horror as Vladimir turns his gun toward them.

In a flash, Nick lunges for the gun, gripping the barrel with his left hand, pushing it downward. The gun fires, boring a small hole into the floor, inches from Daniel's head. Denise and the girls stop, just a few feet away.

With his free hand, Nick rabbit-punches Vladimir squarely on his nose, which makes a disturbing crunching sound. He senses Vladimir losing his grip on the gun, stunned by the burst of pain in his shattered skull. Nick tries to rip the gun away, but Vladimir's grip is still too tight. The gun blasts again, this time putting a hole in the lower wall near where Mina crouches. Nick knees Vladimir in the groin, forcing him to double over in agony; still, his grip on the gun remains firm.

Determined to get control of the gun, lest another errant shot should find its way to Denise or one of his daughters, Nick changes his tactics, now gripping the gun with both hands, pulling, tugging, twisting, applying every ounce of strength he has left.

He feels the air leave his lungs as Vladimir drives his left fist into his solar plexus. As a young boxer Nick had spent hours and hours in the gym strengthening his stomach muscles, training to absorb any type of blow to his gut. But that was many years ago, and Nick's once-washboard abs are long gone. Unable to breathe, overcome with an overpowering urge to vomit, Nick wavers. Much to his horror, he feels the gun torn from his grasp.

Blood pouring from his nose, chest heaving, wincing in pain, Vladimir stumbles back a few feet, sliding the heels of his shoes across the floor. He raises the gun, as if it has suddenly acquired the burden of extra weight, struggling to aim it at Nick's forehead. Nick can see that he's weak and delirious. But he can also see the unmistakable resolve of a man now determined to kill.

"Enough," Vladimir says, shaking his head, trying to ignore the excruciating pain. "Time to say good-bye."

Just as Vladimir starts to apply pressure on the trigger of his gun, the front door bursts open.

"Drop the gun! Now!"

Nick, Mina, and the girls all dive to the floor.

Automatically, though with reduced speed, his reflexes compromised by the extensive damage to his body, Vladimir turns and swings his gun in the direction of the open door.

Two cops, standing side-by-side, knees bent, arms stretched out in assault mode, fire their automatic weapons. Eight rounds of hot metal riddle Vladimir's body.

# Chapter 39

## THURSDAY MORNING

The hospital room is cold and sterile: white hard-rubber flooring; white plastic-paneled ceiling; harsh, intrusive fluorescent lights; two cheap-looking metal-framed posters, one of ripe oranges in a blue ceramic bowl, the other, an impressionist woodland fern; no chairs for visitors; a view of the parking lot from a window long in need of washing.

A vast array of medical equipment surrounds the back of Daniel's bed, looking haphazardly arranged, like the makeshift invention of a mad scientist slapped together using odd gadgets and gizmos from his garage. A cardiac monitor beeps constantly in time with his heart. A plastic container gurgles like a small ornamental waterfall, sucking air and blood from his chest cavity. Three bags of clear liquid, each dangling from individual metal poles, connect to intravenous lines dripping vital fluids into his body. Blue plastic boxes with dials and digital displays control the IV rates. An outlet on the wall delivers cool, pure oxygen to a small plastic tube strapped below Daniel's nostrils.

"The doctor told me you're lucky to be alive," says Mina.

Daniel is propped up in his electric, adjustable bed, conscious but weak.

"She said the bullet went clean through, right here." She points to the right side of her chest, well below her shoulder. "He said it missed your heart, your lungs, no main arteries."

Mina grabs hold of Daniel's left hand and caresses it.

"She said that *that*," pointing to the half-inch diameter plastic tube stuck in Daniel's chest, "should be able to come out in a few days. And then you'll probably be home within a week. But you're going to have to take it easy for a while."

Daniel closes his eyes and grimaces. "Head hurts."

"You hit it when you fell. Pretty hard. That's what knocked you out. I thought you were gone." A crying gasp escapes from her throat. "You're still concussed," she says, struggling to regain her composure.

Daniel lowers his eyelids. His expression turns grave. He looks deep into Mina's eyes, without words, for an answer to the question that's now most vitally important to him, but one that he's also most afraid to ask. Seeming to understand the source of his anxiety, she softly strokes his hand.

"Everyone's fine, Danny. Nick, Denise, the two girls. Everyone."

"Am I the only one in the hospital?" he asks, his voice slow and strained.

"'Fraid so," she says. "You're on your own."

Daniel's eyes swell with water and overflow, draining teardrops down the sides of his face.

Mina swipes a tissue from a Kleenex box sitting on the side table next to his bed and gently dabs the streams.

"Yurovsky?" he asks, trying to focus through his wet, blurry eyes.

"Gone. To where he belongs—hell, no doubt," she says with no hint of remorse or sadness.

"How?"

"Cops. They arrived just in time."

Daniel closes his eyes, overcome with joy and relief. He did the right thing after all; he made the right choice. Thank God. One of the few he's made in his life—and certainly none more important.

"That was a stupid thing you did yesterday," she says gently, looking down upon him, appearing to read his mind.

He closes his eyes, searching his memory, reliving the moment, once again feeling the fear, the confusion, and the pain he experienced back at Nick's home, back in that entrance hallway where everything now seems so surreal. "I know. It *was* stupid." He takes a deep breath, which irritates his chest wound, causing him to wince in pain. It takes him a few moments to recover.

"When I was a kid my hero was James Bond. I always wanted to be like him. Hell, every kid did. He was *so* cool. Handsome. Strong. Confident. Brave." He chuckles with difficulty. "An amazingly capable guy, with just a tinge of ruthlessness. He was everything I wasn't. Everything I'm not." He struggles to catch his breath. "Things somehow always worked out for 007. No matter how reckless he was, he never got a scratch. Sometimes his suits got a bit dirty. That was about it. He'd brush them off and move on. But of course, in real life, you press your luck, you take foolish risks, you get hurt. I'm no James Bond. What I did was stupid. And I'm lucky to be alive." He looks into her eyes. "But you know what?"

Mina shakes her head.

"I'd do the exact same thing again." What he doesn't tell her is that he believes there's nothing he wouldn't do to protect her. For the first time since seeing Mina, he registers the bandage on her right cheek. "What happened?"

"It's nothing."

"You okay?"

"Fine. A few stitches. I've been hit harder," she says. She pulls his hand up to her lips and kisses it. "Thank you, Danny."

"For what?"

"For saving our lives. For saving my life."

Daniel shakes his head. "Me? If you hadn't thrown that knife at —"

"Shhh …" Mina strokes his left arm.

Daniel can see from the expression on her face that she would prefer not to debate the merits of anyone's actions, his or hers—actions that only beg questions, questions about decisions that can never be clearly answered or fully understood.

"I gave my testimony yesterday afternoon. They seem to be satisfied I'm telling the truth. The recording sure helped. Apparently, the FBI had their suspicions about your Agent Salter. And guess what? Turns out, his name is mentioned more than once on the recording. I never made the connection. Anyway, I need to go back this afternoon for some follow-up questions. Getting into the witness protection program isn't going to be easy."

Sadness consumes Daniel. He doesn't want to lose Mina—can't lose her. Not yet. At least not before they're given half a chance to explore things further. There's something there. He feels it, deep down. Not like the others. No. Not like the slew of post-marriage disasters he keeps repeating year after year. He knows he's impetuous, prone to make emotional decisions that defy logic or reason. And he knows most of these decisions are bad, sometimes even harmful, to himself and others. But dammit, this feels different. And it deserves a chance.

As these thoughts race through his head, Daniel realizes for the first time that he's staring at the poster of a bowl full of oranges on the wall at the foot of his bed. "Did you know—" he allows himself time to capture the insight. "Did you know that the best part of the orange is the part no one eats?" His speech has become more deliberate, slightly slurred, as one of the mechanical ghouls looming above his head automatically administers his next dose of morphine.

Mina looks at him quizzically, uncertain as to the cause of the sudden slurring of his speech.

"It's the tasteless white part inside the peel. That's where the nutrients are concentrated," he continues.

"And?" asks Mina.

"And that's what my life has been—ignoring the good part, always going after the juicy, sweet part."

"What are you trying to say, Danny?" she asks.

"I don't know. Probably some lesson in it." His voice trails off.

"You think too much."

He nods, conceding the point. "The irony—the irony—is that I've always gone after what feels good. Not what's good *for* me." He closes his eyelids as his dilated pupils float to the top of his head. "The source of all my troubles."

"Welcome to the human race."

Daniel opens his eyes again, taking a moment to regain focus. "Yeah, but humans are supposed to be able to exert free will. That's what separates us from the rest of the animal kingdom. Right?"

"What's this all about, Danny?" Mina leans forward and strokes his forehead.

"I'm not sure."

She pauses for a moment, turning her head to the poster of oranges. "Am I what feels good ... or what's good for you?"

"Both, I think."

She looks out the window before responding. "I'm not sure, either."

"But I'd like to find out," says Daniel, sounding like a schoolboy asking a girl to the senior prom.

She answers with the smile he was hoping for. "Me too."

Daniel and Mina turn their heads toward the entrance to the room, responding to three rapid knocks on the side of the opened door.

"Danny? Danny!" Denise, followed closely by Nick, hurries over to the side of his bed. "You're all right. Thank God, you're all right."

"A little worse for wear. But I'm still here," he says.

"We've been so worried. You did a crazy thing, you know."

"I know." He tilts his head toward Mina.

Eyes still locked on Daniel, Denise shakes her head and takes his right hand in both of hers. "We just saw the doctor. She said you're going to be fine. Thank God." She bends over and kisses his forehead. "How do you feel?"

"Like someone shot me in the chest."

"Very funny." She swats his hand and then moves aside to make room for Nick, standing behind her.

Stepping to the side of the bed, Nick first looks at Mina, across from him. He nods to her without expression, barely acknowledging her presence, then reaches out and grips his friend's right hand, their thumbs firmly interlocked in a power grip reserved for true soul mates. No words are spoken. Nick is content to communicate telepathically, speaking without the encumbrance of language, relieved and thankful that his best friend is alive. There will be time—time enough later—to talk about what happened, to converse upon the almost unspeakable incident that will no doubt transform both of their lives. For now, though, he's happy to require no more than this.

Denise moves along the side of the bed on Nick's right, and addresses Mina. "Hi."

"Hi," says Mina.

"You okay?" Denise asks.

Mina looks down at her shoes. "I told Daniel everything … at least all he needs to know, for now, about what happened yesterday."

"Thank you," says Denise.

Nick jumps in. "How'd your statement go?"

Mina looks up from the floor and into Nick's eyes. "Fine. Yours?"

"They seemed to buy everything I told them. I'm sure they're going to crosscheck my statement with yours. Just to be sure."

"Hmm. There's only one thing that might be different," says Mina.

"What's that?" Nick sounds surprised.

"I told them ..." she glances toward Denise, "I told them that you and I met in a bar in Denver. That you were sitting alone, minding your own business. That I approached you. And that you turned me down. Said you were happily married."

"And?"

"And that we then struck up a conversation. I explained my situation, that I was in trouble, in danger, and that I asked for your help—and that you generously offered to help."

"What about the hotel room?"

"Never mentioned it. I thought that might help you—you know, protect your reputation. I know how important that is around where you live, and in your work. Keeping up appearances and all."

"Christ, you shouldn't have done that. I told them the truth," Nick barks.

Mina shrugs. "Sorry, thought I was helping. You can always change your story."

Angry that she lied, concerned that the authorities now have conflicting stories that might call the veracity of their overall statements into question, Nick also feels a hint of appreciation at her small show of generosity. It was sensitive of her to understand that public awareness of his attempted dalliance with a prostitute in Denver, regardless of the outcome, could, and probably would, compromise his professional and some of his social relationships. He'd have to think about that—whether he might not change his story to match hers. It would certainly save him from some potential negative repercussions, she was right about that. It might even help save his job, his promotion. How he'd change his story to hers, he wasn't sure. But it's certainly worth further consideration. His demeanor softens.

"Are they going to provide you with protection?" asks Mina.

"They don't think I need it. Neither do I. Yurovsky told me it was just between the two of us, that no one else even knew about his vendetta. It was his personal business. The feds don't think any of his partners in crime," he says, "will take any interest in me, especially since I don't know anything about them or their business dealings. I'm not a threat—unlike you." He pauses, a tinge sorry for the sting in his last remark. "What about you? What's next?"

Mina turns toward the poster of oranges on the wall above the foot of Daniel's bed. "Redemption."

"What do you mean?"

"Oh, nothing." She turns to Daniel with a conspirator's grin.

Nick looks back and forth between Daniel and Mina, trying to discern her meaning, before realizing that her answer wasn't intended for him.

Mina continues, turning her attention back to Nick. "Sorry. Inside joke. I'll be fine, I'm sure." She shakes her head. "They said they're going to put a Marshal on me round the clock, starting tonight."

"Good. Then what?" asks Nick.

"In theory, I go into witness protection. But it's not that simple."

Nick nods. "How so?"

"I learned this morning that I need to first *qualify* for witness protection." Her fingers form quotation marks around the word "qualify." "The whole thing's pretty complicated. *Very* complicated, actually." She closes her eyes and shakes her head. "I should have done some research. Should have thought this whole thing through before I got into it."

"You did the right thing," he says.

"Maybe." She probes his eyes, as if searching for any hint of insincerity. Appearing relieved to find none, she continues. "Anyway, it's going to take some time. They told me that first I need to give a detailed testimony to the Feds. Fine. No problem.

But that's just the beginning. *Then* they have to put together an application—a fucking application!" She looks to Denise. "Sorry."

"No need to apologize. I've heard the word before," says Denise, with an air of maternal support, appearing to sense that the young woman before her, despite attempting to appear self-confident and self-sufficient, is alone, lost, and confused.

"Right." Mina's cheeks flush.

"Don't worry, Mina. I'm a friend." Denise gives her a smile.

Mina smiles back guardedly.

"Okay, so the application *then* goes to the OEO." She scratches her head. "What's that stand for again? Oh yeah, the Office of Enforcement Operations. The OEO *then* arranges an interview for me with the U.S. Marshals' Office. If they buy my story, they turn around and recommend me to the U.S. Attorney General. Can you believe it? The fucking Attorney General." She looks again at Denise. "*He's* the one who decides. Can you believe it? The Attorney General! I'm starting to think I might just decide to disappear on my own."

"Stay with it. I'm sure it'll work out. And I'll do everything I can to help."

She looks at Nick, bewildered, surprised to be on the receiving end of any show of kindness from him.

Daniel squeezes her hand. "He's not so bad."

Nick asks, "Where are you going to stay in the meantime?"

"With Daniel. For a while." Mina looks down at Daniel for any hint of objection. "He's going to need some help getting back on his feet." She reaches out and strokes his left hand in both of hers.

Daniel smiles at her.

Nick's eyes widen as he looks at Daniel in disbelief. He wants to object, to yell out and warn his friend that he's making a terrible mistake, that this woman is nothing but trouble. How could she be anything else? The girlfriend of a Russian mobster? A thief? A prostitute? About to go into a witness protection program? It's one thing to help Mina get back on her feet and entirely another to support the demise of his closest friend—and it is his demise that she will surely bring upon him. Why can't he see this? *Daniel, open your eyes!*

Nick feels a sharp, forceful kick to his right shin. He turns to Denise, who leaves no doubt that she's capable of reading his mind and that she believes he has no business interfering. He bends down, rubs his shin, stands again, and looks at Mina. "I'm sure he could use your help."

"What are you going to do for money?" asks Denise.

"Haven't figured that one out yet. I can tell you what I'm not going to do." She lowers her head; a return to prostitution is not in the cards.

They both nod.

"Well … I've got to go," says Mina, regaining her composure. "I need to go back and talk to the feds this afternoon."

She leans over and kisses Daniel on the cheek. "I'll be back later."

"I'm counting on it."

As she steps behind the back of the bed and heads to the door, Denise reaches out and cradles Mina's right hand. "Mina, you're not alone. Not anymore."

Mina probes Denise's eyes. "I'd like to believe that's true."

"It is." Denise squeezes her hand.

Mina's expression softens. "Thanks."

On her way out the door, Mina stops, turns her head, bites her lower lip, and looks back at Denise, as if seeking validation that what she just heard, and felt, and wants very much to believe, is indeed true.

Denise answers with a simple, graceful nod of her head. Mina smiles and walks through the door with a little extra spring in her step.

A few moments pass in silence before Nick speaks. Despite Denise's objection, he feels compelled to warn his friend that he's making a mistake getting involved with Mina. "Danny, I wasn't going to say anything, but —"

"Good," says Denise, cutting him off.

"Two against one, huh?" Nick says, realizing he's outnumbered, and that, regardless of his concerns, now isn't the right time to press the issue. It can wait. Celebrating his friend's very survival, taking comfort in the positive prognosis of his return to health—that's all that matters, at least for the moment.

"Danny, the girls would like to see you. Is that okay?" asks Denise. "We thought it was best for them to stay in the waiting room until we knew you were well enough to see them."

"Please, I'd love to see them."

Nick walks briskly down the hallway to retrieve the girls. As he turns into the entrance of the waiting room, at the end of the hallway, he finds them sitting on an old, mustard yellow, threadbare couch, silent, heads fallen, hands tucked snugly underneath their thighs as if to prevent them from wandering about. As Nick enters, they look up and scan his face for any telling signs of Daniel's condition. Nick smiles at them. "Uncle Danny would love to see you both."

The two girls jump from their seats and start racing down the hall. A passing nurse growls at them. "Slow down, ladies." Initially they abide by her warning, slowing to a hurried walk, but quickly, unable to contain the excitement in their legs, they return to a sprint. They stop and look back at their father for guidance on which room is Daniel's. Walking well behind them, Nick lifts his right arm and points like a traffic cop to the door on their left. They make a quick turn and dash through the door.

Shocked by what they see—the strange, ugly, and intimidating medical equipment sloshing and beeping and slurping, the myriad tubes coming out of Daniel's body—they stop dead in their tracks five feet from his bed.

"Come here, you beautiful things. I'm not going to bite," says Daniel.

They step warily towards the side of his bed, as if approaching a fragile object. Daniel raises his right hand. They both grab hold, fifteen fingers interlocking, forming a strange, multi-tentacled sea creature. He steadies his grip, infusing it with force, signaling that he's strong and able, that there's nothing to worry about, that all will be fine, just as it once was—that all *is* fine. Reassured, they gaze down upon Daniel—their champion since birth, their cheerleader, their third parent with no agenda, no judgments—with bright, beaming smiles.

"Shall we slip out for a minute?" Nick whispers to Denise.

"Good idea."

They step out of the room.

"How about a quick stroll around the floor?" asks Nick.

They head down the corridor, which circles the ward, in silence. Nick reaches out and takes Denise's left hand. They pass the nurses' station, watching numerous people in green scrubs going about the business of checking patient clipboards, accessing computer files, sharing medical opinions, and making calls to health insurance companies.

They walk a bit further, still in silence, occasionally compelled by natural curiosity to glance through the open doors, though only briefly, wanting to respect the privacy of patients and their families—the same privacy they would hope to receive in a similar situation.

"I think you should give her a job," says Denise, as if releasing a pent-up thought.

"Who?"

"You know who."

"What, as my personal assistant?" Nick jokes.

"No. I was thinking more in terms of a job where you both have *zero* contact. Ideally, as far away from your office as possible," she says with a hint of mischief.

"Why should I give her a job?"

"Because everyone deserves a second chance, Nick." She pauses. "Even you."

Nick looks at her.

"Just one, though," she adds.

"That's all I need." He squeezes her hand, feeling the great burdens of shame and guilt lift from his shoulders. *Thank you.*

They turn the next corner and see a middle-aged woman lying unconscious on a gurney, a bag of clear liquid dangling on a shiny, thin metal pole rising above her head, looking as if she may have just come out of surgery. Two orderlies emerge from the hospital room on the right and wheel her into her room.

"We're alive, Nick."

Nick sighs deeply and nods.

"Do you know how lucky we are?"

"Yeah, I do," Nick says. He puts his arm around her shoulder.

They walk together for a minute in silence.

"We should get away. Take a trip somewhere. Just the four of us," says Nick.

"That would be nice. I think we all need to be together for a while, you know, have some time alone without distractions or daily pressures. We need to all talk about what happened. Somehow we need to find our way back to normal—if there'll ever be such a thing again."

"Maybe we should just head up to the cabin for a few weeks."

"Any place is fine by me. Any place but Denver," she says.

Nick stops her in the middle of the corridor, grabs her shoulders, turns them toward him, gazes into her eyes, lowers his head, and kisses her on the lips. "Did I tell you I love you today?"

She nods her head and smiles.

"I did? When?"

She points to his adoring eyes. "You've been telling me all day." She stands on her tiptoes and kisses him back. "Don't ever stop."

# Chapter 40

## FRIDAY MORNING

Nick steps into the main conference room at Rohr. It's 11:30 AM. Jim Franklin passes him on his way out, offering a wry smile. "You're up," he says.

Dark wood paneling covers the walls. Straight ahead, large floor-to-ceiling windows reveal brightly lit, towering skyscrapers fighting to break through the heavy fog. Five men and three women, all middle-aged, formally dressed, sit quietly in tall tufted leather reclining chairs on each side of a large, rectangular dark mahogany table. Its shiny surface reflects the looming buildings and gray atmosphere outside the window. Gold carpeting covers the floor.

The board meeting has been in progress for over an hour.

Johann rises to greet Nick. He offers his usual warm embrace.

The board members remain seated, appearing guarded. Most look uncomfortable. None rise.

Nick nods to the group. He knows them all, most well. Today they look like strangers.

Johann guides Nick to an empty seat at the middle of the table, then finds his own at the head.

Johann takes a long, slow sip from his water glass.

"Until yesterday, this was intended to be a chance for the board to ask Nick any questions before we take a vote on selecting a new CEO."

Johann clears his throat.

"Of course, in the best interests of the company, I've asked Nick to start by explaining the extraordinary events of the last few days. Nick?"

Nick looks at the austere faces surrounding him. He peers at Johann, who nods in support—the extra dose of courage he needs.

"We'll, it's a long story—and it's one that needs to start with a confession."

# THE END

Manufactured By:     RR Donnelley
                     Momence, IL  USA
                     April, 2010